Portrait
of a
Woman in White

Portrait
of a
Woman in White

a novel

SUSAN WINKLER

SHE WRITES PRESS

Published 2014
Printed in the United States of America
ISBN: 978-1-938314-83-4
Library of Congress Control Number: 2014933540

For information, address:
She Writes Press
1563 Solano Ave #546
Berkeley, CA 94707

Cover photo ©2012 by Christopher Rauschenberg

To the Stuff of Families

Central Paris, 1939

What I dream of is an art of equilibrium, purity, and tranquility, devoid of upsetting or troubling subject matter.

—Henri Matisse

Contents

Part I: Belle Époque

•1•

France, June 1940

Tomorrow was to have been her wedding day.

They allowed themselves just the few hours before nightfall to pack—a single suitcase for each of them, and only what they could easily carry. Alone in the waning light of the bedroom, Lili stopped to examine the small heap on her bed: extra socks, a warm jacket, a bar of scented soap, a hairbrush. How could this insignificant pile sustain her? She added all of it to the belongings in the worn leather valise and pushed down hard to make more space. Then she turned to the bedside table, where a clock stood alongside a family photograph and two blue sketchbooks lay open next to an empty box of artists' pastels. The radiant colors spread across the table in luxurious disarray. In an anguished motion, she gathered up the pastels and placed them back into their dark wooden box and closed the sketchbooks. She arranged these final items carefully on top of the pile, lowered the lid of the valise over everything, and, with a final, devastating snap, shut the bag. Her dreams went dark.

The Nazis had stormed into France and were sweeping toward them. Tomorrow she would have married Paul. These were the facts, simultaneous and irrevocable. Yet when she tried to comprehend them, she was overwhelmed by a longing for all that had gone before and all that was to have been.

Where was Paul? As strong as she had been during the hour before, she needed him with her now. Outside, she saw that the sky had grown black, and a wave of exhaustion passed through her. Shivering, she curled her body onto the small bed. She could shut her eyes for a few minutes, at least.

With an explosive boom, her uncle's voice reverberated from down the hallway. "No! We cannot risk complications with jewelries. You must choose from your favorites, not everything." Aunt Jeanne's reply was unintelligible. Lili had visions of her frantically attempting to sew her beautiful ruby-and-diamond rivière necklaces into her hemline, dragging it down ridiculously.

From another room, her father insisted that he must bring his radio. "But Maurice, it's too big, and anyway, we can't count on electricity," her mother tried to reason with him.

"Then how will I know what's going on?" he shouted back in bewilderment. Lili shut her eyes in an effort to escape this growing nightmare.

When she opened them again, it was dark and quiet. She sensed Paul's nearness in the shadows by the bed. When he leaned over her to stroke her cheek, she could make out the long outline of his body, so close now that she thought she could hear his heartbeat.

"Lili, it's almost time to leave," he whispered. His warm breath moved across her forehead. "We have no choice. But I hate the idea of it."

"I know. So do I," she said, her voice quavering. He touched her lips lightly, as if to silence them. There was so much to say, but neither dared speak about what might go wrong; there were far too many ugly possibilities.

Paul reached out to switch on the table lamp and sat down next to her on the bed. In the soft light, she could see the tenderness in his hazel eyes, their golds and greens.

"Do you remember when we played here as children?" She took his hands and cradled them to her cheek. "Once, you found me fainted on the floor, and when you lifted my hand to check my pulse, I felt comfort in your touch. Now they are the healing hands of a doctor. I want your hands with me, always."

Drawing her to him, he held her and stroked her hair. "In my mind, Lili, you are already my wife. Soon, I promise you, we will stand side by side under the wedding canopy. I will crush the wineglass and gaze into your eyes before we kiss, and we will be one. Our future will be together." When he put it like that, with such certainty, she believed him.

It was time. The family was gathering in the marble foyer with their packed belongings. Lili could not leave without first taking in every detail of the rosy-hued bedroom. On the nightstand she'd placed a photograph to remind her of their life in Paris—had it been only twelve weeks earlier that they'd fled the city for the safety of the countryside? Nowhere was safe anymore.

Lili picked up the photograph. It had been taken on the happiest of days, when they were gathered together on her mother's birthday to celebrate the portrait Matisse had painted. Sonia Rosenswig smiled serenely from the red velvet chair, almost a mirror image of the elegant portrait newly hung on the wall beside her. In the photograph, as in the portrait, Sonia wore a white dress, and the emerald ring was on her finger. Maurice stood proudly behind her, his hands resting gently on the back of her chair; Henri was to her left and Lili to her right. Jeanne and Eli Assouline stood next to Maurice, and behind Lili stood Paul Assouline, his fingers touching Lili's in the hidden folds of her skirt.

Life had seemed perfect to her then. She'd had a sense that they would look back on this as the golden age of the family Rosenswig. Impulsively, she slipped the photograph into the pocket of the sweater she wore over her dress.

That night the family drove off the property in silence. An Oriental rug had been thrown down over the enclosed flatbed of the borrowed truck, where Lili squeezed in next to Paul, their extended legs touching, hemmed in by luggage and a well-stocked picnic basket. Henri drove, with Maurice and Sonia on the banquette next to him and Eli and Jeanne seated right behind, along with more suitcases. The nighttime temperature was cool; Lili kept her right hand interlocked with Paul's and the other inside the pocket that held the photograph.

It was a long ride to the Spanish border, and beyond that, Lili couldn't bear to contemplate. The main roads were already crowded with refugees, some on foot, some with livestock or carts, and a few others lucky enough to travel in cars or trucks. France was in a political twilight; Paris had fallen, but French soldiers in the provinces were preparing for battle. No one knew how long they would fight or if there would be an armistice. To the Rosenswigs and Assoulines, it hardly made a difference. No matter how profoundly they thought of themselves as French, they were Jews.

Dawn had not fully broken when they arrived; Lili squinted to survey the surrounding scene. "So, we're not the first in line after all," Henri announced, shutting down the truck's motor on the small patch of brown grass he'd staked out for them. Awake and bleary eyed, the family members registered their situation one by one.

With the Germans marching relentlessly toward the border, they'd hoped to be whisked through to Spain a few steps ahead of the troops. Apparently, so had everyone else here at France's final outpost.

"My God! I don't know where I've ever seen so many French. It's like a political rally in Paris. Do you suppose the entire government is leaving, too?" said Maurice, attempting to cover his surprise with sarcasm.

"Look, there. It must be Spain." Sonia pointed ahead, ignoring him.

"Yes, we can almost touch it from here," Jeanne agreed enthusiastically. Sighing, she rested a manicured hand on her breast as though their ordeal were finally over, then took a moment to arrange the waves in her hair.

"But not quite. Believe me, my dear, it looks much closer than it really is," Eli said. In his accented voice, rich and melodious through his mustache, it sounded like a warning, as though he were privy to some secret information.

Lili pushed aside the curtains to peer through the dust-covered window, trying to make out the extent of the confusion around them. She had not prepared herself for what she saw: a procession of wagons and bicycles, horses and oxcarts, all carrying children, parents, and grandparents. Some were in cars. Still others walked, or hobbled with fatigue.

"They can't all be going with us to Lisbon," she gasped.

"Yes, I'm afraid we're all clamoring all for the same thing, to leave France, to cross Spain, to enter Portugal, to make it to Lisbon and onto a boat bound for far away," Paul said quietly.

She thought back to the darker, broader threat in Eli's remark and whispered, "Your father is right. Everything looks closer and appears easier because we are desperate."

It seemed obvious that they were doomed to tire of the confines of the hot, stuffy truck and would inevitably join the hundreds of other refugees who paced the camp anxiously. But for how long? Certainly everyone hoped to be let through first, and surely there were those who felt they deserved to cross before the others. In the end, they would discover that they must wait, and wait, and wait, together—first for their turn to pass inspection by the officious French police, then for inspection by the Spanish, who took their time to open every single bag.

Hours passed slowly in the camp, overcrowded with hungry and cranky, dirty and exhausted bodies, engaged mostly in complaining and bickering. "Where did it go, the civilized behavior that we French pride ourselves on?" Lili wondered aloud.

"Let's get out and look around," suggested Paul. It was the only thing to do.

Henri had used his extensive contacts to obtain for the Rosenswigs and their Assouline relatives the Portuguese transit visas that were required to enter Spain. The Rosenswigs were called up first. It was early the next morning, when the camp was still enveloped in fog. They were to pass French inspection at the guard booth, then cross the wooden footbridge into Spain. Paul seemed to sense Lili's nervousness and walked alongside her, carrying her bag.

Everything depends on this, she thought with each step. The knot in her stomach tightened. She could have run to the border, so anxious was she to reach safety. Eli's voice replayed in her head: *It seems much closer than it really is.* She imagined the border receding to infinity, always a little farther, just beyond reach. As they neared the inspection area, she wanted to grab onto Paul and pull him through with her.

They walked past a small unit of French soldiers—one of them looked no older than sixteen. Paul remained next to her when the French border guard leaned his head out of his booth to glance at Henri's paperwork.

He looked up sharply at Paul. "You! Are you a Rosenswig?"

"No, I am not. I'm only here to help my fiancée." He held up Lili's leather valise. "My name is Paul Assouline. I'm crossing with my parents, back there." He put down the bag and gestured behind them.

There was a sudden commotion. Five of the young French soldiers burst forth to surround Paul, and in a swift, aggressive action they shoved him back to the refugee waiting area, out of Lili's sight. Her face paled in alarm. Henri shot her a dark look, warning her not to protest.

"Sometimes they think they can sneak through like that, but we always catch them," sniggered the guard, who had decided to examine the Rosenswig papers more closely. Lili held her breath as he took his time to finger through them, backward and forward, staring into the face of each Rosenswig.

When at last he was satisfied, he grunted and nodded that they could pass. Across the footbridge, the Spanish border patrol barely glanced at their visas.

Lili kept looking back, scanning the landscape for Paul. Something had detained the Assoulines on the French side. It was difficult to make out through the fog, but Eli appeared to be arguing with several of the soldiers and was pointing to the hem of Jeanne's skirt, where her jewels were hidden. Eli threw his arms in the air, gesticulating wildly, but the soldiers ignored him, uninterested; they pressed Jeanne and Eli through to the next checkpoint.

Where is Paul? Lili looked miserably to her brother for an answer. Henri's face was tense, but he only shrugged. Teetering between fear and nausea, she thought she might vomit.

From a distance, the Spanish border guards appeared to be interested in what Eli had offered, even if the French were not. Eli was on his knees at the Spanish checkpoint, tearing at the hem of his wife's skirt and handing over the contents, her precious jewels. "Oh my God," said Henri. "What gives them the right . . . ?"

At last Jeanne came over the bridge, squeezed between two soldiers who pushed her onward against her will. Tears streamed down her cheeks. She caught sight of Lili and called out breathlessly, "It's Paul. They won't let him pass! Those boys are drafting him into the French army. . . . He's been conscripted to fight the Germans!"

Lili's stomach plunged when she caught sight of Paul. She watched in disbelief as the French soldiers held him back, surrounding him, and pressed Eli through to Spain.

"No! Wait!" she shouted, so alarmingly loudly that they momentarily stopped short to look at her, waiting for an explanation.

In that instant she ran, right past the astonished Spanish police, across the footbridge, and back into France. She flew by the French border guards and stopped only when she reached the soldiers who guarded Paul, keeping him from her. Panting, she planted herself in front of them, stood tall, and took a deep breath.

"He must be allowed through!"

The soldiers had the insolence of youth. They leered at her and blocked her way to Paul. The youngest of them stepped right up to her, patted her cheek, and said with an arrogant grin, "Hey, your boyfriend's going to help us fight the Germans. Don't worry. With his help, we'll win."

"I'm a doctor. I could never fight," Paul said, shaking his head, his eyes flashing.

"A doctor?" the soldier repeated snidely. "That's even better. We're short on doctors." He positioned his bayonet in front of Paul, keeping Lili away. The border patrolmen who had watched Lili zoom past only a moment before caught up with her now. They were upset and yelling in Spanish and in French. They grabbed her by both elbows and started pulling her backward toward the bridge.

"No! No!" she screamed, trying to shake herself loose. But it was useless.

"Messieurs, that's no way to treat a lady," Paul upbraided them. They came to a stop. Then he held Lili's frantic gaze in his steady one. Her hair had fallen loose from her chignon, and through the strands and welling tears, she watched his shoulders fall. He opened his mouth to speak. At first no words came out, but then he recovered and said to her confidently, directly, "Lili, it's no use. Go back to your family. I will find you wherever you are. Don't worry, I will find you." Still, his words, his voice, did not achieve their usual calming effect.

"Wait! Let him take this . . . please." She jerked an arm free and reached into her sweater pocket. The photograph taken on Sonia's birthday was still there. She held it out toward Paul, silently beseeching him.

The youngest soldier grabbed it from her and studied it, before passing it on. "Here, Soldier—I mean, Doctor—your girlfriend's in the picture. You'll need it."

Paul grasped the photograph without taking his eyes off Lili and slipped it inside his coat. He watched while they forced her back across the border into Spain. Her tears flowed uncontrollably.

"Survive, Paul. Survive and come back to me," she prayed aloud.

I will find you wherever you are. Don't worry, I will find you. Paul's words echoed through her, imbuing her with his strength and faith.

"Yes," she whispered, as though he could hear her. "We will find each other. The war will soon be over. I will write you from America. All of my life, you've been with me in my heart, and you are a part of me. If I lose you, I lose myself. A story that begins like ours can never end."

•2•

Paris, Years Earlier

Paris in the 1920s was at the center of the world.

And the rue La Boétie was where everything important happened, where all news was urgent news, and everyone was involved in the arts.

Looking out onto that street from her bedroom balcony, Lili felt like a part of it all. She and Henri were nurtured there, under the cheerful but diligent eye of their mother, just above their father's antiques shop.

Electrifying canvases by Braque, Matisse, and Picasso, on display in the windows of neighborhood galleries, greeted her as backdrops to her early forays into the streets of Paris. And the grown-up talk around her was of the adventuresome modernist painters of the time. The rue La Boétie was surely the center of art, not just for Parisians but for everyone.

To enter the Rosenswig apartment was to step back in time. Lili's parents, especially Maurice, had the somewhat reserved manners of that generation, and Lili grew into a happy, thoughtful child who was raised to look closely at things. After school and her *pain au chocolat*, she would settle herself into a comfortable old chaise in the salon, her skirt patted down over her knees, to think about the day's adventures. As she aged, the room continued to beckon, its intimate seating arrangements host to cozy conversations with friends and daily familial exchanges. There were a few austere and (to her) frightening pieces carved with gargoyles that were meant to be beautiful but that she would always avoid looking at directly. Henri found her hiding from them behind a chair one day and teased her so mercilessly that she taught herself to smile and look away when she walked by them.

Lili and Henri were raised in unusually fortunate circumstances, of which she was aware from her earliest years—namely, that her parents were truly in love, still and forever. She never tired of hearing her father tell the story of how Cupid's thunderbolt struck directly into his heart on a warm evening long ago. "It was my *coup de foudre*, love at first sight," he would say—striking words for a man not normally given to the display and discussion of sentiment.

Maurice, then a young antiques dealer, was striding purpose-fully one balmy evening, already late for an important auction, when the accidental touch of a stranger on a crowded street sent a bolt of electricity up the back of his hand, startling him. At his feet a young woman bent over, searching desperately for something on the side-walk: an emerald ring.

Sonia told them about the ring that had come into her father's fash-ionable pawnshop that afternoon, how its blue-green darts had leaped out to her, offering the promise of something irresistible. Impetuously, she had put it on her finger before closing the shop, then wandered the streets, until she felt a jolt like a thunderbolt and the ring slid to the ground. In a panic, she had stooped to follow it. When she lifted her face to Maurice, she was smiling and the emerald ring was on her finger. She was struck by how handsome he was.

"I saw only her, a woman in white, her reddish curls a bit mussed, a pink blush to her cheeks, her eyes as blue-green as the emerald. By the time she said, 'Thank God, I found it!' I had already decided: *If she is Jewish and she doesn't have a fiancé, I intend to marry her.*"

Maurice and Sonia were married three months later in the syna-gogue on rue Copernic. The bride was radiant in a simple white satin dress shaped by corsets and crinolines, a chic little hat, and the emer-ald ring that had so cleverly brought them together, a wedding gift from her parents. Henri was born on their first anniversary, and Lili six years later.

As children, Lili and Henri did not embody a central sun around which their parents' marriage circled. It was Sonia, that strong beam of light, toward whom they turned as they grew. Maurice, too, basked in her radiant glow, and everyone accepted that he had to be right next to her when they were together. If not, he would roar. "He's old, with old-fashioned habits," Henri whispered to his sister whenever Maurice inserted himself between them and their mother.

It bothered Lili far more that Henri was always trying to push his way in, to be the center of attention. He could be such a bully that she felt safest next to her mother, who would speak up for her when necessary. Henri had only to whisper in her ear, in a high voice that mimicked their mother's, "*Lili l'Épine*," Lili the Thorn, and she would dissolve into tears. Sonia did not like it one bit, and to compensate for Henri's attempted dominance, she bestowed on her daughter the title "*Lili la Brave*," Lili the Brave. Perhaps even more than intended, it gave Lili courage, and she taught herself to smile and hold back her tears. She could not disappoint Maman.

In many respects, the Rosenswigs were unusually insular, keeping their social ties more or less commercial, by choice. Their exclusive circle was readily open only to their adored relatives the Assoulines— their sole family after the deaths of Lili's grandparents soon after she was born. Lili worshipped Uncle Eli and Auntie Jeanne and had a childhood crush on their handsome and gentlemanly son, Paul. Henri appeared to be as much in awe of their distinctive elegance as of the glamorous life they led. Every few months they arrived in Paris, producing a whirlwind of shopping excursions and art shows and touring the sights for a week or two until they returned to their magnificent country château, leaving the Rosenswigs exhausted. Before each visit Sonia would sing out, "Thank goodness they're coming soon. Life isn't the same here without them." But by the time their driver came to take them home, and their luggage and packages were stuffed into the car, and they had waved their vigorous good-byes, all Sonia could manage was, "Oh, to take a nap and go back to living our normal lives!"

Like her parents, Lili cherished normal life; Henri, maybe less so. It was quite different for the Assoulines. Uncle Eli had the soul of an outsider and was a collector of many beautiful things. This made him all the more wary of the evil eye, a superstition known to every youth in Constantinople, where he had grown up, and that persisted in complicating his existence even in France. The evil eye was the envious glance of others, one that inevitably caused misfortune. Elizar Assouline, born into a line of wealthy Turkish bankers, with his glamorous wife and beloved son and the privileged life he had made for them, was certainly not prepared to renounce their happiness or their luxuries, but he was prepared to conceal those things from the world much of the time so they wouldn't bring him trouble. Around his neck he wore a simple silver talisman to ward off the eye, and, at his insistence, so did Jeanne and Paul.

In reality, Jeanne and Sonia were second cousins, but as two only daughters of the same age, and because their mothers were first cousins who had also been close, they'd been raised like sisters. The two had managed to maintain their bond even when circumstances distanced them, continuing an unbroken chain of letters and calls, and finding reasons for regular visits even after Jeanne married her idiosyncratic Turk, who further protected his family from the evil eye by insisting that they live reclusively.

When Jeanne and her family were not gallivanting about with Sonia and the Rosenswigs in Paris, they were sumptuously ensconced in their own world in the countryside.

Their estate was aptly named "*Le Paradis*." Paradise. While one heard whisper of many marvelous châteaux in France, hidden away here and there, to Lili, Le Paradis was always the most special of all. Her first visit there became a cherished memory, immutable and infused with magic, like a dream. It became her standard for all that followed. So perfect that it was destined to be only a moment in time.

•3•

Le Paradis, 1928

Lili lolled drowsily between her parents on the red banquette of the Paris–Lyons railway, glued to the scenes of nature rolling quickly by her window. Henri, who had been chastised for bolting from car to car, suddenly jumped up, shouting, "We're here! We're here!" Never had they traveled so far from Paris.

It wasn't hard to spot Jean-Pierre, the Assoulines' chauffeur and the only uniformed driver at the tiny village station. Henri's eyes popped as he walked the length of the sleek black Bugatti, unable to refrain from touching it.

"Why haven't we seen this one before?" Henri asked the driver.

"Ah, it's unique in the world," said Jean-Pierre, letting them know that the car had been made to Eli's specifications. "But he allows it to be driven only here, in the countryside." Lili was sure that her uncle made a grand effort to hide his family from the evil eye, which he must have believed resided mostly in Paris.

It was late in the day. They left the main road and drove through fog into a landscape of thick forests and grassy fields; to the children, it was wild, untamed nature, full of possibilities. The drive was long, but Lili did not feel restless. Their mother, though, was noticeably excited, and when she reassured them, "It won't be long now. We're almost there. And when we arrive . . . " Lili strained her imagination in anticipation.

At last they turned onto a tree-lined drive, the Bugatti crunching over pea gravel. By then it was dark, but they could make out in the distance the contours of a seventeenth-century edifice. The lovely structure was enrobed in a white stone facade, with a terrace across the front, lit up for their arrival—but the dark and fog cloaked her in modesty, obscuring the details of her shape. As the car pulled into the courtyard, double wooden doors opened on the terrace and out stepped Jeanne, Eli, and Paul, all in their nightclothes, against a backdrop that glowed as brightly as the exterior of the house. Jeanne seemed to float out to them, carrying an electric lantern, while Eli volunteered to help with the luggage, as the staff were by now in bed. Paul joined him, smiling shyly.

It was difficult to tell who was more excited, Sonia or Jeanne, as they rushed toward each other with girlish grins. After they had all kissed everyone on both cheeks, and Henri, red with embarrassment, had whispered to Lili, "It must be only our family in all of France who behaves that way," they were escorted up the grand staircase to their rooms, where Lili fell straight to sleep on top of the bedcovers.

The next morning's rays of sunlight shone through slight openings in the shutters onto strawberries embroidered on the satin quilt. More strawberries covered the walls of her room, which were padded like the coverlet. She delighted in the thought that she had slept inside a jewelry box in the middle of a strawberry field.

"Liliane, are you awake? Get up. This place is fantastic. Paul is taking us on a tour to see everything. Come at once!" It was Henri, revved up into high gear, and his enthusiasm was contagious. She slipped on her shoes and rushed out to meet them. She glanced in a mirror on her way and saw that her chestnut curls were a wild halo framing a sleepy face and dark eyes. Like her brother, she loved an adventure.

Henri never did wait for her. He lacked patience and hated to stand still. Already he had a strong build and the broad, sturdy shoulders of a natural leader. His hair was neatly brushed back, forming light brown waves above his mother's eyes, blue-green and always alert.

Paul stood behind him. He was taller, though younger—twelve to Henri's fourteen—and Lili, even at eight, could tell that Paul admired the confidence of his older cousin.

Paul cleared his throat and assumed his best posture as guide. As an only child living away from other children, he seemed to relish the experience. Lili had been told that his father could not abide the village school, so Paul was kept home with tutors. His thick black hair was combed straight back from a high, pale forehead, emphasizing an aristocratically long profile and soft hazel eyes set under heavy brows. Paul had always been kind and gentle and a bit awkward with them in Paris, and Lili loved him for that. They were to discover his territory now.

They set out as explorers in single file, Paul first, with Henri close behind, then Lili, who was determined to keep up. She did not want to be lost in what seemed a fantastical maze.

Paul stopped underneath a suite of immense tapestries hanging side by side along the length of the hallway. "Do you know these?" he asked. In their fading images, illuminated by the morning sunlight streaming in from across the hall, she recognized the fables of La Fontaine, taught to every French schoolchild.

"Look!" She pointed with excitement. "There is my favorite, 'The Hen Who Laid the Golden Egg.' See the greedy owner and his magic hen? She laid him a golden egg every morning until he killed her to look inside her for more gold." The three studied the ugly, forlorn face of the owner sitting on the steps of his farmhouse, the dead hen in his lap. "I don't understand why he didn't appreciate the poor hen," said Lili.

"Some people just don't understand what is important and what is not," said Paul. "My parents have hung these here so I would pass by them every day and think about their stories." Henri snorted, but Lili thought his parents must be right, because Paul seemed the finest boy she had ever known.

Sometimes he stopped to explain the story behind an object: "These silver sconces were originally made for Versailles" or "Here is a painting of gondolas my father found in an abandoned passageway beneath Venice."

Lili twirled around, trying to take in all she could in what Paul called the "jungle room," filled with palms and paintings of faraway lands. "See these masks in the cabinet?" he said with a mischievous sideways glance. "They're from a tribe in Africa who would dance nearly naked when they wore them." His knowledge seemed to her very adult and far-reaching.

Oh, the rooms he showed them! Bedrooms like Lili's, reflecting nature, their walls covered with butterflies or romantic young couples romping in the countryside, and filled with the sorts of beautiful old furniture her father loved. As Lili, having been surrounded by her father's trade, was already somewhat worldly about these things, much here appeared to her to be exceptionally old and unusual and not to be touched. But she was her father's daughter, and never tired of looking.

At the end of the hallway, they came to an ornately carved door. "This is the only room we're not allowed in, my father's study," Paul said, urging them past it to the gilded wrought iron of the spiral staircase that would take them to the reception rooms below.

Downstairs they entered an airy kitchen, covered in shiny white-and-blue tiles like those in a Turkish sultan's palace. A stern-faced cook and his smiling wife worked in white aprons to prepare lunch. The cook glared when his wife, Annie, took time out to serve the children bread and warm milk on a wooden table set up in the middle of it all. Paul raised his brows discreetly to his cousins; he had already warned them about ill-tempered Boris.

Boris carried a tray holding a single silver jam pot to the table. Staring at Lili, he said, in a raspy voice that matched his compact, wiry body, "Blueberry jam. I picked them myself in the garden yesterday. Take some." He thrust the pot down in front of her. A block of fear settled in her chest. She had a memory of having become ill from the smooth, round berries once in Paris, but, afraid to upset him, she could not bring herself to answer.

"We don't really like him much, because he isn't at all friendly.

There's something odd about him. My mother talks about letting him go. But he's a really good cook, and we don't want to lose Annie," Paul had confided.

Boris fastened his intense gaze again upon Lili. Her good manners, laced with fear, compelled her to put just a tiny spoonful of his blueberry jam on an end of baguette, and she chewed. Paul seemed to sense her discomfort and saved her when he stood to say urgently, "Let's go now to see the pond."

They walked out and through the garden to a large, round body of water. Its murky green was surrounded by rough-hewn stones—an invitation to play. They spent the rest of the morning inventing all sorts of games that called for a pond that was cold, deep, and dirty. Out came Paul's well-worn armada of little boats on strings. Later, in the garden bed, the pirate Henri found a net on a long pole that he refused to abandon until he captured every boat in Paul's fleet. Henri put up a fuss when the parents called them in to prepare for Sunday lunch.

Back in the strawberry room, Lili pulled a fresh dress over her just-cleaned hair and body. The white cotton dress with pink peonies outlined in red had been laid out for her, and it carried the scent of the lavender soap she had bathed in. Sonia stopped in to gather and tie Lili's damp hair in a red bow and, when she stood back to admire Lili, said, "You look just like a prima ballerina, darling," before she disappeared onto the terrace for *les cocktails*.

Down the long hall to the dining room, Lili concentrated on her best ballerina carriage. She had only recently been allowed to attend dance classes, and now, as the ballet mistress had instructed, she called upon an imaginary string to pull her up from the top of her head. A door had been left open on the right, and she saw herself in a wall mirror inside. She imagined herself older, onstage, and pretended to pirouette into the room. Pushing off with one foot, turning precariously once, twice, she felt dizzy. The room was not familiar. Red felt walls above dark wooden wainscoting surrounded her. Bookcases were everywhere, filled with volumes covered in various shades of leather, their titles embossed in unfathomable gold letters that she guessed must be Turkish. Two globes of the world, one of them gigantic, sat on a long table next to piles of paper maps. A tall telescope on legs pointed out the window.

In one corner stood a large wooden desk decorated with carvings of lions' heads—surely the desk of Uncle Eli, whom her father called "a learned man." On it were books, a compass, and an assortment of tiny covered boxes. She was drawn to the boxes, decorated with pictures that looked like scenes from Japanese gardens, and she stepped closer to peer at the loveliest of all, a swan floating under a cherry blossom tree.

No one would know if I reached out to pick it up, she thought. The temptation was overwhelming. The box was lightweight, like holding air in her palm. As if of its own accord, her other hand dared to lift off the lid. Inside was a powder the color of sepia. When she carried the open box to her nose to sniff, powder flew everywhere, enveloping her head in a dark, dank cloud that grew dense around her, drawing her in closer and tighter to blackness.

When she opened her eyes, she was on the floor and Paul was kneeling next to her. He clasped her hand in his and appeared to be searching for her pulse. His expressive brows widened from concern to relief. "You're awake! My little Lili. What has happened to you?" She wanted to answer but didn't know how to explain herself.

She watched his eyes dart along the carpet to the snuffbox lying open beside her, its contents spilled everywhere. He picked up the delicate box and twirled it in his fingers, studying it a moment before putting it back exactly as he had found it. Lili was still thinking about how to answer him, but his expression had turned grave and he seemed to have forgotten the question.

"That box holds my father's favorite tobacco. It's very precious to him. If you've sniffed it, don't tell him. Anyway, I'm sure it was an accident."

Just then, Lili's father found them. She thought he looked as worried as if one of the lions on the desk had come to life and eaten her.

"My God, Lili, we've been looking all over for you. What has happened?" By now everyone had gathered around. Lili looked up at their trusting faces, and her voice trembled when she said, "I was practicing ballet, and I must have fallen down." She did not elaborate, and in that way she convinced herself that she had not quite told a lie.

Her uncle Eli stared at the tiny container overturned on the carpet while she prayed he hadn't figured things out. But his dark mustache twitched, and his even darker eyes seemed to pierce through her. Then his gaze softened. In a voice filled with concern, he asked, "Lili, do you remember how it happened? Did you sniff from the box?" But, of course, it was too late to change her story, even with the evidence right there on the floor, broken.

"I'm sorry, Uncle Eli. I knocked over one of your boxes during my pirouette practice." Her stomach churned with this deceit.

His eyes narrowed as he considered her; then he flashed his toothy white smile. "Don't worry. I have plenty of little boxes, but only one Lili."

"That's right," said her father gently, and he picked her up and carried her to the strawberry bedroom and laid her down on the bed, kissing her forehead. Her mother and Henri followed behind, but their concern only made her feel more guilty. Suddenly, she vomited blueberry jam all over her pink peony dress. She was never sure what had caused her upset: the jam or the lie.

Sonia helped her to change into clean clothing, giving her an extra-long hug before she joined the others for lunch. Lili had no interest now in food, or in answering questions about what had happened in the study. She sat up on her bed and opened a book, but she was thinking about how Paul had helped her, and the advice he'd given her, when Henri, who had hung back in the hallway, stepped into her room. He had a sly look on his face when he said, "Lili, have you ever heard the legend of the Japanese snuffbox?"

She looked up with anticipation. "Tell me, Henri. Please."

"Well, according to the legend, any girl who sniffs its contents will fall in love with the first man she lays eyes on afterward."

Lili wanted more than anything to ask Uncle Eli if that were true, but obviously she could not.

•4•

Paris, 1928–37

"My dear girl, you have a propensity for light-headedness. We can't have you falling down whenever you make a turn," her father told her when they returned to Paris. Lili understood that she had stupidly trapped herself in her own lie and that her father knew it, too.

Maurice had never approved of his daughter's studying ballet, and the unfortunate incident in the library gave him an excuse to forbid her to return to her ballet school. He considered the ballerina's profession beneath the Rosenswigs' social station, subscribing to a nineteenth-century prejudice against dancers as women of few means and little virtue, anxious to attract wealthy admirers. The gossip sheets constantly alluded to such indiscretions, and Maurice did not want his daughter to end up as more fodder for them. So, as Lili's enthusiasm had grown with each class, he'd regretted it more and more.

But Lili knew that Sonia had always chafed at the limited confines of home—in those younger days spent in her father's pawnshop, and now, as she helped her husband in his antiques business—and was pushing Maurice to allow more freedoms for their daughter. Lili had overheard him complain recently that her mother was far too enthusiastic about an "artistic" life for her. This comment had provoked a full-blown argument, not intended for Lili's ears, which she had witnessed through their bedroom door, left ajar.

"I suppose you would be happy to see our Lili as another Josephine Baker, prancing around a stage in a few banana peels!" Maurice snapped.

Sonia's eyes blazed at the angry slap of his words. "But that's absurd. How can you even suggest it? A few lessons would never lead her to that. Who do you think she is?"

"You're asking me what I think? My dear, this is not about me, it's about you and your romantic ideas about the life you want for Lili. Maybe you'd like her to become the next Ida Rubinstein, who scandalizes her family and everyone else by dancing around in not much more than a tiny top and a skirt made of beads." Madame Ida, the grande dame of the Ballets Russes, was Jewish and from a highly respectable and wealthy family.

"She will never become a real dancer. You've watched her. The girl is so clumsy, she could benefit from a few lessons in grace and movement."

"You know as well as I that even the ballerinas of the corps de ballet make ends meet by becoming the mistresses of wealthy patrons. It's a dangerous world, and I will not allow her to associate with any of it. I will not have her compromised."

"Oh, for heaven's sake, that is revolting, and you know it would never happen with our Lili."

"No, it will not. Because she's done with ballet classes." In a huff, he turned to leave.

"Then what *do* you want her to grow into?" Sonia called defiantly after him. "I mean, other than a wife and a mother?"

Maurice spun around to face her, his expression tight. "I would be quite satisfied with that. Until then, she can work in my shop, with me, where she will associate with the right kind of people and I can watch over her."

He pushed open the door, nearly knocking Lili over. "Sonia. Do you see who's here?" A look of parental consternation passed between them, and Lili was relieved to see them reunited.

She had always known that the ballerinas who studied with her, especially girls who had given up regular schooling for a life on the stage, were quite different from her schoolgirl friends. For all the discipline they showed at the barre, the instant the ballet mistress dismissed them, the older girls with the most stem-like bodies would charge to the dressing room to slump their shoulders and dangle their legs while they smoked cigarettes and discussed their romances without restraint. It was these overheard conversations in the rooms backstage that introduced Lili to all types of scandalous behaviors that her father would have kept from her. Naturally, she was fascinated.

Though not quite nine, she already imagined herself as a ballerina dancing before an audience at the Palais Garnier. Her mother's innocent remarks about her clumsiness, though, had spoken to her deepest fears, those that Henri never failed to remind her of. She wanted to be prima ballerina only, not in the corps de ballet.

When Maurice told her unequivocally that she had no choice but to quit, she didn't argue. Her eyes welled with angry tears, and she ran to her bedroom to commiserate with the small collection of porcelain miniature ballerinas that danced on her windowsill. Each one, caught in her own graceful movement, seemed utterly free—a thought that caused wet drops to rain down Lili's cheeks.

But Maurice, who hated to be the source of her distress, had thought of a way to redeem them both. It wasn't long before he came to her room to suggest, in the most encouraging way, that she take up drawing.

"You have a good eye, Lili, and that's what it takes. It would teach you to see as though you were looking through a magnifying glass. When your eyes are very well trained, you might even come to help me in my antiques shop." She was deeply flattered that he might want to include her in his important business affairs, and she did not want to provoke arguments between her parents. Maybe she could give up the stage if they allowed her to pursue drawing.

Sonia's brows raised in surprise when she heard the news. But she was clearly pleased to see Lili smiling again. "Fine. Tomorrow, Lili, I'll take you to Sennelier." Sennelier was the art-supply shop that all the best artists frequented, just across the Seine, near Beaux-Arts, Paris's most famous art school.

When Lili stepped inside the shop and detected the fresh scent of turpentine and paint, and so many wooden shelves jammed to accommodate all variety of colors, brushes, papers, and other stuff of artists, she felt giddy with possibility. It was a world waiting to be created, the origin of those works she admired hanging in the windows along La Boétie.

Sonia set off with her to locate the most basic pencil set and drawing pad, but Lili came to a sudden stop in a row that pulsated with the brilliant hues of giant pastel crayons.

"Look, Maman! Colors! Please don't let Papa make me draw in dull gray pencil, when the beauty of the world is here," she pleaded. Sonia, in apparent acknowledgment of her daughter's headstrong nature, allowed Lili to leave Sennelier with her first blue sketchbook and a set of six pastels that day, holding them close to her heart all the way home.

They became her intimate companions and accompanied her on the daily errands. At the market, while Sonia chatted with every *commerçant*, Lili was busily recording in her sketchbook interesting details that caught her attention—a kaleidoscope of greens turning to yellows to ripening reds in an artfully arranged display of apples, or the somber grays and silvers of fish scales, culminating in a luminescent, open eye. Sonia knew just how to engage everyone in lighthearted conversation until she saw the blue cover close on the sketchbook, the signal that Lili was done. Then they'd be off, no one the wiser.

Lili was proud that everyone seemed to know her mother. Sonia's beauty—russet curls, a wide smile, and eyes as blue green as the changing seas—turned heads as she moved down the street. As a young artist, Lili longed to capture her on paper, but Sonia's exact loveliness continued to remain elusive.

Over the years, as Lili's eye and hand developed artistic

sophistication and she learned to turn out accomplished drawings of most everything else, she was disturbed that she still fell short in her attempts with her mother. Nothing could explain it. In frustration, she turned to Henri, who wisely predicted, "It will take a master painter to capture the essence of Sonia."

•5•

Paris, 1937–38

"**P**apa, I've decided to open a gallery for modern art. What do you think?"

Lili detected a tremor in Henri's voice, even in his attempt to seem offhanded. He had waited until the family was seated in the salon, after dinner, to lower the boom.

Maurice stared at his son, too horrified to answer. He scowled, then growled, "Modern art, as everyone is aware, speaks directly to freethinkers, foreigners, and the nouveau riche. Personally, I find most of it ugly. It will never last."

"But surely you don't expect me to follow in your footsteps and warehouse furniture for the whims of future generations of minor aristocracy. I could never do that, Papa."

Maurice was so affronted that he did not speak to Henri for days.

Henri didn't flinch at his father's judgment. Instead, he went out on his own and was soon able to secure the financial backing of certain "American friends," whose names he was not at liberty to reveal.

At twenty-three, Henri had grown into his own. Lili guessed that he had developed a more independent and personal side to his life when he'd moved to the top-floor rooms in the family building on the rue La Boétie, where he had a separate entrance and staircase. It was from there that he started to deal in the style of artistic canvases that made the quartier pulse with modernity. He had a keen eye and an exciting way of talking to people that made them want to be part of the future.

"The boy is far too brash. Can't you see that? His scheme will never work," Maurice said, throwing his hands into the air in a gesture that Lili took as both offensive and defensive.

Maurice, as Lili and Sonia were aware, had never entirely understood Henri.

Maurice was from a world where change was neither necessary nor particularly desirable. Born into his antiques trade, he was happy to sell the same eighteenth-century writing desk that his own father had sold before him, sometimes purchased back from the same family when their children wanted to update just a bit. He did not subscribe to a world that changed.

It took every bit of cajoling Sonia could muster to convince Maurice that Henri had a strong sense of modern aesthetics, that his brashness could turn out to be an asset, and that they should trust him to succeed. Eventually, Henri worked out an agreement to rent a ground-floor space from his father. It had invitingly large windows flanking the entrance on the rue La Boétie and in no way interfered with Maurice's antiques on the other side of the building, at rue d'Argenson.

Lili was delighted with the growing stream of customers circulating through the art gallery that Henri had established under the family living quarters, and with the fresh air that blew through their lives when the door was opened to new ideas. Maurice merely shook his head, mystified that so many could be drawn to such "disagreeable" works.

"Henri, I simply don't understand why an artist who sees something beautiful can take it apart to make something that's quite ugly. And these new works of Picasso? What is all this fuss?"

"Papa, this is modern, and some of us find it quite agreeable," Henri retorted. The Galerie H. Rosenswig was decidedly modern, just like Henri. It comprised several rooms that were calm, spacious, and elegant. Lili was proud of what her brother had accomplished but also sad for Henri. As much as he wanted his father to approve of and even applaud his enterprise, she doubted that Maurice ever would. Maurice looked around the gallery with an unsettled expression, hoping his eyes would find something familiar and comfortable to rest upon. But all he seemed to see were paintings hung side by side at the common eye level, not stacked in traditional salon style, from the ceiling to the top of the molding, as in the Rosenswig living quarters above.

In the middle of each of three rooms was a grouping of new furniture that stood out in its simplicity, upholstered entirely in leather—the latest trend—with a piece facing in the direction of each wall. Henri explained that he had arranged it this way so his clients could be seated "to quietly view and to live for a few minutes" near the paintings under consideration.

"You know what would really help me out, Papa? If we could bring down just a few antique pieces from your storage room, not even the best ones. I want to set them around the gallery to give people an idea of how it looks to add new art to the older furnishings in their homes." Maurice grimaced, but how could he say no? Henri's idea worked—even Maurice had to agree, overhearing Henri's clientele exclaim in excitement at seeing a colorful modern piece hung above a baroque daybed. And the traffic at the Galerie H. Rosenswig continued to stream in.

Success became Henri. Lili watched him grow to be as capable of charming clients as his father was, though Henri was undoubtedly more aggressive. No one in Paris would ever have disputed his reputation as an affable, handsome young man. *He shows his impatient side only to us, his family,* she thought. His circle of friends had expanded, and he was out every night; he seemed to know everyone and had talked about joining an exclusive men's club on Saint-Honoré.

Whether his social adroitness was to enhance business or just a result of his feeling so comfortable in his own skin, Lili didn't know. Probably it was that everything was happening at once for him and he felt completely confident in his chosen path. Though it was hard for

Lili to see it herself, her school friends divulged to her that they found Henri quite good-looking.

Almost seventeen, Lili had nearly finished her formal schooling. She had emerged from her awkwardness a graceful beauty, even without ballet, and was on to deciphering relations between men and women. Hundreds of hours spent drawing had helped shape her into a reflective, self-reliant young woman, often content to be alone, in contrast with Henri.

Henri the visionary, who did so well in directing his important clients to the smart choice, the painting that would be sure to grow in value and set its owner apart as a person of great taste and style, continued to have difficulties with his own father, who did not regard his son's opinion as highly as did the Swiss industrialists and American bankers who traveled to Paris to seek him out. So Henri knew it was not with complete confidence that Maurice one day came to him for his advice and guidance in choosing a piece of art for his beloved wife on the occasion of her birthday.

Maurice approached him cautiously. "Henri, now, I don't want you to think of me as just another of your clients. I don't care about future investment value, or rounding out a collection, or how well it matches in a room. And I don't care what it costs . . . within reason, of course. Business is good. Better than I had ever imagined possible when your mother had us make the move to La Boétie."

Maurice turned his head and cleared his throat—no doubt, Henri thought, at the sad reminder that his son had passed on the opportunity to join his father in business—before he went on. "I want to give your mother a gift on her birthday that is really quite special, quite meaningful. Not a bauble, but an enduring piece of art, as a tribute to her and to our life together. Ever since I met her and was struck by the *coup de foudre*, I've been in love with her."

He smiled benevolently at his son. "We've been very lucky, you know?" Then he frowned and shook his head. "No, I doubt that you do understand. I hope that someday you will."

Henri suppressed a groan, anticipating how difficult, if not impossible, his assigned task might be. "I will help you only on the condition that you promise to remain open to everything. Even the modern, Papa. I'm not suggesting that you lower your standards, but this is the twentieth century and you will have to adapt to what's available—and besides, Maman likes modern art."

Maurice scowled but did not disagree. "But nothing too . . . modern. Please, Henri."

Henri fully expected to spend many afternoons touring his father through the neighborhood galleries where Henri was recognized and where all was familiar to him. Typically, Henri and the other dealers exchanged news daily about their trade, often over a meal or adrink, discussing who had signed up which new artist for his gallery, what was selling, and who was buying. This was a business that relied on honest gossip and the goodwill of neighbors to send clients to one another, and Henri benefited from his dealer friends.

They stopped first at the nearby Galerie Claude Bessett, just down the rue La Boétie.

"Ah, the Messieurs Rosenswig. To what do I owe this honor?" Claude Bessett greeted them with the impeccable manners he was known for.

Claude was one of Henri's close associates; between them flowed an open and frequent exchange of helpful information. They shared the same knowledgeable clientele, but Claude sold the older works that might appeal to Maurice, while Henri's inventory was purely modern. If they were to pass in the street, Claude might say, "Bombart was in today, but the Courbet left him cold. I suggested he visit your gallery. He's looking for something new."

Today he said, "A gang of noisy Germans dropped by this afternoon. They've suddenly changed their ideas about art. It's the Hitler factor. He tells them impressionism is no longer beautiful, and they believe him. Now they want older, pastoral pieces. When they asked for Dutch still lifes, I told them I would see what I could find. . . . Monsieur Rosenswig, have you seen anything like that at the estate sales?"

"No, certainly not." Maurice dismissed the idea with a snort of disgust. Whether he had or hadn't, he did not jump to sell to the Germans, as Claude seemed to. To Claude they were distasteful but could pay, so he would work with them. But to Maurice the Nazis were intolerable, just as he knew he was to them.

"I do my best to avoid all Germans," Henri said. "I'm just thankful they're not in the market for my modern pieces."

Lili had witnessed an incident that had surprised her recently in Henri's gallery. A young couple—likely German, as she gathered from their expensive-looking but austere attire—had mounted the steps to enter. Henri had gone pale, then, rushing to the door as if to greet them, blocked their entry with a broad gesture of his outstretched arms. With an unaccustomed stutter, he'd lied, "I'm so very sorry, we closed early today. My entire inventory has just been promised to an American gallery." As soon as they had gone, Henri had pulled his handkerchief from his pocket and mopped his face, which Lili could see was covered in droplets of perspiration.

"Henri, I've never seen you turn away a customer!" she chided.

He glared at her, his cheeks bright red. "I don't know those people, and I don't want to. Do you have no idea of what's going on out there, Lili? They don't print all the news in your precious *Vie Parisienne*. Jews all over Europe are trembling with fear. Yes, your life is beautiful. You live in France. But your beautiful house is made of glass. Those Nazis are relentless. They will try to come after us here, too. And if they make it, God help us."

He made her feel guilty, like a stupid child, and her chin jutted forward as she defended herself. "Of course I'm aware of things, but I don't dwell on them, as you seem to. I was raised not to speak of distasteful matters beyond our control."

"Yes, our family can't seem to face reality, unless it's sugarcoated." He appeared lost in thought. "In today's world, one cannot be too careful—especially me."

"Why you? Is it because of your gallery? What makes you so special?"

Henri only sighed. "Please, Lili. I don't want to discuss it. Go home now. I'll be up for dinner."

The Galerie Bessett was more established than Galerie H. Rosenswig, not just because it was older, but also because the Bessett family had aristocratic connections. Claude's grandmother had been the last bright beacon in a line of rich and influential women whose spark was dimmed by several generations of marriages to those duller, less beautiful, and less demanding of life. Claude, who savored the luster of his family's former history and position, continued to convey a sense of hauteur that some took for snobbery. Henri accepted Claude for what he was, not forgetting that he needed Claude as a professional ally.

"Ah, I'm in my element here," Maurice confided with a sigh to Claude.

Henri overheard. "Yes, Papa, that's why I suggested it." He was pacing the gallery, studying the ornately framed pictures on its walls.

Claude was at his most affable, presenting lush landscapes and romanticized scenarios, one after another, to tempt Maurice, who would look closely at each with an air of hopeful enthusiasm, then brush his hand over his salt-and-pepper waves, pull his fingers slowly down the side of his face, and shake his head no. None felt quite right for his lovely Sonia. Henri worried that his father would never find the perfect piece of art to present to her, and that the search would drag on until its ultimate end in futility.

When it became clear that Claude was unable to locate the ideal something to please Maurice, Maurice was ready to give up his search in exasperation. "That was a waste of time and it's entirely your fault," he said to Henri afterward.

"Oh, and why is that, Papa?" Henri said flatly.

"I'm afraid you just don't understand what I'm looking for. I want to give your mother a gift that will be a testament to how I feel about her. Not a painting about just anything. . . . " His voice trailed and his head hung.

Henri did not want to fail his father in this, his area of expertise. They walked back toward his gallery in uncomfortable silence and had almost arrived, when Henri suddenly lit up. "Papa, I do have another idea. Please, just listen."

Maurice looked up, but without great enthusiasm. "All right. Go ahead. Tell me your next *brilliant* idea." "Brilliant" was the term that Lili and Sonia had begun to attach to many of Henri's ideas of late, but when his father used it, it did not inspire confidence.

"I think everyone is fond of the paintings of Henri Matisse. Certainly Maman is. Even you don't object to his modern work, do you?"

"No, not really," Maurice conceded.

"You know that his reputation is well established as far away as America. He's not so young anymore and spends most of his time in Nice, but he has a show coming up at the Rosenberg Gallery, our friend just down the rue La Boétie. I heard that Matisse will be in Paris for a couple of months before the show. Papa, I really think that if we go together to explain your situation to Rosenberg, and I suggest that Matisse do a portrait of Maman while he's here, Rosenberg might go for it and talk Matisse into it. Rosenberg has always seemed sweet on Maman, and Matisse loves beautiful women. In fact, I heard he just had a falling-out with his latest Russian model. He could be very happy to have an arresting redhead like Maman sit for him. Tell me, what do you think?"

"A portrait of my uniquely stunning wife? " Maurice cocked his head and looked at Henri, considering. His lips pursed, then relaxed upward into a grin. "Yes. We can try. Why not?"

Henri went himself to talk to Rosenberg, and a few days later they got word that Matisse had agreed to do a portrait of Sonia Rosenswig, to be delivered in time for her birthday. Henri was so relieved that he no longer cared that Maurice didn't fully appreciate the thought and maneuvering that his son had contributed.

All Maurice could think about was that he would present his wife with a painting by a renowned artist whose work was not too abstract. And it didn't hurt that Matisse was a traditional Frenchman, like he was.

He smiled to himself when he imagined how it would be to direct Matisse to execute a portrait of Sonia looking just as Maurice remembered her when they first met. He would describe it like this: *She must be in a white dress, the emerald ring on her finger, smiling her special smile.* Surely when Matisse saw her, he would understand that no other woman in the world had the special look of Maurice's Sonia.

"It will be the golden age of the family Rosenswig," Lili proclaimed joyfully when Maurice announced his gift. The Matisse portrait, with all it entailed and signified, felt like the beginning of a new era, and Lili was as excited as her mother.

Sonia was to have sittings with Monsieur Matisse, and for that she would need the perfect white dress. Like all Parisian women, Sonia took the time to admire the rarefied designs of haute couture, those luxurious made-to-order fashions supplied to the very wealthy by a few renowned designers. This was a world outside the everyday reach of the Rosenswigs, but Sonia had let her daughter know that it was the magnificent draping of Adèle Normande that had captured her heart.

It was a contented afternoon in the family salon, shortly after the announcement of the portrait, when Lili whispered a small suggestion into her father's ear. Maurice looked up from his newspapers with a sly smile and said, "Sonia, I'd like you to get yourself something at Adèle Normande—a very special white dress to wear in your portrait."

Sonia made an appointment, and the next afternoon Lili walked briskly alongside her to the Normande Couture showroom on the Faubourg Saint-Honoré. Lili was seventeen years old, as enthralled with the world of high fashion as her mother was, and equally delighted to have its mysteries opening to them.

When they reached the entry, through an interior courtyard, Sonia gave Lili a conspiratorial smile; then she rang the door buzzer with a gloved finger. In those few seconds that followed, Lili felt her mother transform, by burying her insecurities behind a front of pride and entitlement. Sonia pulled herself up to her fullest height, threw back her head, and entered as an aristocrat. Lili trailed her, trying to look dignified, trying to remember how she'd been taught to move in her ballet classes long ago.

Lili forgot all about how she wanted to present herself the moment they were greeted by the showroom assistant, an elegant woman whose body appeared wrapped in a single piece of fabric that moved gracefully when she did. She indicated, with a mere tilt of her sleek blond head, that they take seats in plush modern chairs the color of sand, then excused herself to find Mme Normande. They watched her walk out.

"See, Lili, she has the true style Normande: a body liberated from stays and corsets—freeing yet shapely."

"It's marvelous, Maman, what can be done with a bit of fabric. I see now how a drawing can fly off the page and become something, anything!" said Lili, her mind filled with swirling shapes, colors, and textures.

The assistant returned with Adèle Normande herself, and Lili was surprised to see a very different sort of woman, with a plump body sheathed discreetly in one of her creations, intense blue eyes, and short gray waves close to her head. Her manner was pleasant but blunt.

"Please stand for me," she directed, and Sonia rose self-consciously. "Now turn. It's good that you're well built, because my gowns are very architectural." While Madame Normande elicited Sonia's ideas in planning the design details, most of which Sonia had already determined, Sonia appeared quietly flattered. The couturier took notes and promised to incorporate them into the final design.

They settled upon a white gown in silk satin, tight but low across the bodice, bias-cut with a dropped skirt, princess length. When a bolt of fabric was brought in for Sonia's approval, Lili could not resist running her palm down its length. "It's like water," she said.

"Yes. This creation must be in silk. Nothing cuts and looks like pure silk. It's the best fabric to capture the folds and drapes that mold to the body," insisted Mme Normande. "I always order two yards wider, to accommodate the draping."

The session took not more than thirty minutes, but by the end, both Rosenswig women were reeling from the impressive experience, and Lili had gained enormous respect for the profession. They were ushered out just as Madame's next appointment, a tall fashion plate of a client brushed by them, speaking German.

A week later, they returned for the first of what should have been several fittings. Sonia's eyes reflected her pleasure and anticipation.

The showroom assistant greeted them with a far more pleasant manner than before. "Madame Rosenswig, I'm sure your gown must be ready to fit. I've been away. Let me call Annette, the head seamstress. Annette is the only one Madame Normande would allow to work on this extravagance."

"I think we're insiders now," Sonia said with a wink when she had gone.

When she returned, something had changed in her demeanor. Her voice attempted coldness, and she seemed to look through and beyond Sonia when she said, uncomfortably, "I'm sorry, madame. Your dress cannot be produced this season. Madame Normande sends her apologies."

Lili watched her mother's face fall and her eyes deepen from a gay Mediterranean blue to a dark navy green, a storm of slate gathering beneath her brows.

Sonia sat rigidly and squeezed every drop of courtesy into her voice to say, "But surely there must be some mistake. It was designed for and promised to me."

"I'm very sorry, madame. There is nothing I can do. We'll reimburse you immediately, of course." Sonia was silent and controlled when the girl handed her an envelope and leaned in to say, in a hushed voice, "Madame, I shouldn't tell you, but one of the house's most important new clients wanted the same dress, unfortunately. Her husband is

Speer, the architect for the German pavilion at the Paris World's Fair, and she will wear the dress at the opening next week." The assistant could not hide her pride, despite the apology.

Sonia shot her a black look from the bottom of the sea and acknowledged the envelope with a brief *merci* and a half smile. She was already on her way out. Lili knew what she must be thinking. Not only had the dress been promised to her, but she had also added to its design, and Adèle Normande had appropriated her ideas. She recognized anger and humiliation in the quick, determined clatter of her mother's heels on the sidewalk.

Sonia stopped abruptly at a newsstand on the street to buy a packet of Balkan Sobranies, long, slender cigarettes filled with dark tobacco. This was the first time Lili had seen her mother desire a cigarette, and Sonia, silent and fuming, offered no explanation. Lili could feel her mother's tension mounting and knew better than to try to mollify her. They were forced to wait in line at the crowded newsstand, where the whole world seemed to have come for the latest edition of *Paris Soir*, piled in stacks behind the newsstand and along the shelves around them. A bold photo on the front page created the flurry of excitement. It showed a tall, pompous tower, crowned with an eagle and a swastika flag, under the headline "Parisians in Awe of German Pavilion at the Paris World's Fair." Lili watched a dark cloud pass over her mother's face. Next in line, Sonia grabbed her cigarettes, lit one, and with the first exhale muttered hotly, "Perhaps anti-Semitism is back in fashion."

With that jolt, Lili realized that her mother must be highly aware of what had been an unutterable subject in the Rosenswig household. She cringed inside, feeling Sonia's indignity and disappointment.

And they still had to find an appropriate white dress for the portrait. "If only I knew how to design it for you myself, Maman, I would," Lili said, thinking how much she would enjoy that.

"And how I wish you could!" Sonia smiled back, drawn out of her anger.

Lili resolved to open a new sketchbook dedicated to fashion.

The day the master Matisse was to come for Sonia's first sitting, Lili managed to remain home from school. She imagined he would arrive holding a splattered paint box and a color-stained easel, his white beard falling over a flowing smock. But she opened the door to a dignified figure in a gray suit and necktie, round glasses perched on a long nose under a receding hairline, his beard trimmed just below the chin, holding in one hand gloves and a cane, and wearing a fedora; he was a study in contrasts. Could this be the same artist who created such exuberant and colorful works? His expression was kindly, and the blue sketchbook he held was not unlike her own. He cleared his throat and returned her to polite reality.

"Monsieur Matisse?" she asked, as if she still couldn't quite believe it. His blue eyes smiled, then darted around the room, taking everything in. Lili was too awestruck to begin a conversation.

Sonia emerged momentarily with a nondescript white dress thrown over her arm. "Monsieur Matisse!" Her voice was lilting in her attempt to remain casual. "I'm honored that you have agreed to paint my portrait. Very much so."

Matisse looked back at her, studying her, then said, "It will be my pleasure to paint you, Madame Rosenswig. What do you have there?" he asked, referring to her armful.

"I've brought out something from my closet for our sittings. An old and boring dress. You'll have to improvise upon it for the portrait. Shall we begin?" she said, and ushered him into the salon. When Lili followed, Sonia said matter-of-factly, "Darling, don't you have exams to study for? You don't want to fall behind."

With stubborn reluctance, Lili closed the salon door. It was her mother's moment, not hers. But she did not want Matisse to think of her as a mere schoolgirl. She was nearing the end of her schooling and already thought of herself as an artist. She was dying to watch him work. She had to find a way. She would wait on a chair just outside and try to concentrate on her schoolbooks.

After what felt like an eternity, they emerged. Lili startled to her feet in anticipation, but Matisse walked right by her with a courteous nod. He appeared preoccupied and moved to the door, as though to leave, but at the last minute turned back brightly.

"Ah, Madame Rosenswig, it just came to me. I have the perfect white gown for your portrait. A silk taffeta with puffed sleeves and organdy ruffles that will set you off quite beautifully. It's one of a closet full of dresses that I pick up for my models at the sales. It's perhaps a little big, but we can pin it around you so it falls properly. Maybe your daughter here would be able to help us?" He didn't wait for an answer. "Tomorrow afternoon, then. In my studio on the Boulevard du Montparnasse?" His hand touched his hat in a good-bye gesture.

When they set out the next day for his studio, Sonia looked distraught. "Lili, I'm worried about the dress he wants me to wear. It will be something old and used now, maybe a rag from his closet that's not me at all. I'll look like a country girl or, worse, an old witch. I could have had anything. Oh, how could I have let it come to this? Your father will be so disappointed," she lamented.

"Don't worry, Maman. No one understands beauty and shape better than Matisse. Did you know he designs costumes for the Ballets Russes?" Lili reached for her mother's hand. "He will have the perfect dress, and you will be as lovely as the day Papa met you. I will make sure of that."

Sonia gently squeezed Lili's fingers, and Lili sensed a subtle shift in their roles. She was taking care of her mother.

Matisse was in a cheery mood when they arrived. His studio was large and set up like a salon, and it glowed with color and light. Paintings hung on warm-hued walls, and everywhere were piles of textiles—pattern on pattern, texture on texture—that he collected to use as backgrounds and props for his compositions. Lili's eyes were wide with excitement; she could imagine being inside one of his paintings, moving within that paradise of shapes and colors.

"Welcome to the cinema of my sensibility," he said endearingly, as he adjusted the heavy frame of his eyeglasses higher up on his nose. Then, with a chuckle, "I'm afraid I might go blind from having flirted too long with my enchanted colors." Of course, everyone who cared about such things had heard the rumors that his long marriage was faltering. Lili had the thought that maybe his wife had more to fear from his love of colors than from his lovely young models.

Across the room was a wide armoire that he opened to display an array of dresses and costumes in every color. He shuffled through them intently, then lifted out a white gown in duchesse satin, with shaped sleeves and frothy ruffles running down a fitted bodice, and presented it to them with reverence. Lili gasped at its delicacy.

"Ah, yes, it does have a certain quality, doesn't it?" he said, stroking the fabric. "Madame Rosenswig, it's yours to wear now. Please. You can step behind there to slip it on." He motioned toward a painted Japanese screen standing in the corner.

When Sonia stepped out she was an angel in profuse white folds. "How do I look?" she asked timidly, for there was no mirror.

"Oh, Maman!" Through the excess fabric, Lili could make out the vision that had so profoundly moved her father long ago.

"Ah . . . yes, the effect is correct," Matisse nodded. "Madame Rosenswig, I doubt that you have changed since the day you met your husband. I hope he will feel the same when he sees your portrait."

That was what Sonia needed to hear. The muscles of her face relaxed, and she settled into a pose that radiated self-assurance.

"Now for the perfecting details. Help me with this, Lili," said Matisse.

Under his direction, Lili learned where to pull a little here, pin a little there, until it fit, not snugly like the clothes of Adèle Normande, but sensually. "I adore this on you, Maman, especially for the portrait. It's not too modern. Papa will be able to recognize you. But let me just adjust here. . . . " Sonia by now put herself entirely, confidently, into her daughter's hands.

While Lili took some last-minute stitches, Matisse talked of his love of textiles and how he looked forward to designing the costumes for the next season of the Ballets Russes.

Oh, yes, she wanted to tell him. How strongly she shared his passion for color, fabric, and costumes. But wouldn't it be presumptuous of her to reveal her own interests, those of a dilettante, in the same breath as those of the maître Matisse? Her childhood shyness returned in his presence, but she did not want the moment to pass without saying anything; she must tell him something, engage him somehow, or she would never forgive herself.

"Monsieur Matisse, I had dreamed of studying at the Beaux-Arts. But, seeing your work, I'm afraid that art school would be entirely wasted on me."

"Really?" he said, rearranging his eyeglasses to pin another stitch. "Did you know that I failed my first entrance exams at Beaux-Arts?"

Lili nearly pricked her finger. "No. How is that possible?"

"Oh, yes." He seemed to relive that disappointment in the sigh that followed. "Fortunately, my mother had taught me to listen less to the rules of art than to my own emotions, so I managed to continue to draw and paint on my own, and finally I was accepted. But by then it was too late—I was already formed as a painter . . . And, do you know, it continues to bother me to this day that I do not paint like everybody else."

With that revelation, she felt the distance between them narrow.

The next time Lili visited his studio, Sonia's portrait was almost complete. "Come have a look at it," Matisse invited Lili.

"No, no," Sonia admonished from her perch. "I'm afraid she's not allowed to look yet—not before the vernissage! Lili will see it then for the first time, the night of my birthday, along with all of the family."

"Keep talking, madame; it animates your smile," said Matisse, choosing a paintbrush. Embarrassed, Sonia hesitated. "Please go on," he encouraged.

"Our cousins will come from their country home for the celebration. It will be like a gallery opening in our home."

"You mean the Assoulines, Maman?" Lili had not seen Paul since he'd entered boarding school, six years earlier. She'd heard he was studying to be a doctor.

"Why, of course. Jeanne and Eli, and Paul, if he can leave his studies in the provinces for a few days. Jeanne says he's very determined to do well."

Lili tried to imagine an older Paul. Would she recognize him? Could he have changed as much as Henri? The idea was interesting, even exciting. But she could not linger on those thoughts now.

Matisse was brandishing his paintbrush like an appendage to indicate a spot near him. "Come, stand here behind my easel, Lili." He placed her a little to one side behind the canvas, facing him. "From there you can watch me, and your mother will still be happy." The portrait was hidden entirely from Lili's view, yet she could watch him work.

The painter began to paint; he leaned back and squinted, then came forward to dab with the brush. He did this, many times.

He worked quietly, while Lili could only imagine what was taking place on the canvas. Then he withdrew his brush, sat back again in his chair, and focused on her.

"For me, you see, the entire arrangement of the picture is expressive. The place the figures occupy, the empty spaces around them, the proportions—everything has its share. Everything must balance, always."

Equilibrium, balance, proportion. She memorized his words, knowing instinctively that they would be important to her. She listened, taking to heart the lessons she learned from him about what was there and what was missing, and how to make the elements work together as a whole. Much later she tried to remember exactly when it was that she first understood how meaningful his advice had become to her, not just to her art, but as a way to think about her life. Up to the present, she had thought of her life as emotion, to be expressed with colors. Hearing Matisse, she had the first inkling that no matter what strong emotions she might experience, she could move them around; she had the ability to space and balance them in her mind and in her memory, to create an equilibrium for herself. He made it sound so easily accomplished, but she imagined figuring it out could take a lifetime.

A week later, Lili passed her final exams at the girls' school she'd always attended. That night, Maurice celebrated with an extra cocktail and an enthusiastic toast at the table.

"To our Lili. Congratulations on the successful completion of your formal education." He stood and raised his glass higher. Then he looked over the table with a nod to his wife, past Henri, and settled his proud gaze on his daughter.

"Next week we will begin your advanced education, with me and our antiques. My dear, you've no idea how happy it makes me to have you join me in our family business."

The exuberance in his demeanor, his booming voice, and his broad, lingering smile felt like a weight slowly crushing her.

"Thank you, Papa," she said quietly.

Frustration welled up inside her. Would she never be treated as an adult, free to make her own choices? She didn't want to disappoint her father, but was she now obliged to follow in his footsteps because Henri had turned him down and was making such a success of his own gallery?

"Papa, a long time ago you suggested I take up drawing. You were right about me then. I've filled up hundreds of drawing pads since. During all this time, did you always expect me to finish school and then join you in the shop?"

Maurice gripped tight before lowering his wineglass. When it passed in front of his face, it pulled the corners of his mouth downward and landed audibly on the table.

"Of course," he said. "Your mother has always helped me and finds it quite satisfactory." Lili well knew that Sonia spent as little time as possible in the shop—only when necessary.

But Maurice had suddenly hardened into a classic figure of parental sternness. Earlier, Lili had been so afraid of hurting him that she could almost have gone along with his plan. But his intransigence angered her. She looked right through him, focusing instead on her mental image of Monsieur Matisse working in his studio. It emboldened her.

"Papa, I don't want to work in a shop. I want the life of a serious professional artist who studies at it every day." Gaining courage, she dared go further. "One who has been trained at Beaux-Arts."

"No, no, *no*! I will not have you thrown into that world, Lili. In antiques, I know whom I'm dealing with. But as an art student, you never know whom you'll brush up against. It is not a suitable environment for a girl of your background. It is out of the question. You know that."

"I think you should let her, Maurice. You can see how much she wants it." Sonia looked nervously from her husband to her daughter.

"Absolutely not," Maurice nearly bellowed. "I won't hear any more of this nonsense. Have I made myself clear, everyone?"

Lili didn't dare answer him. She longed to be free. To stay at home all day and work for her father . . . It was not possible.

Henri turned to her with an amused smile and said in a drawn-out voice, as though addressing a child, "Papa is only trying to protect you—his little girl."

This was too much. Lili's cheeks flushed. She stood abruptly, turned away from the table, and walked out of the room. Her plate sat untouched. She felt her parents' shocked looks burn into her back, and she cringed inside for hurting them, but she couldn't help herself. It was time for her to grow up.

Convinced she had the most ridiculously overprotective father in the world, she plopped onto the seat of her bedroom vanity. Still fuming and physically agitated, she automatically picked up her hairbrush and began the brushing ritual, a habit that had always allowed her to relax and think clearly. Admittedly, she admired Henri, who had forged his own path regardless of their father's wishes, but why had things always come so easily to him? And would she always be treated like a child? She sat up straight to consider her reflection, then sighed and slumped again, disgusted to see that she continued to resemble a girl more than a woman. She was tall enough but had the face and body of a child. She would have to rely on the strength of her personality to portray the grown woman she wanted to be.

Throwing herself onto her bed, she reached for her most recent blue sketchbook on the side table, as though she might find the answer in its pages. She ran her soft palm lovingly over its rough, familiar surface, opened it, and flipped aimlessly through sketches of dresses, hats, and coats she had been working on since her visit to Adèle Normande. Then once again, this time more slowly, paying attention to the details. It could pass for an entire collection, and it was not so bad. "So, why not this?" she said aloud. The decision came easily. She would find a position in the world of fashion that would teach her the art of clothing design.

Early the next morning, Lili crept into the cool, dark kitchen to make herself a large and fortifying café au lait, then carried it back to her room. She would need time to prepare herself. She riffled through her wardrobe, then her chest of drawers, but after an exasperating effort to put together something impressive, nothing seemed quite right. In the end, she opted for simplicity and dressed classically in a black flared skirt and white sweater, then threw a double strand of false pearls around her neck. As soon as the shops opened, she left the house, carrying her latest blue sketchbook and trying to imagine what she could say to convince a stranger to hire her.

By the time she turned off the Faubourg Saint-Honoré to enter the interior courtyard of Sabine Rouelle—the design house that copied so well the draped Grecian styling of Créations Adèle, Adèle Normande should have been flattered—Lili knew what to say.

"And exactly what experience do you have, Mademoiselle Rosenswig?" the assistant head of design, a small, well-tailored woman who sat behind a large desk, asked her bluntly. Lili folded her hands protectively over the sketchbooks in her lap and took a deep breath.

"Why, madame," she answered, looking the woman straight in the eyes, "I have been drawing and playing with colors all my life. My mother has, in fact, been a client of Créations Adèle."

Possibly impressed, the woman nodded toward the blue book cradled in Lili's lap. "Well, are you going to show me some drawings?"

Like a mother reluctant to hand off her children, Lili passed the top sketchbook to her and held her breath. The woman opened to the latest drawings, a series of dresses that exuded charm and simplicity, and slowly turned the pages, taking so long that Lili had to breathe again. "Well, well, mademoiselle, your drawings are adept. You have a strong eye and a sense of how to use the fabric on the body. You have a sophisticated restraint that's unusual for a novice, but you have much to learn." She looked up and handed Lili back her blue book. "We may be able to use you, part-time. An apprenticeship. It barely pays, you understand, and requires hard work. But in the end you'll know something."

At home they were not as averse to her plan as she had expected. Her father rolled his eyes, thought about it for a minute or two, and said, "I suppose it could be good for you to work for someone else for a while. It will be demanding. Let's see how long you stick with it." It was as if he had thrown down the gauntlet to challenge her. She was determined to prove herself to him.

•6•

Paris, 1938

At the end of Lili's first week working at Sabine Rouelle, she came home exhausted. Still, she loved her new life and thought nothing else mattered.

Sonia was waiting for her. "You'll never guess the news. Jeanne called. Paul has just moved to Paris to continue his medical studies. He's in an apartment on the Left Bank, near the medical school."

Lili's heart came to a stop. Had her gentlemanly young cousin really grown mature enough to be in medical school and living on his own? When she'd last seen him, in Paris on his way to begin boarding school, they had still been almost children.

Sonia continued, "Jeanne asked me if we would look in on him occasionally. So I sent him a note inviting him to dinner here whenever he likes. 'We are your family in Paris as much as you want us to be,' I wrote. 'But we don't want to interfere with your studies.'"

Lili wasn't listening. She was reflecting on the times they'd spent together at Le Paradis and remembering how she'd idealized him then. No boy since had matched her high-and-mighty prepubescent standard or been as kind and honorable and handsome as she'd believed him to be.

"Anyway, a good-looking boy like that in the heart of bohemian Paris will want an independent life, free to do the things young men do. I won't pressure him into spending his free time with us," Sonia was saying.

Of course, she's right. How silly of me, Lili told herself. Paul would be twenty-two now, and a man. Best to prepare for the worst. Most likely, the aristocratic boys at his boarding school had made quick work of his extraordinarily gentle nature and had turned him hard and self-satisfied or, worse yet, priggish. She had never cared for those types, though she was very aware, and even disappointed, that she had little experience with any type of boy.

Yet the more she thought about it, the more she convinced herself that Paul hadn't changed at all. The boy she'd known would be an assiduous pupil, living and studying in a studio near the university and its medical library, content with that monkish sort of life.

After so many weeks had passed that Lili was afraid she would never hear from him, Paul contacted Sonia to accept the dinner invitation.

The thought of seeing him again left her feeling giddy. *I must make it clear to him that I've grown up, too,* she thought, as she searched desperately through her armoire for something that might make her look more mature and possibly even alluring. Of course there was nothing there that she hadn't seen before, so she settled on a plain, dark dress with a discreetly draped neckline set just below her collarbone, which seemed to her suddenly too white and slightly protruding.

In exasperation, she examined her reflection more closely in the full mirror of the armoire. Though she'd just turned eighteen, she looked barely sixteen, especially when she smiled. When she wasn't smiling, she looked rather too serious. Her mouth was small, "like a perfect pink bow on a beautiful gift," as her mother had once said to reassure her. Her skin was a pale cream in contrast with the dark hair and eyes. Her curls needed constant attention because, if left untamed, they could make her look like a Medusa, as her brother never hesitated to remind her. No, she told herself, she was not especially pretty, and definitely not alluring. That wasn't new, though, so why did she feel so terribly disappointed with herself tonight?

When the doorbell sounded, she couldn't stop herself from rushing to answer it. Heat burned her cheeks, and when she opened the door she wondered which of them blushed more deeply. Paul's hazel eyes looked down into hers, and for a long, embarrassing moment she was transfixed by their colors, the green becoming yellow brown. To relieve the awkwardness, Lili had no choice but to reveal her baby smile and blurt out that her mother had sent all the way to the baker in the Marais for a challah for him tonight, and it wasn't even Shabbat. Paul grinned and said, "We all know that the Rosenswigs have never been as observant as the Assoulines, and now your *maman* is trying to make up for it in a single night." They both laughed. It was understood that Uncle Eli had come from Turkey to France and considered himself essentially Jewish, while the Rosenswigs preferred to think of themselves as French first. As when they were children, Lili and Paul were in cahoots now, and from that moment, she knew they could be friends in a way that had nothing to do with the family.

By the time they were called to dinner, the warm flush that tinged her face had traveled down over her chest. For that reason alone, it was a relief that Paul was seated on the other side of Henri, who was next to her. For most of the meal, she couldn't see his face as he answered all of her parents' tediously polite questions about medical school, his living quarters, and so forth. But from time to time, Henri leaned back in his chair and she caught a glimpse of Paul. He was tall, and his face had filled out nicely, with the surprise of a slight dark shadow of beard on one so fair. She recognized from their childhood his elegant profile and long lashes under a pronounced, curved brow. His straight, nearly black hair was brushed neatly into place. He was really quite handsome, with a natural dignity that hid behind his unchanged modest and gentle demeanor. For one moment, he caught her eye and they exchanged glances, before Henri leaned forward again and Sonia came up with yet another silly question to interrupt their silent communication.

"Maurice, don't you think we should introduce Paul to the Solène family? They're good clients of our antiques," she confided to the rest of the table. "Suzanne de Solène and her brothers are about Paul's age, and I heard the boys are almost ready to begin their medical studies. Their father is a renowned surgeon, and I think you would enjoy him, Paul. In fact, you would enjoy all of them. Suzanne is a beautiful girl. Don't let me forget to make an introduction," she said, beaming.

Lili wanted to accompany Paul to the door the minute the dinner was over. By some miracle, he seemed to be waiting to be with her, too. They walked together in awkward silence to the foyer, but at the door he turned and said, "Let's step out into the hall for some air." They crossed the threshold, out of earshot of the others.

"Have you been to the art deco brasserie La Coupole, on Montparnasse?" he asked. It was the largest and most famous restaurant in Paris; she'd walked by it just to peek inside. She shook her head, her breathing shallow, and waited to hear what he would say next.

"It's extraordinary. I'd like to show it to you. Would you want to meet me there tomorrow afternoon? I mean, if you think you could . . . get away on a Saturday." She nodded, not knowing how to sound as casual and sophisticated as she longed to be at a moment like this. "Can you be there at three o'clock, on the terrace? My classes are over by then."

"I can be there," she said, quietly thrilled, sure she could work out the details.

"Good. I'll find you there. Until tomorrow," said Paul. He bent over her hand, took it in his, and brushed the air above it with a kiss, with great formality. When he looked up he was smiling in jest, and she again recognized the boy she had grown up with.

The next day at La Coupole, Paul led her through its striking domed interior, across the mosaic floors, and past red velvet benches and columns painted by artist friends of the restaurant owner.

"This has always been a gathering place for artists. I've seen Matisse in the corner there, sipping his beer. And the exotic dancer Josephine Baker comes here with her pet cheetah. I remember when you wanted to dance," he said, suppressing a smile.

"That was ballet. I was terrible at it." She frowned at the memory.

"And now you're working in fashion, really working. I'm proud of you, Lili. What do you want from it?"

She tilted her head and thought before answering. "I want to create, to bring my ideas to life. I can't just stay at home. And you, Paul . . . I never expected you to become a doctor."

"No one did, especially my parents. But I couldn't allow myself to end up a selfish rich boy like so many at my boarding school. We're alike, you and I."

By the time they were seated, they had eyes and ears only for each other. After that, they met every Saturday afternoon. It was understood that these were secret rendezvous, and they mentioned nothing about them to Lili's family. They were both a little nervous during their private encounters, though any observer would have seen merely a proper young couple passing the time quietly at a corner table, but it wasn't long before even their silences no longer seemed awkward. Hesitantly at first, then in a more relaxed and honest way, they began to discuss all sorts of things. Away from Henri's dominant presence, they were able to open up.

After a few weeks, Paul asked her directly, "Lili, where do you tell your family you go on Saturdays?"

She blushed and turned away, then said confidently, "I tell them I'm at a special etiquette class for girls, offered by my old school, to learn to become a lady. Papa is delighted with that."

"Really?"

"No, of course not!" Already she was sorry at having teased him. It was terrible enough to lie to her parents. "I say I'm at the cinema with my girlfriends. I've had to make up entire movie plots to tell them."

"You really are very creative," he said, staring at her with what she hoped was admiration.

"And what do you tell people about *your* Saturdays?" she asked.

"I've no one to lie to but myself. And I've stopped doing that." He paused, watching her, and his hand moved onto hers under the table. "Lili, I care for you. You're much more than a cousin to me. Tell me that you feel it, too."

His hand squeezed hers, and tingles became stirrings of romantic excitement that surged through her in anticipation of something that she dared not imagine in detail.

"Yes." It came out as a whisper. "I do."

Over a short time, they began to discuss a future together obliquely, but it seemed certain. It felt natural to fall in love, and a future together was the only one Lili could imagine.

Her days at Sabine Rouelle were exhilarating and occupied her completely. But when she came home at night, exhausted from her new routine, her thoughts were of Paul. She lived for their Saturday afternoons together and longed to see him more frequently. "Couldn't we meet some weekday evening? I'm sure I could find a pretense to go out," she asked him one day.

He pushed aside his glass of red wine and put his hand over hers. "I'd like that, too. But I'm afraid it's not possible, not right now. My studies don't allow for it," he said gently.

Embarrassed that she may have been too forward, she covered up by throwing back her hair, then said lightly, "Your studies shouldn't take up all your time. It's not healthy. You doctors should know better."

He opened his mouth to speak, hesitated, closed it again, and looked away uncomfortably. When he looked back, his eyes were steady and intense.

"Lili, I have other obligations that have nothing to do with medicine. That's all you need to know. Please don't ask me about it again."

"But, Paul," she protested, unable to stop herself. He put his index finger to her lips to quiet her.

Abruptly he stood and reached into his pocket for change, which he flung on the table. "Let's go, Lili. I'll walk you across the river."

He was serious. Could it be another woman? If not, what could he be so reluctant to tell her? She knew such thoughts could drive her crazy. She must trust him—hadn't she always? In time, she hoped, he would tell her.

As they walked, she talked about how much she liked her work, a neutral topic. Inside, she felt nervous and tight, but when she looked up at Paul, his strong profile was reassuring. He held her hand and listened quietly as they crossed over the Seine at the Pont Alexandre III, with its bird's-eye view of last year's World's Fair site. He stopped her midway and pointed to the specter of the massive German pavilion, whose swastika and giant bald eagle had been dismantled but cast a permanent shadow of Nazism over the city. She watched his jaw clench and his hazel eyes narrow before he spoke. "We can never allow them here, Lili. I'll do everything in my power to keep them out of France and far from us."

Paul seemed lost in thought, and Lili was quiet the rest of the walk, troubled and confused by the threats to their future. She insisted that Paul leave her several blocks away, to avoid being seen together by her family. While she was protective of the secret she and Paul shared, she hated being left out of his. She needed this time alone to think about it and to loosen the knot in her stomach.

The apartment was quiet—unusual, Lili thought, for this late time of day. She heard hushed voices coming from behind the shut salon door. They must be gathered there for cocktails. A woman's voice dominated, gaining strength. It was unfamiliar, accented. When Lili entered, the voice quieted, and she saw that two guests were with her parents and Henri. A diminutive woman, her graying hair pulled back into a bun, looked apprehensively at Lili through wide-lensed spectacles. Next to her stood a pale-faced man, slumping slightly, his arms dangling at his sides. He smiled politely and nodded toward Lili. She felt like an intruder.

Henri broke the silence. "Lili, these are our friends Frieda and Emile Leiben. They were just telling us about their experiences . . . in Germany."

"The Leibens became clients of mine soon after fleeing Berlin for Paris. After Kristallnacht. But I will let them tell their story," Henri said, looking to Frieda Leiben to continue.

She spoke a genteel French with even German rhythms, in a tone that seemed to belie her words about the Night of Broken Glass.

"It was terrifying. At first we didn't understand what was happening.

None of us. The night was dark. Without warning, organized Nazi mobs ran riot. They destroyed a synagogue, then a Jewish-owned business, a Jewish school, Jewish homes. It went on and on, the pogrom. Our German police turned the other way. They did nothing to stop it. Many of the Jews who were attacked were sent to concentration camps, where they're forced into labor and treated with extraordinary cruelty. And this is not just in Berlin. It's happened throughout Germany." Her steady voice began to crack, and Lili shuddered. Until now, she hadn't believed the rumors she'd heard.

Emile Leiben continued the story. "I knew we had to leave right away. Anything could happen now. The next day, I was able to trade some of our fine art collection back to a sympathetic Aryan dealer, whom we'd worked with for years. Somehow he was able to arrange our quick exit to France, where we arrived with nothing but a tiny Rembrandt rolled into my coat pocket. This was the treasure that I brought to Henri, who managed to sell it for us the next day, taking no fee. Naturally, we are extremely grateful." He put his arm around his wife and regarded Henri warmly.

Lili understood how lucky the subdued couple had been to escape the fate Hitler would have had them endure. She looked from her mother to her father to Henri. Their complexions were almost gray in the early-evening light. Each one returned her look, signaling their complicity. The Rosenswigs were aware of the Leibens' story now, but no one would bring it up again.

After that, discussion at the Rosenswigs' home centered on the grand event quickly approaching: Sonia's birthday and the unveiling of the portrait that none of them had yet been allowed to view. It was an effortless topic of conversation that avoided other, less promising realities.

When the much-anticipated day finally arrived, they were all there: Henri and Lili; Maurice and Sonia; Jeanne and Eli, who had arrived from the country; and Paul. In the past, they would have celebrated at a chic restaurant, undoubtedly the family favorite, Maxim's. But, in a nod to Eli's superstitions about making a grand splash in public—which they certainly would have, as Henri was already quite a regular at Maxim's and becoming even more notorious in general—they chose to remain at home. Sonia requested a spectacular menu from the cook, Lucie, and the mysterious painting awaited them on the wall of the salon, behind closed doors.

That evening at eight o'clock, Maurice asked the group to assemble outside the door of the salon while Sonia was inside with Lucie, arranging herself just so in the red chair next to her portrait. The fact that this scenario ran contrary to the rules of a usual surprise party made it all the more exciting.

As befit a night of celebration, they were dressed to the nines, perfumed and coiffed. When the clock in the entry chimed, Lucie opened the door to the salon just enough to reveal her small face, framed in tight black curls, beaming broadly.

"*Entrez, tout le monde*," Sonia called.

There she sat, posed like a queen on a big red throne, wearing a new white dress, her elbow resting on the gilded wood frame of the chair, her head leaning on the index finger of her left hand. Her right hand was placed in her lap and showed off her emerald ring, which glimmered in the last rays of the sun setting through the window. Behind her a small table was hidden, a prop for a vase of jubilant yellow mimosas with dark-green stems, which framed her head and the warm, reddish waves of her soft hair. Her clear blue-green eyes tried to remain serious as she looked at her family, waiting for their reaction.

On the wall just to her left, inside a heavy gold frame, was a vision of the image they had in front of them. It was Sonia, certainly, but seen through a prism that filtered out any imperfections, any marring of the perfect balance of color and form. It was clean, pure, and calm, charming in its elegant composition of body and chair, the sensual, arabesque shapes that were the expression of Madame Rosenswig. This was her home, seen as faultless through the eyes of Monsieur Matisse, where she was at the center and accommodated perfectly.

A single "Aah!" emerged from them in unison. Maurice had been the first to enter the room. He walked right up to the portrait. Slowly and deliberately he stepped back, then walked to one side, then to the other, never taking his eyes off the woman in the frame. "Look. Her eyes follow me wherever I go. It's like the *Mona Lisa*. The *Mona Sonia!*" He looked at his joyous wife and released a laugh of glee, tinged with relief.

"Sonia, my dear, it's you! It's as though you'd stepped into the canvas. Matisse has captured your presence in body and in spirit." Elated, he bent to kiss her on the cheek. She radiated her contentment, and they stood together to admire the portrait. Monsieur Matisse had succeeded. But unlike the Mona Lisa's, Sonia's expression hinted at no wicked secrets. She was a model of purity and love.

With his arm around his wife's waist, Maurice turned them both to face the others and said, "This is something that will be in our family forever."

Letting go of Sonia, he approached Henri and placed his right hand on his son's shoulder. "Henri, thank you. Thank you for making this possible. I shall always remember this moment."

"And so shall I, Papa," answered Henri, clearly surprised and deeply moved by his father's expression of gratitude.

In the next room, the table was set with the same delicate Limoges porcelain that had been with Sonia since her childhood. Lili, too, loved the pretty little birds on the exquisite plates. When she was young, she was sure she heard them chirping, and she always felt cheerful around them. Next to each plate was a champagne flute. Tonight they poured only Veuve Clicquot, which Lili adored. Anyway, champagne was in vogue, and it was so much easier than switching from whites to reds to Sauternes. How they were in heaven with their flutes and their bubbles, Lili thought, stealing a glance at Paul.

Sonia was in the seat of honor; the red chair had been brought into the dining room so she could continue to reign and mark her end of the table as the most grand. Next to her, of course, was Maurice; he always insisted on sitting next to his bride, even when Lili and Henri had been small children and also wanted that spot. Eli was on the other side of Sonia, next to Jeanne, then Paul. Lili, predictably, was between her father and Henri. She and Paul exchanged looks across and down the table, hoping next year they would be placed side by side, and tried to flirt behind their smiles. Did the family guess anything, or were Lili and Paul forever children in their relatives' eyes?

"So, Henri, tell us," teased Eli, "is Albert still *maître d'hotel* at Maxim's? I could almost return there just to see that wonderful fellow. I think he deserves full credit for returning the restaurant to its place of glory. Does Hélène de Montesquieu continue to hold forth in the upstairs room?"

"Yes, Uncle, Albert is, thankfully, in charge, and the place is, as always, the cat's meow. You really should go back one day. But"—he winked slyly—"as for what scandals happen in the upstairs room, I really couldn't say."

Dessert was Lucie's own version of the Bombe Maxim's, a delightfully layered ice cream confection that she decorated with pink rose petals and carried in on a huge platter. "Ah, I've forgotten something," said Henri, and he stood and left the table, returning with his newest *appareil de photo*, a camera that took colored pictures. He wanted to take a portrait photograph of the whole family gathered around the new painting—"a portrait of a portrait," as he said. After the final coffees, Henri herded everyone back into the salon, with Sonia in the red velvet chair, carried back to its place, and the rest of the family arranged so that the portrait was visible behind her.

When they were set in place, Lili looked around at the family: Uncle Eli, strong, worldly, if a bit eccentric, the charm against the evil eye—a traditional filigreed hand with a blue lapis eye embedded for extra protection—hanging from a slim chain onto his chest; fun-loving, innocent Auntie Jeanne, always so glamorous and cared for, wearing for this special private occasion one of her magnificent jewels, a rivière necklace of diamonds and sapphires; Maurice, at this moment particularly proud and patrician, his hand resting gently on the back of his wife's chair; Sonia, a vision of loveliness; Henri intently setting up his new photographic equipment, leaving himself just a moment to run to his position on one side of his mother. Lili stood on her other side, in a well-cut sheath dress with a discreetly dropped neckline and a modest string of pearls. Paul stood behind her, their hidden fingers touching, almost entwined. They were smiling when the camera went off, caught in a frame of blissful innocence. It was a scene they would all remember forever, even without the help of a photograph.

•7•

Paris, Early Fall 1939

It was a glorious, sunstruck morning. Bombs were falling in Poland, but still the threat felt most keenly to some in Paris that day was from brilliant-hued autumn leaves, just tinged with brown, on the verge of taking flight.

Jeanne was visiting again, this time without Eli, and Sonia had planned for them what was to be a perfect day—luncheon in the frescoed tea room at Ladurée, then off to the ultrastylish Salon Antoine, where Sonia had recently secured a "standing," a weekly rendezvous where Monsieur Antoine himself would supervise the continued sheen and curl of her titian locks. Jeanne was fortunate to be squeezed in for an appointment at the same time.

The scandals of the tabloids were often leaked here first, for Antoine's regulars were among the most fashionable and worldly in Paris, and sometimes those women, linked to powerful men, were privy to bits of information that took wing at Antoine's. It was also here that Jeanne heard more in an afternoon than she ever had in the countryside. She was anxious to bring the news back to the rue La Boétie.

A cool gust, a hint of the inevitability of winter, blew into the apartment when she and Sonia returned in the late afternoon. Lili and her father were perusing auction catalogs together in a corner of the salon. Discarded brochures of nineteenth-century antiques lay strewn at their feet. Lili looked down at them, thinking how the whole world of the last century was truly gone.

"Thank goodness you're home!" Jeanne entered breathlessly. Maurice, startled, rose from his chair. A classic beauty with shoulder-length, light-brown waves, Jeanne had always succeeded in resisting trends and maintaining her own elegant style, even under the pressure at Antoine's. But where was her usual calm and warm smile? Her dazed look made clear that her perfect day of beauty, barely ended, was already in the past. Sonia came in right behind her, looking grim but unsurprised. "You won't believe what I heard today at Antoine's, will they, Sonia?" Jeanne stepped into the center of the room.

"Well, all the talk, as you might well imagine, was about the monstrous behavior of Germany and whether it would dare to invade France. In the chair next to mine was a woman whose husband, it is whispered, was a government minister during the last war. She leaned over and quietly told me that this morning at breakfast he'd said to her that the worst thing that can happen is that we all become German. 'I can tell you,' he said, 'that I'd rather be a living German than a dead Frenchman. And others agree with me.' Then she winked, as though I were in conspiracy with her and her idiotic husband. Unbelievable! Is this really what others are thinking?"

Maurice rolled his eyes at her naïveté and said, "Maybe not everyone. But we cannot allow ourselves to be too complacent." She wasn't listening.

"Then I heard something else equally unbelievable. An important Jewish family in Vienna had all their possessions seized by the Reich, and even then they had difficulties in leaving the country. The family had tremendous collections, including Old Masters." Her words came at a gallop, reaching an increasingly higher and faster register.

"'Oh my God,' I realized. 'That is I. It could be us! I must tell Eli.'" The look of indignation she wore began to crumble under the weight of her realizations. She stood before them on the verge of tears. Sonia looked on her cousin with empathy, but it was Maurice who rushed first to lift an arm to comfort her.

Lili knew what her father was thinking: that Eli had admirably protected his wife. Until now, at least, he had kept her hidden from the reality of a world beyond.

Could Jeanne be the only one who didn't understand that with the German invasion of Poland on September 1, World War II was now official? Had she not heard about the outrageous Nazi art confiscations throughout conquered Europe, especially from Jewish collections? Or the rumors about Hitler's grandiose plans to build a giant museum in his childhood home of Linz, Austria, to be filled with the finest art that he could get his hands on? No one in the family wanted to break this news to her, so they said nothing.

On the third of September, France had followed England to declare war on Germany. Now all of France was waiting for something to happen. Parisians held their breath, expecting the Germans to advance, but there was not so much as a gunshot. The next weeks dawned unseasonably warm, and in the lingering heavy heat, the tension built to near bursting.

"Lili. Lili!" Henri hissed. She'd just arrived home from seeing Paul and was standing in the dim foyer when her brother stepped out of the salon, startling her. Why hadn't he already gone up to his rooms?

"What now, Henri? It's late and I work tomorrow. Let me go to bed, please."

He grabbed her shoulder and steered her to follow him. "This is important, Lili. Really. Come with me," he whispered. With a deep sigh of inevitability, she let him lead her down the hall to the dark kitchen, where he switched on the bulb and indicated that she sit in the simple wooden chair at Lucie's small table. She could see blackness outside the narrow kitchen window. Lucie had gone home, and their parents had retired to their bedroom for the night.

Henri pulled up Lucie's work stool and sat across from Lili. She saw that he was agitated; he was squinting, thinking, and drumming his fingers on the tabletop. She rarely saw him alone outside of family dinners; they each had their own life now, and she spent most of her time either at work or in secret with Paul.

Henri stopped his fingers and focused on her. It was his old trick to make her wait before he spoke, but this time she could see he was serious. It frightened her.

"You've met my friend Rose Valland, the curator at the Jeu de Paume?" he said. Henri had invited Rose to the Rosenswig home for dinner and to see the Matisse portrait not more than a month earlier.

"Yes, I liked her very much." Lili remembered her as pleasantly serious and entirely committed to her work at the museum. At the time, she had wondered if Henri was seeing Rose—they had so much to discuss and obviously enjoyed each other. But when she'd asked him teasingly the next day, he'd dismissed it with a shrug of his shoulders.

"Today Rose asked to meet with me in private, in my gallery when it was closed." He hesitated. "I'm going to tell you something that you must never repeat, ever, as you will understand the consequences to her and to France." The drama of his words caused Lili to look at him with skepticism. Rarely was he this serious.

"And?"

"Rose confirmed as true all the nonsense that we've heard about the museum Hitler is planning to build in Linz. He is voraciously hungry for great art to fill it with and will stop at nothing to get it. He plans to call it the *Führermuseum*, after himself, and it has already been designed by his favorite Nazi architect, Albert Speer, who designed that hideous German pavilion. The museum is to be built as soon as he wins the war, so he'll have somewhere to show off his wartime acquisitions." His fingers tapped again nervously.

Lili stared at him. "And he wants French art, of course."

"Of course. And so does that other Nazi imbecile Hermann Göring, Hitler's number two. Göring jumps at every opportunity to grab up the very best of European art and keep it for himself. He may already have amassed more than Hitler; at least, he's trying to. They say he's a megalomaniac, that as his political clout grows, so does the size of his stomach and the magnitude of his country home, a monstrous residence in Germany that's filled to bursting with stolen art. He calls it "Carinhall" as a memorial to honor his late first wife."

The thought sent a shiver right through her. How could any woman love the monster who was credited with coming up with the idea of concentration camps?

"Is that why Rose wanted to meet with you in private? To warn you about him?"

"No, not just that."

"What then?"

Henri bit his lip. She sensed his legs were looking unsuccessfully for a comfortable position under the table.

"Henri, you must tell me." His agitation would not distract her. She would stare him down if necessary.

"Yes." He cleared his throat. "Rose told me that for the past year, she and her colleagues have been secretly working out the details to take the art out of the Louvre and move it to safety. All this in order to protect it from looting and bombing in case the German army makes it to Paris. They are now beginning the gargantuan task of physically moving nearly every piece of art in the museum, the entire Palace of the Louvre, to various châteaux around France. And through all this, no one else must know."

"But everyone has heard that all French museums were officially closed on August twenty-fifth, as a precaution. How has no one guessed that this is going on?"

Henri shook his head. "The details of such a project must be so complex as to be unfathomable. Rose said there are about sixty of them working now on it. But they need even more help." He ran his hand through his unruly brown curls. "They're trying to pack up an entire palace in just a few days. Rose said to me that they could use me. She trusts me, and I'm an expert at handling art. She's asked me to come by tonight." He looked at her, his gaze intensifying. "She also asked me if I had a knowledgeable assistant with the same convictions as me. 'Perhaps the sister I met at your home,' she said. 'Encourage her to come with you.'"

Lili's heart pounded. To be given this opportunity to do something and not stand by helplessly . . . How could she refuse to get involved? She felt suddenly as if all of France depended on her.

Late on that Indian-summer night, in only a sliver of moonlight, Lili and Henri hurried through the Tuileries Garden toward the imposing contours of the Louvre that rose majestically ahead. Lili often passed this way, but in the near darkness everything once familiar seemed curiously different.

Humid breezes whipped her hair across her cheeks. The daytime heat had not subsided, and she felt damp, but she could not have cared less about that. She cared only that while Hitler's troops were pushing through the borders of Europe, she and Henri had been called upon to do something that mattered, to help keep safe their national art treasures.

As they approached the Cour Carrée, the courtyard entrance to the Louvre, it was blanketed in darkness. They caught a hint of muffled voices, then the idling of truck engines. Without warning, the wide doors of the Louvre pushed open, flooding the courtyard with light. The Cour Carrée was filled with people. Lili looked on, astonished. They were working together like ants in a human chain organized to pass a seemingly endless number of wrapped packages from hand to hand and onto waiting trucks. At once it became real to her, the extent of the conspiracy to evacuate the museum.

Henri took her arm purposefully, and together they skirted the courtyard, making their way to the Louvre's grand entrance. Lili stopped, mesmerized by another scene before them. Inside the museum, at the top of the staircase, half a dozen men carried what looked to be the sacred Greek statue *The Winged Victory of Samothrace*. Her glistening marble body and huge, proud wings were swaddled and strapped into a large and strange contraption, entangled in a web of ropes and dangling from a pulley. The men advanced haltingly and precariously down the many steps to the courtyard. All solidly built, they moved like slow ballerinas, seeming anxiously aware of their cargo's fragility.

"Lili, keep moving. This is not the theater. We must find Rose." Henri pressed her forward.

They climbed the steps to the museum and walked through the first galleries, looking for Rose, then through bare corridors and half-emptied rooms. Where had it all gone? Seeing how many artworks were already off the walls, Lili didn't know whether to feel shock or relief.

"Henri!" a man called out.

Lili turned, but Henri had already rushed from her side to greet a tall figure in the next gallery, half-hidden in the shadow of a column. She watched as the man stretched a long arm around Henri's shoulders and pulled him closer, then kissed him on both cheeks. They stayed close, the man's arm resting on Henri, their foreheads almost touching, and spoke in voices too low for her to understand. She could not make out the man's face but was sure she did not recognize him.

When Henri returned, his face was flushed.

"Who was that, Henri?"

"An American dealer. One of the very best. His name is Peterman."

"Do you know him well? He seemed very familiar with you."

Henri looked away.

They continued through halls and rooms strewn with boxes and wood shavings and bodies hard at work. Soon Rose found them. She arrived smiling beatifically, with her hands pressed together as if in prayer. "Thank goodness you've come. I'll put you to work right away." Rose was a petite and meticulous woman who for the occasion wore a long, loose robe that fell almost to the ground. It was covered with grime. But at that moment she reminded Lili of a nun, devout in her museum calling.

But when Rose looked at Henri, her face softened into a smile of admiration, and Lili could see that whatever her brother thought, Rose had feelings for him. Henri's expertise was required to help with paintings in the next gallery, Rose explained. Her eyes trailed after him as he went, and Lili heard her sigh rather wistfully and murmur to herself, "Why are all the interesting men like that out of reach?"

She turned to Lili and smiled sheepishly. "You can work with me. But you might want to pin up your hair first. The air here is filled with dust from objects that haven't been moved in centuries." She pulled a few hairpins from her pocket.

They walked together into the Galerie Daru, which was filled with two-thousand-year-old statues. Rose threw out her arms expansively. "Look at them all. Most are quite small. Each must be inspected very carefully. It will be your job to record their destiny." Not completely understanding, Lili took the pad and pen she was handed.

Beginning with the smallest sculpture, the staff brought them one by one to Rose. Her intent blue eyes and nimble hands moved deftly over the marble bodies to determine for each a rank in fragility and importance. Rose called out the number for Lili to write down. The pieces were then wrapped and loaded onto tarp-covered trucks that went out in night convoys to the art's various hiding places. Lili later learned that a total of thirty-nine truck convoys departed the Louvre during the art evacuation, each accompanied by museum personnel and surrounded by police on motorcycles. The *Winged Victory* they'd seen that night was on its way to the Renaissance château Chambord, transported on a scenery truck loaned by the Comédie-Française.

They finished the Galerie Daru early the next morning. Henri, who had also worked through the night, came to find them. Like his sister, he was filthy and exhausted but couldn't hide his pride at being a part of things. They went home in the first morning light, talking quietly about how well the French worked together to protect their common heritage.

•8•

Paris, Later that Fall

When Lili was with Paul, everything seemed richer and more vibrant. Their summer romance had fully blossomed on intimate walks in the Garden of Luxembourg; it was there that they shared their first kiss. Lili's once-girlish feelings had raced beyond what she could comprehend or control and into the realm of adult emotion. She would do anything, *everything*, to preserve what they had. To allow the romance to flourish, she and Paul decided that their courtship should remain a secret from their family. Lili was grateful that she did not have to field any pestering questions about where she was going or what she was doing. At home they were quietly preoccupied with more insidious threats.

She knew it was entirely possible that Paul's friends from medical school might have guessed about the two of them, having seen them together so often. But Paul always introduced her as his cousin, without qualification, so did they guess at the truth?

When the couple's need to rendezvous became more frequent and even impulsive, they found a meeting spot more convenient and discreet than the gardens. Lili suggested La Palette, a small café on the Left Bank's rue de Seine that was a favorite of the art students and faculty of nearby Beaux-Arts. She was fascinated by its louche reputation, which reminded her somehow of her young days at the ballet school.

"I'm surprised at you, Lili. You've never shown me your bohemian side," Paul said, amused. "But I'm not taking you there. For one thing, your father would not approve. He'd say I give in to your subversive attractions."

"But my father will never know. We would never tell him. Anyway, you could allow me my subversive attractions if you really cared for me," she said, making her smile so seductive and her words so ambiguous that Paul's expression was shocked, until he realized she was teasing him.

"All right," he said. "The café is far enough from the rue La Boétie that there is little risk of our being recognized here. Very practical."

Walking into La Palette for the first time, Lili saw instantly that it was perfect. Discarded painter's palettes dripping with dried colors hung as decoration above the bar, and the place was packed with students and smoke and animated conversations about art. Laughter drifted from the bar, and Lili looked in time to see a handsome artist type detaching cups filled with a green liquid from hooks on his jacket and passing them around to his friends, who wore kaleidoscope glasses. He flirted with an attractive woman in a long gown with large, naked breasts drawn onto the bodice.

Paul frowned. "It's absinthe in those glasses, Lili. "The Green Fairy," they call it. Those are the young surrealists. You know, this is exactly the atmosphere that your father wants to protect you from." She didn't answer, but she could see why. It was almost dangerous but also exciting and seductive, and she liked that. And Paul couldn't resist her enthusiasm.

At La Palette they always sat indoors, even in the finest weather. Paul agreed that the café's rather dark interior suited their need for intimacy; it was together at a small, worn wooden table in the corner that they began to plan their future in earnest.

One afternoon Paul telephoned Lili at the workshop and asked her to meet him there, though he gave her no special reason. She arrived first and, as their favorite table was taken, stood near the bar to wait for him, examining the dirt on her new black suede pumps, not yet broken in. Her ankles hurt after her fast-paced walk there. She would not have worn the new shoes had she expected to come to La Palette today.

When she looked up, Paul was standing at the door, scanning the room. He didn't see her immediately, and she watched his face fall. But the moment he caught sight of her waving, his expression transformed into a radiant smile. She felt his warmth when he kissed her cheeks. They sat, and he took both her hands between his. His expression was earnest, full of hope.

"Lili, I can't wait any longer. I just want to be with you—all the time. I barely concentrate on my studies, and I don't know what to do about it. Soon they'll have me working on patients, and I'm worried I'll forget to examine something essential because I'll be thinking about you. That would be inexcusable. I want to talk to your father. I will tell him that it's for the sake of medicine that I'm asking for your hand. I'll beg him, if necessary—he will have to say yes. What do you think?" His eyes rested on hers, waiting for her answer.

She searched for the right words. She wanted to tell him she had always known they'd be together, was certain that they would make each other happy. He waited, still holding her hands, his hazel eyes intent on her. She was about to speak, when she saw him wince, as somewhere from behind them came a siren, starting as a low whine, then rising to a drawn-out banshee shriek.

"Air-raid drill!" someone shouted above the din. A rush of bodies rose and fled en masse toward the street, slowing into a crush at the main exit. Without a word, Paul took Lili by the elbow and tried to maneuver out the café's door, but they were caught in the center of the crowd. She was aware of scuffling and a powerful movement behind her; a big burly fellow, his large backside turned sideways, fell heavily against her. Lili's ankle twisted in her new shoe. She stifled a cry as the man threw her painfully off-balance. She fell to the floor as white dots played behind her eyelids.

Within a moment, Paul was holding her upright, balancing her with a steady arm around her waist. He looked at her swelling ankle and shook his head. "I'm afraid it's a sprain. Don't try to walk. Let's go to my flat; I have my medical bag there." The siren was just another practice drill, and the crowd would scurry to an air-raid shelter, much farther away. It only made sense to go to Paul's instead.

Her knee was bleeding. He picked her up over her valiant but impractical protests and insisted on carrying her all the way to his building, on the rue de Buci, and up the flight of stairs to his flat, while her ankle pulsed with pain. He nodded at the concierge on the way in and managed to wrestle his key from his pocket and into the lock without putting her down. Inside, he deposited her gently in an armchair that he pushed up next to the bed so she could elevate her feet. He left her there and went to the kitchen alcove to get his medical supplies. He was oddly quiet throughout.

It had become a private joke between them that she had been begging him to allow her to see his flat. His strong sense of propriety had not permitted it until now. She looked around at the spartan decor. The essential chair, bed, and small kitchen were out of balance with the extremely large writing table, covered with medical books and papers, that anchored the opposite half of the room. The ornate desk reminded Lili of the one in Paul's father's study at Le Paradis.

"A monk could live here quite happily," she called out from where she sat, to break the silence.

She could see Paul through the doorway. He must have heard, but instead of answering, he concentrated his attention on filling a deep tub at the sink with scalding water. When he came back, he placed the steaming tub next to her, then brought in a clean towel and his medical bag.

"Or an extremely dedicated doctor could live this way," Lili said, again hoping to renew conversation. Paul just smiled. *Could he really be this shy?* she wondered, watching him dip the towel into the hot water and hold it out for a moment in the air to cool. She saw his muscles tense when he gave it a strong twist and reached out to wash the blood gently from her knee with the warm, damp cloth. It felt surprisingly soothing.

"An extremely dedicated doctor can also appreciate a beautiful knee," he finally said, somehow avoiding looking directly at her. He knelt so that his hands could move more easily down to her red and swollen ankle, eased her pump from her heel, and carefully peeled off her short stocking. She tingled while he explored the swelling with his fingertips, lightly touching her ankle, her foot, then her toes.

"It's just a sprain, and not terribly severe. But it will take some time to heal. I know it can't feel good," he said professionally.

"But it does," she whispered. As she watched him touch her, the warmth from the tub seemed to envelop her in a rising heat that climbed slowly but relentlessly up her legs, turning them almost pink, and settled there at the top, causing her to quiver almost unbearably. She reached out and placed her moist palm on Paul's hand, pulling it up her calf to her thigh.

He looked at her, astonished. No longer thinking, she drew him up toward her. She could feel his breath on her neck, and they kissed—but not the timid kisses they had shared in the gardens. These were longer, deeper. She shut her eyes, not wanting him to stop. His breath came more quickly. Suddenly, he pulled away.

"No, Lili. We can't; we shouldn't," he said, moving backward, shaking his head.

Their bodies separated, but his gaze never left hers. Day was darkening to night, and a shadowed light radiated in from the street. It was *l'heure bleue*, the hour of blue twilight, between daylight and darkness, when everything felt otherworldly. Lili rose to stand on her good leg. "Our world may end tomorrow," she said. "Yes, we should."

"No, don't stand!" He moved toward her again, cupping one hand under her derriere to steady her as his other arm wrapped around her back. He held her close to him; her head dropped back, and she shut her eyes. They stayed still like that for nearly a minute. Then his lips grazed her cheek, her neck. "You're so soft," he murmured, and, lifting her, carried her to the bed.

There was no question now, no turning back. She watched him pull off his shirt. When he lay down next to her, he picked up her hand

and placed it on his bare chest. His skin was warm to her touch, and she could feel his torso rising and falling to the rhythm of his heart. She spread her fingers and pushed against its firm muscles, feeling his heartbeat quicken. Then he lifted his head above hers, and she lost herself in his golden eyes while he unbuttoned her blouse. He kissed her collarbone. His lips, his tongue, his touch, the scent of his hair . . . She closed her eyes to anticipate each new sensation as he moved down her body. She held his head between her hands and pulled him to her. She was not afraid.

After, they remained curled up together, held in each other's thrall. When Paul spoke, his voice was husky. "Do you have any idea how long I've cared for you? When we were small, I was nervous around you, a little girl, and I didn't understand why. You were exciting, and at the same time I wanted to protect you. I didn't care how domineering Henri acted or what mad adventures he took us on—I wanted to be with you. I still do. But I won't think of you as a little girl ever again. Our bodies were meant for each other. There will never be anyone else for me."

She touched his cheek and gently drew his face close to hers, then lightly brushed back his hair so she could look into his eyes. His black lashes seemed to float over calming pools of caramel flecked with olive as he returned her gaze with a look that was steady, unhesitating. She had no doubts. "Nor for me, Paul. I've never wanted anyone but you." Saying it, finally, she felt completely sated and closed her eyes.

"Lili, there's something more you need to know about me." Maybe she'd been asleep for only a few seconds, but his words startled her out of her trance. Involuntarily, her body pulled away from him.

He reacted with a gentle smile that she knew was meant to appease. "I don't want to scare you; I just want you to understand me completely, so there are no big surprises. Have you been to the Catacombs? I will tell you there."

"You can't mean the underground ossuary, where they keep bones from the dead." Her eyes widened, and Paul kissed her.

"Yes," he said, reaching over and entwining her hand with his. "Don't worry. It's actually quite beautiful."

The next day they met in the public square, Place Denfert-Rochereau, at the entrance to the Catacombs. Paul seemed to delight in not offering any further explanation until he had taken her inside. Lili was far more concerned about what Paul needed to tell her than about why he had chosen to bring her here, the resting place for bones unearthed from overflowing Parisian cemeteries of past centuries. He took her hand and began to lead her down a narrow spiral stone staircase that continued deep into a world that quickly became dark and silent. Lili felt dizzy until they stopped and Paul pulled a flashlight from his pocket and flipped it on. They had arrived in a twisting hallway. He washed the light over walls of mortared stone. She could smell the dampness.

"We won't see much, yet. Not for a kilometer or so. You're not too afraid?" He grinned.

She shivered from the cool air, the prospect of dirt and bones, and especially in anticipation of what Paul was going to reveal about himself. She already saw aspects of him she hadn't known existed: an ability to lead a secret life, and a taste for the macabre. She was frightened, but she would not let on. "Of course not. I like it here," she lied, knowing he couldn't believe her.

"Good. It will get more interesting when we arrive at the bones."

They continued, Lili putting one foot before the other behind Paul, pulling her coat tighter around her. Water gurgled just beyond.

"That's the aqueduct. We're almost there." Paul sounded excited. A minute later he flashed the light on a stone portal, trailing it up to an ominous inscription: "Halt! This Is the Empire of Death."

We can't be going in there, she thought, shooting Paul a bleak look.

"Ignore the sign, Lili. We're here!"

Paul pulled her with him into a chamber with walls of carefully stacked bones. Skulls, tibias, femurs, all shades of white and precisely arranged into patterns. A skull face, embedded between thighbones, seemed to watch her.

"It goes on and on like this," he said, shining his light to illuminate halls and caverns that lay ahead, all lined with bones, neatly organized. "It is extraordinary, isn't it?"

"Yes, it is," she said, turning around slowly, trying to take it all in despite the dim light. "The beauty, the geometry, of the bones—I've never seen anything like it. How far have you explored?"

"I come here several nights a week."

"But why? Is it for school? To study bones?"

Paul suppressed a laugh. "No. Something else, which is what I brought you here to tell you. When I first arrived in Paris and began my practicum, I met some patients in the hospital, young refugees of all sorts from Germany and Eastern Europe. We talked about their lives; I liked them. One day they invited me to one of their meetings, here in the Catacombs."

"Meetings? About what?"

"I don't think you'll like what I have to say." She felt her chest tighten and her body brace. "We arrange for the smuggling of refugees out of Nazi territories and provide shelter and medical attention to illegals, and we plan what we'll do when the Nazis make it to France. That sort of thing." He was trying to make it sound trivial, but how could he?

"Paul, I'm astounded. I had no idea. . . . You never told me." She bit her tongue. Of course he hadn't told her; he had known she would object.

But now she felt angry. "Why are you associating yourself with that? What you're doing could be terribly dangerous. Don't you know it's safer to stay away from such activities, such people? Why do you endanger yourself, our future? Why get involved?" She heard herself speaking like a wild shrew across the cavern and couldn't stop, although she had to wonder: Was what he was doing really so different from her work at the museum?

Paul's eyes softened, but there was conviction in them. "Lili, you have to understand something about me. I can never forget that I've been handed so much good fortune. I feel responsible—not just for you and for me, but for everyone. It's in my nature. There's nothing you or I can do to change that. You must accept that about me."

Paul stood firm; his strong chin was set defiantly, his dark hair waved in the dampness, his thick brows pulled together. But his eyes implored her. She could not return his look. Instead she let her gaze fall over his broad shoulders and down his long, lanky body, and by the time they reached his dust-covered shoes, she had relented.

Of course. Paul has always done what is right, what's best for everyone. He has always been noble. Would she want to change him, even if she could?

She took a step toward him. "I just want us to be together. Is there something wrong about that?"

"Not at all. I hope one day soon to live with you at Le Paradis. But nothing is inevitable, especially happiness. I see death every day at the hospital, people struggling to hang on. Look around us. These bones represent six million lives, layer upon layer, all forgotten."

Lili felt the tears welling in her eyes. "Promise me you'll never go to battle or do something stupid."

"I'm a doctor. You know I could never fight. And I hope you don't think I'm stupid." He lifted his hand to wipe away her first tear. She knew he was trying to humor her.

"I don't know, Paul Assouline. You may be too heroic for me."

"Lili, I just want to make sure you know me. That you'll be able to tolerate me. It's you who has always known how to make the best of things. Without you, I'm not sure what hope I'd have left." His brows furrowed, and his eyes were deep and serious as he watched her. "Are you with me?"

Lili nodded. "Yes, I'm with you."

"Good," he whispered, and she saw his face relax. "Tomorrow I will go speak to your father, to ask for your hand."

It was no secret that Maurice thought of his daughter as still a child and Paul as a precocious young nephew. The perfect moment to approach him to ask for Lili's hand would be when he had no time to think of a reason to say no, when her parents didn't care that the two were distant cousins or that Lili was young and Paul had years more as a medical student before he could establish a practice. The moment when everyone could immediately comprehend that the couple's lives could make no sense to them until they were married.

But the moment they stepped inside the Rosenswigs' apartment, Lili was aware that something was not right. The heavy double doors to the salon were closed for only the third time in her memory, and Henri's muffled voice was audible from where they stood out in the hall. She let go of Paul's hand to knock on the door softly, with growing trepidation. "Hello, Henri? May we come in?" She pushed on the handle.

Sonia was seated stiffly, as though at attention, in her red chair; Maurice stood nearby, leaning his elbow on a large bureau. Their attention was focused on Henri, who stood across from them, framed by the gray silk curtains of the wide window as though he were the only actor on a stage.

"Lili, you've come home just in time. And Paul is with you? So much the better," Henri spoke with unfamiliar gravity. "Please sit down for what I'm about to tell you. You too, Papa."

She felt her heart sink into her stomach. The heavy mood in the household took up all the air, leaving no room for her and Paul. She could tell by Paul's expression that he recognized it, too. For a fleeting moment, she felt only exasperation and wondered how Henri's news could possibly be more important than her own.

"You have heard rumors of what is happening elsewhere in Europe," Henri began. "We seem to prefer, as a family, to dismiss them without much discussion, as though that will keep it far away from us. But I have heard so much disturbing news that I can no longer dismiss it. We cannot just sit here comfortably and wait to see what might happen next." He paused to assure himself of their full attention. "Paris and France are already taking measures against a possible invasion by the Reich, and so should we."

Henri looked at his father. "We cannot continue to live in an eternal present. For us as Jews, especially, it is a far more serious situation. The Nazis are moving toward us. We have to consider that the worst may happen, and prepare ourselves. We must talk about leaving Paris as soon as possible."

Maurice took in a deep breath of air that filled his cheeks, and then blew it out. "Nonsense!" he said indignantly. "We lived through the last war, and we'll live through this one."

"Papa, this one is different," Henri said quietly.

Lili felt her exasperation turn to shame. How foolish, how selfish she had been to put her own desires first, as though she could defy the inevitable.

As could be expected, Henri had planned everything out. Having gained his ground, he moved around the room like an impresario, talking quickly, leaving no time for questions. "I think the family would be safer, and I would certainly feel better, if you joined the Assoulines at Le Paradis, if Paul's parents will have us. It is remote enough to remain out of the fray, at least for a while. You should take the essentials and leave unobtrusively—in the car, if they're willing to send it. I'll stay here long enough to pack up my gallery and arrange to have the art shipped to Le Paradis for safekeeping."

"But what about my antiques? I can't just leave them here. What will happen to them?" Maurice, in bafflement, threw out his arms and waited for an answer.

"Maurice, we may not have much time. Let Henri put them in his basement or try to sell them quickly, as a lot," said Sonia, reaching her hand onto his knee to calm him.

He gaped at her. "*No!* People would think we were desperate. They'd go for too little, and then when we return to Paris we'll have nothing! What are you thinking?" He turned to her angrily; she glared back.

"Papa, we're not sure when, or even if, we'll be returning to Paris," Henri added cautiously. "I heard that the Leibens left Paris last week for the South. And they are our voice of experience."

Paul spoke up. "The Leibens were right to leave, based on all I've heard, and I'm relieved that you are considering it, too." His eyes met

Lili's briefly. "I'm certain that my parents would want you with them in the safety of Le Paradis. In fact, Auntie Sonia, my mother may never let you return to Paris!"

"Then it's settled," Henri said, with a false finality that seemed intended to end further discussion. He slapped the closest piece of furniture, a shiny mahogany desk, for emphasis.

"I'm not convinced that this is at all necessary. Maybe just for a short time . . . until things blow over," Maurice conceded gloomily.

The next few days were spent packing things up for storage in the suddenly inadequate basement at the rue La Boétie. In the past, the Rosenswig retreats to Le Paradis had been preceded by joyful anticipation, but now the situation was different. They picked their way around wooden containers, half-filled and strewn about once-perfectly appointed rooms, destroying both their geometry and their familiarity. Sonia was quiet as she and Lili packed the Limoges dishes, wrapping each piece carefully in newsprint to keep downstairs safely and indefinitely. Lucie helped them, trying to hide her worry and lift the mood with her chitchat. "Madame, now I can give these shelves a good cleaning before you come back to Paris. I've wanted to do that for a long time. Wait until you see them gleaming!"

Meanwhile, Maurice attempted to direct the fate of his antiques. At first he wanted Henri to ship them to Le Paradis, but finally he settled on keeping them in the basement. He hadn't liked it at all when a couple of less distinguished, and in his eyes disreputable, antiques dealers from another quartier had approached him slyly and asked to buy up his inventory for disgracefully low prices. His face had reddened as he struggled to maintain control, before responding in a deep and determined growl, "Gentlemen, I'm not selling . . . and I'm not leaving!"

How dare they try to take advantage! To add to the insult, he had thought his family's departure from Paris remained a secret.

Lili continued at Sabine Rouelle's, telling them nothing of the Rosenswigs' plans, even though Jean-Pierre and the car would come for them that very week. Though she kept silent, she wondered for how long she would have to say good-bye to her childhood and the familiar surroundings of her home? She and Paul well understood that this was not the right time to approach Maurice about their betrothal; he was already beside himself at the prospect of change. Because she was needed at home every day right after work to help with the packing and closing up of the house, it was impossible for her and Paul to be alone together. She felt the carefree days of their romance slipping away, and it was not clear to her when, or how, they could ever return.

From the time they decided to leave Paris, Sonia made sure that Paul was included at the family dinner table, and Lili was silently thankful that for those few days he gave up his evening meetings. Still, now that the Rosenswigs were preparing to move in with the Assoulines at Le Paradis, her parents were treating him more like a young nephew than like the grown son of her mother's cousin, and insisted on taking care of him. Lili worried that her parents would transform her questionably distant blood relationship with her third cousin into a closer kinship in their minds and would therefore frown upon a wedding.

To be able to speak alone together during those days required furtive planning. One Friday evening when Lili said good-bye to Paul at the door after a family dinner, they quickly arranged to meet the next morning at La Palette.

It was jarring at first to breathe in the fresh, cold air of that early winter morning. As she made her way through a dusting of snow to meet Paul, the route seemed twice as long as it had in the summer. When she reached the café, she saw right away that their special table in the corner was waiting for them—a good omen, she hoped, as she positioned her chair to watch for Paul.

It was unusual for him to be late, and she passed the time tracing his silhouette with her finger on the wooden tabletop. When she looked up and saw him walk through the door, his expression was serious. He had the look of a grown man, one who could be a doctor. His camel overcoat was dusted with melting snowflakes; his dark hair had taken on waves in the moist air. His smile when his eyes found her reassured her that nothing had really changed in their lives. He loved her. They would be married.

When he kissed her on both cheeks, his were a shock of cold against her warmth. He sat in the chair across from hers, took her bare hands in his gloved ones, and studied her gravely. She waited for him to speak.

"Paul?"

"Liliane," he started, "I can't travel with you quite yet to Le Paradis. I need to stay in Paris and continue my studies for as long as possible. I'll come later, I promise you."

He'd told her of the entire medical faculty's concerns that the university would be closed if the Germans approached Paris, and what a difficult interruption to the students' medical education it could be. But now she felt numb.

"My practicum has only just begun," he went on. "This is my opportunity to put my knowledge to use and work on patients. They're going to rotate me through all the Paris hospitals. I'll be able to do my work at last. This is what I've been waiting for." He batted his fist excitedly into his palm, and his brows mounted his forehead, but she scarcely heard what he was saying.

"You must go, Lili, but it's not right that I go now. It would look like I was running away. I'm a doctor, and it is my chosen duty to put others before myself. Besides, as things worsen, the university is expected to come to a forced halt, and that will put my career on hold. Staying here until the situation becomes truly impossible is the only thing I can do."

She wanted to plead with him that he must go with her. Everything around them was changing. She was face-to-face with a dread so deep, she had kept it a secret even from her conscious daytime thoughts. In the coming instability, they could lose each other.

But Paul was so good, so determined. She felt her eyes brimming with tears; she tried to hold them back and not show him the frightened and selfish girl she feared she was at that moment. She remembered Lili the Brave.

"Don't worry," Paul said. "I will join you at Le Paradis. In all likelihood, Henri and I will travel there together for weekend visits."

"Of course," she said, forcing a smile. She wasn't happy to leave Paris, but now to leave Paul, too? As for relying on Henri's schedule, she knew better than that. No matter what Henri said, who could even guess at what her self-important brother would eventually do and when he would decide to join them?

She bit her lip, determined to remain composed. She could see that his mind was made up; there was nothing more she could, or would, say. No matter how she felt inside, he was right.

Paul was expected back at the hospital shortly, and when she rose to leave, her demeanor must have betrayed her, because he took her by the arm and held her back. "Lili, you must believe that I want to secure our future together as much as you do. I want to marry you, and if we don't find a way very soon, we could lose the opportunity. Given the uncertainties, our chances might become even worse. Let me try. I'll go tomorrow to your father."

That evening when Lili answered the door to Paul, she meant to explain that her father was in a bad temper. The stress of packing the family and arguing with Sonia about how much luggage she was attempting to bring had taken its toll on him. But before Lili could warn Paul, he squeezed her hand confidently, then took determined steps past her to the salon, where Maurice paced from window to wall. Most of the beautiful Rosenswig furnishings, including the red chair, had already been carried to the basement for storage, along with Maurice's inventory. The family gathering place was no longer either comfortable or welcoming.

Maurice was lost in thought as Paul entered, followed by Lili. He paused noticeably before he regained his bearings to greet them with a cursory nod and say, as though to himself, "Good. The children are home."

"Papa, speak with Paul. I'm helping Lucie to set the table, if it's still there." Lili shut the salon doors behind her, leaving the two men standing uncomfortably.

Between the pantry and the table, she was of no help at all to Lucie and could not even bring herself to make idle talk. Once, she ran across the wide hall, emptied of its tables and lamps, to listen at the door of the salon for a sign. Nothing.

Paul emerged a few minutes later. He looked discouraged and was shaking his head. "Your father said that he has no time to think about the matter now. That we are young and have our whole lives before us, that you are under no pressure to make such decisions, that I have years of school and practicums ahead of me. And . . . I can't think what more. The main idea was that he doesn't want to even consider it at this time. He's too busy trying to keep everything as it has always been. The poor man. I'm not sure what to do."

Through the dim light, Paul watched for her reaction. She was not good at hiding her feelings from him. True, Papa was not at his best, but could he not understand their urgency, especially given the uncertainties? She was afraid of what might happen if they were separated. If they could be married right away, she could stay with Paul in Paris.

"Papa doesn't understand that we are not children, that we know what we want. Did you tell him that we are ready to be together through those years of school and practicums? Oh Paul, when can it begin?" Her composure failed her.

He reached for her and held her so close that when he spoke, she felt the calm of his words vibrate through her. "Try to be patient. It will happen. I will make it happen. You must believe me."

You must. Her ribs tightened like a cage around her heart, and she could not answer. When she was with Paul, she saw the world through his eyes and wanted to become a better person for it. What would she become without him?

•9•

Paris, A Week Later

If anyone had come to visit the Rosenswigs on the rue La Boétie the day before their planned departure from Paris, the visitor would have questioned whether the family was actually still living in those desolate rooms. Lili felt the emptiness that surrounded her. Only the basement was occupied, and it was piled high with the cheerful cups that held their morning café au lait, Lili's well-loved books, Henri's prized photo collection—she didn't like to see their daily props and long-held treasures displayed so meaninglessly.

This would be, she hoped, her final trip downstairs. She carried with her to storage a small picture book of animals she'd rediscovered behind where her bedroom armoire had stood, one she'd passed many happy hours with as a child. Holding her mouth tightly shut, so as not to breathe in the dust and memories that lingered there, she ran in, placed the book with the others, and turned to run out as quickly as possible, slowing down briefly to pick up a photograph that she saw had fallen to the floor. Back in her room, which held only her bed and her packed luggage, she examined the photo. It was the one Henri had taken the night of her mother's birthday. There they were—all together, happy and unconcerned—with Sonia, beaming, seated by her Matisse portrait. In a swift motion, she tucked it away in her valise.

It was their last day together in Paris, her final meeting with Paul at La Palette. They didn't have long; Paul had stolen a few moments from his shift at the hospital. They shared the same somber mood. Under the table's well-worn wooden top, carved with the initials of other, anonymous pairs of lovers, their fingers touched and their hands caressed, but they spoke little.

"I wish there were another way," Lili said quietly. She looked down, afraid she might cry.

Under the table, Paul squeezed her hands between his own and leaned forward on his chair. When she looked up at him, his face was so close that she could see the green flecks swimming in his eyes. He was gentle, comforting.

"You'll be safe at Le Paradis, and that's what's most important. I'll come to you as soon as I can. We can be married there." He brought her hands to the tabletop and kissed her ring finger. "Lili, I won't let you down. After this mess, we'll live happily ever after—I promise you that."

When she rose to go, they embraced without words. He caressed her hair and then her face. Lili felt him retreat into the silent fears he tried so hard to conceal from her. They walked out together and went in their separate directions.

Outside the café, the skies were gray. It was almost dusk. A newsboy carrying the latest copies of *Le Matin* shouted out its headlines: "Germans Plan Invasion of Norway; Britain Is Said to Be Next—Then What?"

She was determined not to engulf herself in sadness during the long, dreary walk back to the rue La Boétie. She would close her mind to her separation from Paul and to her uncertain future and would concentrate instead on capturing views of her beloved Paris. She stared wide-eyed, like the open shutter of a camera, and chose a different route. Setting off down the narrow rue de l'Université to the Palais Bourbon, she crossed over the riled waters of the Seine to the Place de la Concorde. To her right was the vast palace of the Louvre, and just beyond it the Tuileries Garden, which was flanked on the Concorde side by the near-twin gallery buildings of the Orangerie and the Jeu de Paume. She stopped at the Champs-Élysées and looked up to the Arc de Triomphe; at the Rond-Point she took a detour down the Avenue Montaigne for a last look at the Tour Eiffel, until it almost disappeared in darkness. When she turned to go home, her cheeks were cold and wet and tears blurred her vision.

• 10 •

Paris, Winter 1940–
Le Paradis, Spring 1940

They were up before dawn the next morning. Lili hadn't slept at all, and, from the looks of him, she doubted her father had either. A grayish cast circled his eyes, and his skin appeared pallid and dry. Sonia joined them in the foyer, attempting to show a bright spirit with her halfhearted smile. Of course, no one would admit to having slept badly.

Only Henri reacted with typical bravado: "A stay at Le Paradis is always renewing. Even as short as this one promises to be. How I wish I could go with you!" Lili guessed he was happy to be rid of them for a little while.

Lucie had prepared a nice lunch of baguette sandwiches with roasted chicken and gruyère, a basket of fruit, and a bottle of red wine for the first leg of the trip, and together they waited for the Assoulines' driver, Jean-Pierre, to arrive in the newest black Bugatti. They certainly did not feel as if they were going on a picnic; Lili was already filled with nostalgia, acutely aware that she was being uprooted from the scenes of her childhood and could never again rely upon its cocoon of complete protection. Underneath it all was the private burden of leaving Paul.

Jean-Pierre pulled up to their door while the streets were still quiet and dark. With Henri's help, he methodically crammed most of the luggage into the trunk of the car, minus a couple of Sonia's suitcases, which she implored Henri to send down to her right away. The mood was gloomy, despite the would-be glamour of a car and driver. Sonia, Maurice, and Lili settled themselves behind Jean-Pierre on the soft maroon leather of the backseat. None of them knew quite what to think or say as they waved good-bye to Lucie and Henri. Even Sonia was at a loss, and Maurice could only nod his farewell. Lili leaned against the window and half-closed her eyes, and until the first shimmers of daylight cast shadows on the road, none of them even attempted polite conversation.

"The Germans are stupid, but let's hope they would never be so foolish as to attack France." Maurice spoke suddenly, as though they had been in the middle of a long discussion. He was gazing out the window, perhaps engaged in an ongoing conversation with himself, as he often seemed to be.

"Monsieur Rosenswig, the Germans will never find us at Le Paradis, even if we send them a written invitation. We may as well be in a castle in the sky," said Jean-Pierre, with a scornful gesture of his gloved hand.

"Let's certainly hope not, on both counts. That would spoil the vacation. We're not to discuss it anymore," Sonia said firmly.

This was the end of it, and they made only small talk for the rest of that long day, traveling deep into the Loir-et-Cher. Jean-Pierre stopped the car from time to time for a "picnic" or to allow one or another of them to "take some air."

Late that night when they arrived at Le Paradis, it was too dark to see the beauty of the place. They rushed from the car to the staircase into the house to get out of the rainstorm that had been threatening all day and had suddenly unleashed. When they came into the foyer, they were dripping, and the luggage left small puddles on the marble floor.

"They've arrived, the refugees from Paris!" Eli's heavily accented voice resonated in greeting from where he stood on the mezzanine in his blue robe and matching pajamas, quite dapper. His white smile flashed briefly under his dark mustache, newly flecked with gray.

"Hello, Eli. I suppose we're all refugees now," Maurice answered wearily.

Even at that hour, Jeanne came down to greet them in her nightdress and robe, and with a sleepy smile kissed them each on the cheek. The way she kept glancing into the shadowed corners of the entry, Lili was sure her aunt was hoping to see that Paul had surprised them by coming along.

"Jeanne," said Maurice, "winter at Le Paradis is not exactly the springtime in paradise that we are used to, but we are very happy to be here."

"And we are always glad to see you," she said firmly. "Let's get you to your rooms, and tomorrow I'll ask you if the rest of Paris is really so worried as Paul and Henri."

At Le Paradis, life went on for the Assoulines as it always had, as though the rest of the world didn't exist. And why not? Why should they agitate about something over which they had no control? Were they not better off simply prolonging their beautiful life as it was? Lili could appreciate her aunt's attitude.

Jeanne continued to dress every night for dinner, working her way through, one by one, all her sensational jewels. Annie and her difficult husband, Boris, still presided in the kitchen, and Annie supervised the well-trained staff, who seemed to work invisibly to accomplish everything that had to be done on the estate. There were so many objects to dust, tapestries and furniture that needed covering this time of year to protect them from fading in the sunlight, and clocks that needed to be wound, as well as the daily cleaning of bedrooms, bathrooms, and kitchen to think about. For the family's mealtimes, which were a grand focus, there was the garden to tend; wildlife and fish to be caught; the many plates, crystal pieces, and service dishes to be kept clean and to set on the elaborate dining table; and silver to polish.

It was an enormous job to run Le Paradis, yet it operated like clockwork. The only jarring note was the frequent bickering between Annie and Boris. It was not news to anyone that he sometimes spoke harshly to her, but Lili noticed that Annie no longer made any attempt to hide her irritation with him. They were openly critical of each other when they didn't think they could be overheard, which disturbed Lili enormously. When she brought it up to her mother, Sonia said, "I've heard them, too. This morning Annie called him a money-grubbing coward. I've no idea what she was referring to, but Jeanne doesn't seem to notice."

"Auntie Jeanne has a special ability to overlook things."

"Yes, she does. And Eli allows it. But you, Lili, can be too sensitive for your own good. Try to ignore it, dear. I do. Remember, we're all on edge right now."

To add to their frustration, communication with Paris was typically unreliable in the country. For every ten attempts that Maurice made to call Henri, maybe one went through. Paul didn't even have a phone.

They did have Eli's shortwave radio, and listening to it was Eli and Maurice's favorite indoor activity. During the sacred nightly news broadcasts, they all gathered around the simple pine table in the kitchen. Eli and Maurice sat in rapt attention, but if Lili, Sonia, or Jeanne tried to interrupt the broadcast with their talk, Eli's mustache would twitch and he would make a shooing motion for the women to leave the room.

With the radio in the house, even Jeanne could no longer ignore the situation. She would pour herself a Dubonnet on ice and grit her teeth before joining them. Every night it was the same depressing news: the Germans were marching toward them, invading their neighbors one by one—first Denmark and Norway, then Belgium, the Netherlands, Luxembourg. Wherever they advanced, there was a quick surrender. Slowly but surely, they were approaching Paris.

Lili couldn't help but notice that Eli spent much of his time alone in his library, behind a closed door. When he opened the door to rejoin them, a cloudless scent of smoke followed him, and his lids were half-closed. She had learned by now that Eli loved his hashish, which he kept in the Japanese snuffbox on his desk that she knew so well. Maurice scoffed at what he called "Eli's Oriental affectation."

"Your uncle did not indulge to this extent until now," Sonia told Lili. "We all cope in our own ways."

Eli was insistent that no one wander from the property and risk being seen. He was always one to plan ahead, anticipating the worst. Fortunately, the skies cleared and the weather turned warm, and they could get out to explore the pine forests of the estate. Lili distracted herself by learning the names of wildflowers and counting the deer, which all looked alike until her eyes became trained to note their markings.

One afternoon well into springtime, Sonia, Jeanne, and Lili were deeply sunk into the burgundy velvet sofa in Uncle Eli's study, drinking their aperitifs. Lili was almost at ease for the first time in the long weeks since their arrival. Eli stood like a professor by the large wall map, attempting quite seriously to show them, with the aid of his pointer, the exact progress of the German troops—a topic that depressed them all—when a jubilant Maurice burst into the room.

"I have reached him at last!" he announced gleefully, looking at his wife. "Henri and Paul will be driving here on Friday morning, both of them. It may take a long time, because they're not the only ones leaving. Henri said the train stations and the roads are already jammed. Everyone is in a panic, expecting the Germans to arrive any day. They're driving a truck full of work from Henri's gallery, and I told him he must bring our Matisse!"

Sonia rose, covering her mouth with both hands, but a broad smile spread under them. Watching her parents, Lili realized that in all her missing of Paul, she had hardly given a thought to her capable older brother. Maurice's words drew a delicate shriek of joy from Jeanne, and Eli's shoulders dropped and he turned his back on his maps and his troops to embrace her. As for Lili, hope welled in her heart, and relief: Soon, Paul would be safely with her.

"When will they be here? How long are they staying?" Eli was the first to ask.

"Well, that is something I'm not quite sure about. Our connection was very bad, and we didn't get to it before we were cut off entirely. I didn't ask in time."

"Let's hope it's soon and that they'll not turn right around again to Paris to pick up more of Henri's inventory," said Sonia. "That would be typical of our determined son, and he would convince Paul that he needed him to go along." They agreed to do everything they could to keep their boys at Le Paradis.

When they did not arrive the next day, or the next, or the next, Lili was as anxious as the others. At every hour she came up with a reason to pass by a front window to see if they were approaching. She saw that her mother had resumed her old habit, which she had previously hidden rather successfully from Maurice. Sonia was in the courtyard below, pacing in red heels and a black skirt, one arm wrapped anxiously around her chest, the other holding a long, slender cigarette. She lifted it to her mouth three or four times, slowly letting the smoke escape between each draw, then dropped it onto the gravel and put it out with an angry twist of her foot before hurrying back into the house.

A few days later, they were drinking tea on the terrace overlooking the pond when a loud commotion came from indoors. Annie's voice was raised in excitement, though they couldn't make out her words. Jeanne and Eli looked at each other in annoyance. If the arguments between Annie and Boris had reached this unabashed pitch, something must be done.

"Wait here. I'll handle this," Eli said. He headed toward the foyer.

"Hello, Uncle. Are we in time for dinner? It's been a long day," they heard Henri say. In a single movement, Lili, Jeanne, Sonia, and Maurice rose to press their way inside. There was Paul. His eyes found Lili while he embraced his mother, his tall figure towering over her. A bit awkwardly, but smiling in front of everyone, he let her go and turned to kiss Lili on both cheeks, gently pulling her toward him by the elbow. "Hello, Cousin," he whispered in her ear. She recognized the familiar scent of his dark hair, savoring it.

Henri swept Paul aside to hug Lili, lifting her a few inches off the ground. "Lili, did you miss me?" he teased, perhaps aware and a little jealous of Paul. Then he announced that he had a plan and would tell them all about it at dinner. Paul threw Lili a knowing look. Undoubtedly he had listened to Henri working out the details all the way from Paris.

The entry doors were open. Outside in the courtyard, a pickup truck was parked, so dirty with road dust that Lili could only guess at its color. Upon a closer look, she could see that inside the truck bed was a cloth of some sort covering a tethered-down heap. "Don't worry. Those treasures will be unloaded and stored as soon as we work out where to put them, including Papa's favorite Matisse," Henri called down to her from the top of the stairs, before settling his private effects in his room.

Lili waited while the truck was unloaded and while Paul bathed and changed into slacks and a jacket. Then he came to find her. Alone at last on the terrace, they exchanged a long, sweet kiss—not the kind he had given her in greeting. Behind them, the setting sun of early summer hung precariously low, its orange glow ready to extinguish as it dipped into the horizon. But before they could really speak, Jeanne rang the dinner bell and the rest of the family joined them for a welcome drink in the twilight.

At dinner, Henri told them the whole story. "By the time we'd left Paris, we had to fight for a place in a painfully slow-moving motorcade of overwrought Parisians trying to make their exit. Last night we pulled off the road into an area camouflaged by trees to sleep in the truck for a couple of hours. I hated to lose our place in that race of snails, but Paul insisted we rest. It was impossible to sleep when that noisy rattrap was bumping over every rock in the road. What a different setting it is tonight at Le Paradis."

The table was elaborately laid with Jeanne's most ornate place settings. She wore the ruby necklace that had been the gift of a maharaja to Eli's late father, who had been a banker in Constantinople.

"Ours is a world of contrasts," Paul told the table. It was something he'd said often to Lili.

Henri stood. "A toast to us all and to all the art in Paris, including those works of art and those Parisians temporarily located elsewhere." He raised his champagne, in a delicate-lipped flute of bubbling pink, upward to the crystal chandelier. Sparks of light reflected from one to the other; he extended his glass to all at the table and then in the direction of the truck outside, bathed in a sunset almost as red as Jeanne's rubies. They watched until it was gone.

Then a barrage of questions shot forth: What was really happening in Paris? Did the neighbors talk about the Rosenswigs' departure? What did they say? And Henri's gallery—what was happening there? Was it closed temporarily without so many works to show, or was an assistant running it? Were all the others leaving Paris? Where were they going? Was everyone in Paris living in fear? Perhaps the only question left unasked was the most delicate: What were they saying would happen when the Germans arrived?

"Our neighbors on the rue La Boétie are most likely unaware that we've left. Like everyone else, they're too busy worrying about whether they themselves should depart, and when and where they should go and how they should get there and what they would do with their belongings. Their annoyance is more evident than their fear. Many Parisians seem content to carry on and express themselves in the grumbling, complaining manner we have always been known for. But fear will come, because Paris will be invaded soon, and who will want to be there then?"

Henri flashed his most charming smile, and appeared to be congratulating himself on his timely exit, when Paul announced that the medical faculty, along with the rest of the University of Paris, had closed indefinitely. It had taken him a full three days to convince Henri that the wise thing to do—in fact, the *only* thing—was to hang a "Temporarily Closed" sign on his gallery and for the two of them to leave Paris, taking with them as many of Henri's pieces as would fit in the truck.

"Did you bring nothing of mine, Henri? And what about the Matisse?" asked Maurice.

"No room, Papa. But I did bring the Matisse, only because I knew you would miss it."

As for the other gallery owners and the artists, Henri told them that Rosenberg had moved to the Bordeaux area and had reportedly sent many of his works to his London gallery, warehousing others elsewhere in France. Picasso, too, had established himself near Bordeaux. Matisse and his beautiful Russian model had made up and left by night train to make their way back to Nice.

"So, you and Henri won't be returning to Paris soon, then, Paul?" Jeanne asked her son.

"No, at least I'm not. There is nothing for me there now. I'm staying here with you," Paul said. He glanced earnestly at Lili and registered her relief; he had chosen her over his clandestine refugee work. "I can't speak for Henri."

"I'll spend a few days here before I go back," Henri said. "Nothing is going to happen tomorrow. I hope to make another run to Paris and back before I return the truck to Claude Bessett. It was good of him to loan it to me at all—especially now. And there are more arrangements to make while I'm there for the inventory that I had to leave behind." While he spoke, he turned over his silver fork to inspect its markings front and back. Having been raised with antiques like those his father dealt in, he could never just enjoy the beauty of a piece without also taking inventory and learning its story.

The evening's first course arrived then: langoustine with caviar in a puff pastry, served in gilt-edged dishes.

"Uncle, if I might ask, how on earth do you get these delicacies for Le Paradis when so much of Europe is so deprived?"

"It's all Boris. I've no idea how he does it, but he has his channels. He's indispensable to us here, unquestionably so," Eli said.

Henri went on to explain his frustrations in trying to make arrangements from Paris for a bank in the region of Le Paradis to store the works from his gallery in one of its vaults. When he and Paul had finally arrived at the bank, two days late and with a fully packed truck, they had been told they couldn't unload it. A flustered bank employee had explained that another party had gotten there first and taken the last large vault. Ultimately, they'd had to make the best use of the several smaller vaults that remained.

"Unfortunately, they couldn't accommodate most of what we brought, and certainly none of the larger pieces. It seems there has been quite a run on vaults over the last couple of weeks. Even those that stood empty for years are suddenly filling up with prized processions, many signed for by families with Parisian addresses, the bank official told me. I couldn't get him to say whom—you know how they are about their confidentiality issues. So, you see, we're not the only ones thinking this way."

"But you can store them here," said Eli, eyeing the next course: plates of stuffed pigeon. "Why not?"

"Uncle, it's not that simple. You must all understand that the Germans will arrive here at Le Paradis. It is only a question of when. After they take Paris, they'll want the rest of France. Consider the following possibilities: They may find us here. They may want to stay here and use your beautiful things. They may want to take your things. They may want to take us prisoner. They might even want to bomb us here."

While Eli and Jeanne studied Henri, Maurice blinked nervously and turned pink, unsure of what to think or say, then burst out, "Henri! You cannot speak to your uncle like that!" as though he were chastising a rude child.

"Now, just wait, Maurice. Let's hear what more Henri has to say," said Eli, his eyelids closed in concentration. He was digesting Henri's words, preparing himself for the next bite. Lili felt Paul's discomfort as he looked away, aware of what Henri was about to tell them. Henri would not hold back in describing a scenario that some at the table were not ready to consider.

"Imagine a Paris that is holding its breath, waiting to see what will happen," said Henri, leaning back in his chair. "Meanwhile, others are planning for the worst, and we must be among them. I can tell you now that many more Parisians will evacuate the city, rather than be held hostage by German invaders."

"So, what will that mean for us?" Jeanne whispered hoarsely. She turned to her husband, but his eyes were still closed. Her own had become large, dark pools, and the waves of her hair undulated as her head wobbled slightly, like a boat adrift.

"As unlikely as it seems to you now, we must be prepared to leave here on a moment's notice. We must hide everything and be ready to exit France across the border to Spain, or farther."

Eli's eyes popped open, and he stared at Henri in astonishment, as did the rest of the group.

"The thing is, it has to be done now. I'm hoping we can start tomorrow."

"But what should we do, Henri?" asked Eli.

"Paul and I were discussing exactly that on the way down from Paris. You have something like your own museum here at Le Paradis. To be safeguarded from the Nazis, it needs to be dismantled and cached. Choosing the most important pieces in your collection and concealing them here on the property is your only option, and that's going to be tricky, finding hiding spots for so many. But we've given a lot of thought to secret places. . . . "

Over the next few days, every able body at Le Paradis worked like mad. To begin with, the paintings on Henri's truck were settled in the basement wine cellar, which consisted of a warren of small rooms for various vintages. The largest paintings were to be leaned against the walls set behind wine shelves that had been pulled forward slightly to accommodate the art. Then the paintings were covered up with dark-stained oilcloths, made to look like nothing special. They were strategically placed behind the least grand labels. With some luck and poor light, they would be overlooked altogether.

"What beauty is hidden here!" Lili whispered to Paul, watching Boris brusquely dress the sacred Matisse portrait of Sonia in an ugly cloth camouflage to position it behind a recent vintage.

Just then, Maurice entered. "No, no, *no*! We'll take that one with us, Boris. Leave the Matisse!"

"But Monsieur Henri didn't tell me . . . ," Boris started, struggling to balance the weight of the portrait in its heavy gilt frame while Maurice called out for Henri to come immediately.

Henri arrived near breathless from rushing around to supervise every move, but in top decision-making form. Even Eli, master of the house, deferred to Henri when it came to moving and concealing these valuable works of art.

"What is the problem here?" Lili saw him stop short at the sight of his overwrought father and red-faced Boris, still trying to balance the half-wrapped portrait, and knew he understood.

"Henri, surely we'll take the Matisse. Tell Boris to put it down. It seems he won't take my word for it." Maurice glared at Boris.

Henri's shoulders sagged a bit, and he took a deep breath. "Papa, it cannot come with us. It's simply too big and too obvious. They'll take it from us at the border, and we'll never see it again. I'm sorry, but it's impossible. The Matisse will be far safer here, I assure you."

"We could take it out of the frame and roll it up. The Leibens did that successfully."

Henri shook his head. "It's far too wide to conceal. Their Rembrandt was tiny."

Maurice stared at his son, his face fallen. In a small, bewildered voice, he said, "Then how will I remember, exactly, the way we lived in Paris? Our lives, and how things were? I can't leave everything behind, Henri. I'm too old for that."

"Papa, Maman will be with you. You'll see her every day. You can ask her how things were," Henri answered impatiently, then softened. "I'm sorry, but we have no time for this now, and there really is no place for the Matisse. You have to trust me, Papa."

Poor Papa, thought Lili. "Henri is right, Papa. We'll all be together, and we'll remind each other how it was. Then, soon, we'll go back home."

"Are you sure of that?"

Paul stepped up and put his hand firmly on his uncle's shoulder. "Yes. You'll have her back. We promise."

They watched Boris rewrap the portrait and slide it in gently behind the wine bottles. Lili noticed he handled it now with extreme reverence.

More and more works that had formerly hung on the walls of Le Paradis descended to the wine caves. Down came masterful portraits and landscapes, Jeanne's romantic collection of Fragonard drawings, as well as a smaller number of impressionist canvases, and even a couple of modern pieces. Each, even the largest, was lifted in its heavy frame from where it was hung and carried by one or two servants out the door and through a concealed, ramped entrance to the underground cave. Once this was accomplished, Boris and one of the gardeners nailed shut the wine cellar's tiny inside entry, which they covered with a paper map. All of this took place under the direction of Henri and Eli. Paul oversaw the team of workers, making sure they caused no damage, that the lifting and placing were very carefully handled, as if by a surgeon.

They were running short on space. Paul pushed up his shirtsleeves and helped to lift the canvases out of their frames, roll them up, and store them in false-bottom trunks designed for just this type of situation and ready for instant transport. Then they brought out some smaller pieces of important furniture for storage in a hastily dug space covered by a false floor, under an unspectacular outbuilding that housed farm equipment. They casually concealed several outstanding clocks and lamps nearby, in boxes full of old objects awaiting repair. Finally, they placed buckets of lime about, to help absorb the inevitable damaging dampness.

Jeanne, with Sonia at her side, was in charge of identifying the smaller pieces to be hidden. Lili was right behind them, working next to Annie, who, with the light touch of a fairy, wrapped tiny masterpieces in bits of cloth to protect them from chips, dents, and scratches. There were at least a hundred ornate snuffboxes, the Limoges enamels, and Japanese porcelains to protect. Certainly they could not hide everything from the invaders' threatening grasp, but they all did what they could.

By now the atmosphere inside Le Paradis had changed dramatically. It was half-emptied of the inanimate personalities that had inhabited its many rooms and corridors, giving them life even when no one was there. As Henri walked down the main hallway, he felt as if he were in an eerie dream. Where paintings had been removed, noticeable discolorations were left on the walls behind—gray shadows of their former selves.

The tapestries were too large and heavy to carry, so the staff had covered them with rough linen to look like supports for removed paintings. If the Germans arrived, they should not be surprised that an owner had thought to send away his valuables in anticipation. The residents of Le Paradis prayed the Germans would not look.

With so much of his cousin's estate now hidden, it was suddenly apparent to Henri what he should have done for himself long before. To make up for lost time, he scrambled to make arrangements to ship a few of his most important pieces to New York, in the care of his gallerist friend Mr. Peterman, to sell or hold until the war was over.

That evening he took Boris aside. "Now, listen carefully, Boris. I will contact you to ship my inventory that remains here to the New York gallery, along with the Matisse. You are to enlist the help of Claude Bessett in Paris to plan the details of packing and transport. Claude knows to send the pieces from my Paris gallery to New York as well. I've given him your contact information, and here is his." Henri reached into his pocket and passed Boris a folded paper. "Do you understand?"

Boris nodded his assent.

Henri had offered to send the Assouline collections as well, but Eli had thrown up his hands at that idea. "I've never been to New York and I'm never going to New York. Why would I send my things there? I've moved once, from Constantinople to France. I've become a Frenchman. If I leave here, it will be only to return to Constantinople to become again a Turk. Please, don't ask any more of me," he said in frustration. Henri was exasperated but chose not to press him.

With all of this going on, Paul and Lili were intent on finding the time to be alone together, to steal away into the forest for a picnic, far from everyone. Since Maurice had dismissed Paul's proposal so adamantly, Paul had not brought it up with him again. Lili could tell that her father had said nothing to Sonia, who would certainly have brought it up with her.

It had been three days since Paul and Henri had arrived, and they were all exhausted from the emotional stress and from the hard physical work. Lili and Paul passed by each other many times between the barn and the main house, often when he was at his most serious, helping to carry something awkward and heavy. Even then, his eyes would cast a spell over her, as they had in their most intimate moments. She longed to be with him. Tomorrow she would be.

The next day was Friday, June 14, 1940. Lili had hardly slept. She felt excited, and a little afraid of her own uncontrolled emotions. She was twenty years old.

She'd risen early. Out the window of the strawberry bedroom, the morning light awakened every shade of green leaf and wildflower in that magical landscape. *How is it that nature can be wild and tame in the same moment?* she wondered, looking out. When she sat at her dressing table, the sunlight that flooded through the window was reflected back to her in the mirror. She had just bathed, and her hair hung in loose, damp ringlets around her face. She felt warm and flushed. Her typically pale cheekbones gave off a burst of rosy color so embarrassingly obvious that she passed over the container of pink powder that Auntie Jeanne had left for her.

She did not go down for breakfast, hoping to stay clear of any demands that the family might try to impose on her schedule. But Sonia had always had eyes in the back of her head. "Lili, pull back your hair. You look quite the coquette," she said, catching a glimpse of her daughter crossing the hallway behind her, in a full skirt plumped up by an unfortunately scratchy petticoat. She did not see the loosely tied blouse Lili wore under her sweater.

On her way out, Lili grabbed a wicker basket and called out

something about picking wildflowers. Henri was on the terrace. He took one look at her, remarked on her "peasant" attire, and raised his brow skeptically, but she ignored him. Nothing could stop her now, and the moment she was out his sight, she picked up speed, passing right through the garden and into the wild.

Paul was waiting for her under the towering plane tree. He looked toward the stream and appeared lost in thought. His hands rested low on his hips, and a light wind blew through his hair and flapped at his sleeves. When he turned and saw her, his expression brightened into a smile, and he walked up to her and grasped her by the shoulders, tilting her face up toward his. His body in all its warmth pressed into her, and the flower basket dropped from her hand.

With every pore, she concentrated on answering him. She crushed herself against him, and they kissed until they were too unsteady to remain standing. No more words. It was only the two of them, together again, inseparable. She trembled to think that it would always be like this.

Later, they lay together under the tree branches. Paul drew himself up on his elbow and gazed at her face. The talisman he wore against the threat of the evil eye dangled from his chest on its silver chain. Lili watched it twirl as though it were winking at her.

"What are you thinking, Lili?"

"That if the Germans were to bomb us right now, in this very spot, I would die content. I must sound foolish."

"I don't want to die. I want to marry you." Paul smiled affectionately, then turned serious. "You know we can't continue like this. It's not right. Tomorrow I'm going into town to find someone, anyone, who is able to perform a marriage ceremony. I'm sure it won't be all that you've dreamed of, but in these times, I'm afraid we can't be particular with the details of our wedding. I hope you're not too upset about that."

"No, but our mothers may be."

"I'm sorry for them, but it can't be helped. Our lives must go on."

"Yes."

Suddenly they were not alone. Henri's voice called out from the distance, getting closer. He shouted Lili's name. It was as though she were awakening from a dream. Paul shot to his feet and quickly organized himself. He helped Lili lift bits of leaves off her skirt before he answered back, "Henri. We're here. By the plane tree."

Henri stared as he caught his breath, seeming surprised to see them together like that. But mostly he was turned in on himself. Lili recognized in her brother a barely controlled anger.

"It's happened," Henri said. "The Germans have reached Paris, and the French government has given up, to spare the devastation of the city. Nothing, they said, could justify the sacrifice of Paris. The Nazis are moving south. They'll be here soon. You're wanted back at the house. Right now." Henri turned back, staying far ahead of them.

Neither Paul nor Lili uttered a word on the way home. At Le Paradis, no one questioned them; no one had been thinking about them at all. Lili found her father in the foyer, pacing and agitated. "The government has fled Paris for Tours—*Tours*, the cowards!" he muttered with disgust. "What will the Germans think of us if there is no one left there to defy them?"

"Maurice, they did the wise thing. Why give them the satisfaction of a formal surrender as soon as they show their faces and shiny boots? I would have done exactly the same," Sonia said. "Lili! Thank goodness you're back. Come with me, both of you." She led them into the salon, where, from upstairs, Eli and Jeanne were engaged in an audible, heated discussion, though their words were elusive.

In the salon, Henri made an effort to appear relaxed, making sure the others were seated before he began. "Well, I don't think I'm going back to Paris after all. So, you needn't worry . . . about that, at least."

"What about my shop, Henri, and what's left of your gallery?" said Maurice.

"I was able to reach Claude Bessett at his gallery yesterday. I told him everything. Claude and I have an arrangement. He has agreed to watch out for our home in Paris, including my gallery and your antiques, Papa. I gave him the information that we are with relatives named Assouline at Le Paradis. He now knows where and how to contact me here, and if necessary he'll be in touch with Boris.

"No one can predict what's going to happen with the Germans in town. Claude said so many French have already left Paris—by train, by car, by bicycle, even by foot—and most at the very last moment, abandoning everything. A nightmare, he called it. Our phone connection was broken before Claude could tell me his plans. But so far, he's stayed put."

"I'm not at all surprised," said Sonia coolly. "Hasn't he always cultivated his German clientele? And now there will be more Germans than ever on the rue La Boétie, just looking for ways to spend their money."

"There's no reason to jump to conclusions. He is, after all, my friend, and a business ally. Under the circumstances, I've no choice but to trust him."

Eli entered, his expression so grim that his mustache seemed a stroke of charcoal over the straight line of his mouth. He led his wife by the elbow. Jeanne appeared smaller and near stricken as he steered her gently alongside his tall, erect frame. Dignity had not deserted him.

"Well? What are you planning for us now, Henri?" he asked facetiously.

Henri didn't seem to notice. "It's time that we decide how we're going to handle ourselves with the turn of events. I would like to point out that our German guests have only just arrived. It's unclear whether France will choose to fight back or settle by signing an armistice. If we sign an armistice, we'll be under German rule, which is a frightening thought."

"Especially for us," Eli said. "We'll be in a more precarious situation than the average Frenchman, and the average Frenchman is already fleeing if he can." He stood facing the rest, with Jeanne slightly behind him, her head bowed. "I, for one, am not going to wait to see what will happen here in France. Quite frankly, I don't see much difference between an armistice and a new German offensive. They're equally untenable to me. I've made my decision. The Assoulines are returning to Turkey."

Lili felt the blood drain from her face.

"But, Father, you haven't consulted me. I could never start a new life in Turkey. I'm a Frenchman, and my life is here," Paul protested.

"This is my wish. And your mother is coming with me," said Eli, as though Jeanne were invisible and not shivering at his side. "She agrees that we cannot stay here."

Jeanne appeared dejected but resigned. She turned to Paul. "We were afraid you would feel this way. If you won't come with us, please, at least leave France. Accompany us partway. We need to know that you will be safe."

Maurice wore a look of shock, and was at first at a loss for words. "But, Eli, I would never have expected this from you. Surely the family should stay together in France, even if we live under assumed identities until this is all over."

"Papa, I don't agree," Henri interceded. "We should have already left France. I've been making inquiries about waiting this all out in America."

"America!" Maurice's jaw dropped. "If the whole world is open to us, why not an igloo on the North Pole, or a mud hut in Africa? This is absurd. Why can't we just rent a small, inconspicuous house somewhere deep in the countryside all together and grow our own vegetables until the whole thing blows over?"

Only at this, when it became apparent that her own father could not face the reality that Henri and Eli had already accepted, did Lili fully appreciate how dire the situation had become. That was the moment the safety net beneath her dropped away completely, and along with it her trust in a future that she could foretell.

She looked to Paul; it might be their last opportunity. He understood. It was the only way.

"I have something important to tell you," Paul announced. "Lili and I plan to be married as soon as possible."

There was silence. It was as though the first bomb had been dropped and had come as a complete surprise. No one seemed to know how to react. "But that's absurd at a time like this," Henri said simply.

Sonia came forward to embrace them both. "I always knew you were meant to be together. We thought it from the start, didn't we, Maurice? Jeanne?" she said, looking to them to continue. "Remember when they were little children how Lili would toddle after Paul around the garden, just waiting for him to say something to her?"

"Yes!" said Jeanne, as she clapped her hands with joy. "And how he would hold Lili's little hand so she wouldn't fall into the pond? He was always her protector."

Eli interrupted. "Yes, we're very happy for you both, but your timing is unfortunate. I'm afraid I really don't see how we can proceed on that right now. I'm sorry. Under normal circumstances, we would be overjoyed, ecstatic, would turn all our attention to festivities . . . but we can't at the moment, really."

"I'm going into town at first light tomorrow to find someone to marry us, and that's all there is to it," Paul said.

"In no way can we risk the delay that could cause. It would put us all in greater jeopardy," Henri said.

"My dear children, I'm afraid that you will have to wait," said Maurice. "Certainly there's no one in the village who would come out here at a time like this. No, far better to wait. I'm sorry—it is out of the question for now."

Lili's stomach was churning. Her father could not know how she felt, but she was certain her mother understood. Sonia pulled them both to her and held them tight for a moment. Releasing them, she said, quietly but with certainty, "I want you to have my emerald ring for your wedding day. I hope that it will bring you as much happiness as it has brought us." She lifted it off her finger and held it out to Paul. "Take it. It will bring you luck."

"Thank you, Maman," said Lili, touched almost to tears. Paul, also moved, nodded and, taking the ring, put it in his inner pocket. He squeezed Lili's hand. "If it does bring luck, then you will wear it very soon," he whispered to her.

Henri stepped in, and what he said put an end to the matter alto-gether. "I heard today that the younger son of old Jezzard in the village shot himself in the foot, on purpose. He didn't want to be enlisted by the Germans if it came to that. Even the villagers are plotting their next move, and so should we. I have a plan."

It was suddenly very clear to Lili that Henri had plotted all along their passage out of France. He'd obtained Portuguese transit visas for them all before he'd left Paris. *What more did he have planned?*

Henri announced that he had decided that they would travel together to the Spanish border, at night, after dark. There they would wait, presumably alongside other refugees also fleeing in panic, many with only vague notions of where they would end up. The Rosenswig-Assoulines, on the other hand, knew where they wanted to go. Jeanne and Eli would seek passage to Turkey, where Eli would request his repatriation. It was agreed that Paul would accompany his parents as far as Barcelona, then reunite with the Rosenswigs in Lisbon, where Lili would be waiting with her brother and parents to catch a boat to New York.

It would work if Paul somehow found them, so Lili tried to focus on that, but her heart was beating so furiously she could hardly think.

The next hours were agonizing. Lili, alone in the strawberry bed-room, moved as though in a dark cloud, trying to determine what would stay and what would go with her in her small, single suitcase. For courage, she kept a photograph visible on her bedside table, the one that Henri had taken on her mother's birthday, of all the family with the Matisse portrait. She lay down on the bed and turned to gaze at the picture. Hadn't it been only this afternoon that she and Paul had lain together under the plane tree, planning their wedding? She shut her eyes for just a moment. Where was Paul?

•11•

French-Spanish Border, Mid-June 1940

Paul Assouline thrust the photograph Lili had given him into his coat pocket and stood his ground at the border, surrounded by the French soldiers who had drafted him as a new recruit. He shoved his way through them, elbowing them so forcefully that for a minute they let him watch as the French border patrol returned Lili, who was crying uncontrollably, back over the bridge into Spain. Midway she broke loose from their grip, just enough to be able to turn her head and look back at him. Her frantic brown eyes met his for only a moment.

"Enough!" said one of the soldiers. They turned him roughly around by the shoulders and pushed him farther into France.

"You can forget all about her now, boyfriend. Don't worry—you won't have the time to think about her anyway. We've got plenty of work for you here in France; we need you to help us fight against the Germans. But first we'll make a soldier out of you." The youngest soldier smirked, looking Paul up and down. "Our new conscript has the look of a blue blood. They're the toughest to train."

The others laughed. "You better catch on quickly, because we don't have a lot of time," the young soldier said warily to Paul. "Tonight we're all going up north by convoy to find the Nazis. And when we find them, we're going to kill them."

That night Paul and the other recruits squatted in three trucks, headed in the general direction of the German offense. Every man in the newly formed troop was aware that the Germans were moving in on them, and they could hear in the false optimism of the broadcast reports that things were not good. They were in limbo, and they feared the worst—that France would give in and declare an armistice.

Paul lay on hard ground that first night in a temporary camp, an issue blanket wrapped around his long body, over the clothing he'd worn for days. Uniforms were in short supply. He was thankful to have his wool coat for when the weather turned. Tonight, though, was warm, and he had folded the coat to use as a pillow. The photograph was tucked inside. He could lay his head on Lili's picture, shut his eyes, and imagine that she was lying with him under their tree at Le Paradis.

Only two days before, he had held her hand and announced their engagement to the family. Then they had packed to flee. In the few spare moments after he'd finished packing, Paul had known exactly what he needed to do. He'd taken the emerald ring from his pocket and examined it close up, his eyes drawn into its deep blue-green. It was extraordinary, he thought, turning it slowly between his thumb and forefinger. Surely, nothing could extinguish its inner light. In the top drawer of his dresser, he had an empty watch box made of black walnut and lined in dark satin, not large, but with a cover that latched tightly with a double metal closure. He set the ring in the box and closed the seal over it, his eyes glistening with faith. He would bury it at the base of their sheltering plane tree. No one would find it there. *No matter what happens at Le Paradis when we are gone*, he said to himself, *Lili and I will come back to retrieve it, and she will wear it as her wedding ring.*

He repeated the vow to himself now. The quiet of the camp was interrupted by shouts of bravado from his fellow recruits, who were gathered around the fire, filled with the flames of patriotism. *So am I*, thought Paul. *But Lili is my country now.* He slipped his hand under his head, into the folds of his coat, and felt for the corner of the photograph.

The next morning they were up at dawn. After a quick meal of boiled eggs and stale bread, the young soldier from the border motioned for Paul to follow him into the surrounding woods. They stopped in a small, circular clearing, and the soldier shoved a pistol into Paul's hands.

"Okay, Doctor, let's make you earn your breakfast. Hold it like so." He moved Paul's fingers around the pistol in a way that felt to Paul terribly awkward, and placed Paul's index finger on the trigger. "See those birds on that branch? Now, shoot! Hit one!" Paul looked at him, aghast. "Don't look at me, idiot. Watch them. Bring one down."

Paul saw what he took to be a family of crows and aimed at the largest, a shiny indigo specimen. He had never been able to endure even the thought of a hunt. *It's not only that I don't want to kill a bird—I can't do it.* The gun shook in his outstretched hand. *What if I actually hit one?*

"That's it. . . . Shoot . . . shoot!" shouted the soldier.

Several seconds later, the gun sent a blast into the trees, throwing Paul off-balance and frightening away the birds.

"No, no, no! You can't sway! You hold it firm, and then you shoot to kill. These aren't birds to you—these are the enemy." As much as Paul wanted to stop the Germans, his deep-set antipathy to violence left him incapable of fighting. It went against his code. That, he realized, was an insurmountable paradox. *So, how long can I hide it, and what should I do now?* he asked himself between practice shots over the next hour of excruciatingly unsuccessful training.

When his young mentor finally gave up on him in disgust, mumbling something about continuing the next day, Paul knew he had no choice. He didn't want to desert, but what they were asking of him was intolerable.

Late in the afternoon, a boy in a red beret, young and carefree, rode past the camp on an old black bicycle. He was whistling. Across the handlebars he balanced a fishing pole and a basket, which was certainly filled with his catch. He turned onto the dirt road leading to a nearby farmhouse. Paul watched. He envied the boy's innocence and freedom.

Very early the next morning, he slipped quietly out of camp, nodding to the soldier on guard as though he were going to relieve himself in the woods. Once out of sight and earshot, he made his way quickly through the forest, ignoring the brambles. When he arrived at the farm clearing, his face and arms were mapped with fine red scratches. It was dawn, and he had to pick up speed.

What he found was more than he'd hoped for—there was the black bicycle leaning invitingly against a shed. *That bike looks better to me right now than the Bugatti ever did.* Miraculously, the boy's red beret was balanced atop the fishing pole perched nearby. Paul grabbed the cap, pulling it down over his thick brows, then snatched the pole and jumped on the bike. Not knowing where he was heading, he started to ride. He was aware that this was the first time he had stolen anything, and he hoped that he would be able to return at least the bike someday.

Remembering that Lili had given him a large chunk of chocolate at the border, he searched his pockets. There it was, wrapped in paper. He left it high on a fencepost in plain view for the boy. Soon it would be a delicacy.

He rode for most of the day, heading south, more or less, back toward the Spanish border. There was still a chance that he could catch up with Lili before he was apprehended as a deserter by the French or as an errant Jew by the Nazis, and before the Rosenswigs sailed from Lisbon. He had no border papers—the soldiers had taken them—but he would come up with something. Lili was waiting for him.

He rode like mad over the hidden roads he confined himself to. He imagined that he and the bike were flying over fields, looking down onto treetops. But when he did look down, he saw filthy leather soles pushing hard against the pedals of a small, rickety contraption that rolled slowly over dirt paths, rutted and strewn with rocks that threatened to jolt him off the track. The day was long and lonely, and at the end of it, he stopped by a stream to drink. When he lay down, his body seemed to fall into the earth and his face went slack. He felt utterly depleted, physically and emotionally.

Then he remembered. He wiped his hands on his shirt, reached inside his back pocket, and gently eased out the photograph. A smile settled slowly on his face as he gazed at Lili. Looking at her standing next to him gave him hope. And there, too, were his parents and aunt and uncle. God willing, they were all out of harm's way.

His hand trembled as he put the picture back inside his pocket. He needed to eat. Some clusters of red gooseberries hovered nearby from a scraggly bush on the embankment. When he reached out to grab them from underneath, his hand would not steady until it closed in on them and their sharp leaves. But they were small and too numerous to handle, so he lost some in the pulling as they fell through his fingers to the ground. He gobbled up what was left, letting the red juice trickle down his chin and throat. It was near to dusk, a good time to fix the fishing pole with some bait and sit next to the stream. *I can survive like this*, Paul told himself, feeling something close to happiness.

And he did, for a while, living from day to day, riding endlessly on his bike, avoiding towns and people, stopping to rest and fish and forage for food. He was cold at night and very hungry, and the water he found to drink was dirty enough to make him sick. When he did inevitably become ill, he ignored it for as long as he could, because first he had to reach Lili. But he was exhausted, undernourished, and dehydrated, and he knew he could not last long in his weakened condition. He laid himself down under the shelter of a plane tree, thinking of Lili, of his parents, and again of Lili. His hand could not be made to move as far as the pocket that held the photograph, but he knew it by heart now, and he saw her clearly when his eyes shut. Then he heard their approach, the barking dogs and the strange voices. He managed to mouth the words "Nazis. But they're too late for me."

Part II: The Spoils of War

•12•

Madrid to Lisbon, Mid-June to July 1940

For Lili, an eternity passed in just a few days. In the mind-numbing hours since she had been forced to part with Paul at the border, time had spun away. The train ride to Madrid rumbled on endlessly, the cars so crammed with refugees that they were lucky to find standing room. She closed her eyes but could not escape the constant, deafening chugging and the strange odors emanating from the train's engine and its sweaty, weary passengers.

When she opened her eyes, she recognized her feelings of bewilderment and loss reflected in every anxious face surrounding her. Despite their conditions and their endless complaints, she was certain that all of them were thanking their God that they'd been allowed onboard, grateful for every meter of rattling track that carried them farther from the Nazis.

It was generally thought imminent that France would declare an armistice with Germany. She and her family had made it this far, but what about Paul? Lili worried about him incessantly.

Her father put his arm around her and petted back her long hair in a gesture retrieved from her childhood. She found momentary consolation in the warmth of his brown eyes.

"You'd be surprised at what a young man can survive during wartime and never speak of again," he said gently.

Of course, she reminded herself—her father had served in the last war. She thought of Paul's patriotic fervor in the Catacombs. But she knew him. He was a doctor and an idealist, and he would be at war with himself if he did what was requested of a soldier. She could not bear the thought of his moral suffering or bring herself to think of him on the battlefield, of what outrages might happen there.

"Don't worry, Lili, he's a smart boy. He'll find his own way," Henri said. "Quiet!" he whispered suddenly. "Here come Uncle Eli and Aunt Jeanne."

Eli, upon boarding, had found for the two of them a prized standing spot where Jeanne had squeezed in and been able to rest, leaning between Eli and the wall of the train car. Since the shock of Paul's conscription, Lili had witnessed the dissolution of Jeanne's elegantly composed countenance. It had aged her quite suddenly; her reliable smile was gone. Eli's face was hardened into an inexpressive gray mask that shattered anytime a recent nervous twitch activated his mustache. Eli had made a hushed request that they not mention Paul; it would be too upsetting for Jeanne. Lili dreaded the silence that made her feel as if he were already dead.

Hotels were jam-packed from the border onward, but Henri had prevailed upon one of his ubiquitous contacts, and when they reached Madrid, there were two shabby rooms in a sad, bare-bones apartment for those in transit awaiting them. "It's not the Ritz, but we're lucky to get them," Henri said, and dubbed them the Rosenswig Suite and the Suite Assouline.

The mattresses looked to Lili like tired, straw-filled gunnysacks, possibly mite ridden. But she sighed in deep relief as her exhausted body and its worn emotions sank down onto one, and the faded and torn lace curtains blocked enough Spanish sunlight to allow them all a couple of hours of sleep.

When Lili awoke, Henri had disappeared. He returned late in the day, smiling like a cat and patting a bulge inside the pocket of his coat. "I've been to the American embassy. We'll be on a steamer departing Lisbon for New York at the end of the week! Thanks to Mr. Peterman, we are the opportune possessors of four American visas." They would join a planned evacuation of American journalists and expatriates who had delayed going back to the States, enjoying themselves until the eleventh hour, but who were suddenly extremely anxious to leave a Europe at war and return to the comforts of home.

"It's a miracle!" Sonia cried out and her hands flew to her face to cradle her smile. She waxed enthusiastic about their "New World adventure," while Maurice was taciturn. Lili was sick with worry. Even if Paul were trained to be a soldier and did survive the war, how would he find her afterward?

The Assoulines had already paid a fortune for two tickets on a cargo ship from Valencia to Izmir on the Turkish coast; from there they would presumably make their way to Istanbul and Eli's family. Jeanne and Eli left the Rosenswigs early the next morning, in an awkward rush to catch the train that would carry them off on their journey. None of them were thinking clearly. In such a state, they were spared the depth of dramatic sadness that they, especially Sonia and Jeanne, would have descended into had they fully realized they might never see each other again.

Jeanne held Lili close, trying to smile, pressing her damp cheeks against Lili's. "The next time we meet, you will be both my niece and my daughter," she murmured in Lili's ear. They had all agreed that as soon as the war was over, they would meet at Le Paradis, where they would celebrate the marriage that would bring their families even closer.

When Jeanne and Eli had left, Sonia excused herself to take a walk. Not long after, Lili pulled aside the heavy lace curtain to check on the status of the rising sun and saw Sonia through the window, seated at a table outside the café downstairs. Her legs were crossed at the knee, and a cigarette dangled from her left hand. Circles of smoke released slowly through her firmly set jaw.

The Rosenswigs pressed on to Lisbon in time to catch the freighter SS *McKeesport*. Lufthansa, an airline controlled by the Nazis, operated the only flight to Lisbon from Madrid. Afraid of ending up somehow in Nazi clutches, they boarded the train instead, for another long and wrenching ride.

At the dock in Lisbon, Lili was the first to spot the *McKeesport* floating ominously in its stall, waiting like a tethered sea monster quietly gathering force. She came to a standstill. Every muscle in her body tensed in resistance, telling her not to board, not to leave Europe, not to leave Paul.

"Move ahead, Lili. Keep up!" Henri and the others were noisy and excited. He shouldered her along, helped by the momentum of the crush of passengers bound home to America. She looked back once before Henri's push sent her forward onto the vast deck.

She was in a new world. These Americans were so obviously at ease with themselves. They smiled their big smiles and waved their happy good-byes to the crowds of anonymous friends who waved back to them from the dock. It all seemed so effortless for them; they were returning home. Almost expecting there might be someone for her to wave to, she turned around to face the dock, but it was already too far off. They had launched, and there could be no turning back.

•13•

New York, August 1940

Years later, all Lili would remember of the journey was her nervous stomach, how it undulated with the ocean's every swell and fall, and the brisk saltiness of the ocean air, which did nothing to revive her. She was so seasick that she sometimes spent entire days below deck, attempting to draw or simply lying on her cot, thinking. She suspected that her never-ending seasickness was nothing but a manifestation of heartache.

When she came up for air, she listened to the sounds of the language spoken around her. At school she had excelled in British English, but these Americans spoke far too quickly to follow. Their staccato accent was not haughty, though, like that of the British who had shopped along the rue La Boétie. She thought she could get along with these Yankees well enough for a while.

Henri spoke enough to converse with his American business contacts and took advantage of every opportunity to use his English. "Look how he seems to know everyone already. He's the center of attention," she said to her father as they watched him in animated conversation with three men gathered round. "He must be thinking about business opportunities in America."

"I hope it's only that." Maurice snorted. "I'm not sure about your brother anymore." He shook his head and walked away.

Sonia spent the eighteen days at sea laughing at herself while she tried to make conversation with her minimal English vocabulary. An American passenger had given her the French-English dictionary he had no further use for.

The sea was not so romantic as Lili had imagined as a child. Nor was it for her father, who frequently stayed below with her.

"Your mother is interested in talking to everyone in the world," grumbled Maurice. "Sometimes I don't understand her at all. These people seem fine—kind, even—but dear God, I hope America is easier for me to manage than this ship on the sea. And I'm afraid I may never learn English." Lili fretted that he spoke so little during the voyage, far less than at home.

The Rosenswigs were among a small handful of foreigners aboard who had been granted the new status of "refugee democrats." In Lili's mind that meant the American government understood that they were going to stay only temporarily, that they would return to France as soon as circumstances made it possible.

She was struggling to accept the idea of even a temporary stay in America when the silence of one afternoon broke into exuberant shouts of wild excitement and thumping from the deck above.

Henri clattered down the narrow stairway, calling out, elated, "You're missing out on something really big! Come up! Hurry!" The SS *McKeesport* was within sight of the Statue of Liberty.

"Oh, Papa! I want my first glimpse of America!" Lili squeezed Maurice's hand and, wide-eyed, bounded up the stairs. But her stomach lagged heavily behind. She slowed to a climb, keeping her hands on the slippery rail. At the top she stopped, closed her eyes, and took a deep breath of sea air; when she opened them she was face-to-face with Madame Liberty.

Jubilant Americans surrounded her, whooping, jumping, clapping, dancing with joy, some shedding tears. *How happy they are to be home*, she thought, and a rush of thanks ran through her that she was among them. A salty gust of wind blew into her face and whipped at her hair, and it felt and tasted like an exciting new world. But when she shut her eyes against the force of it, she saw a vision of Paul, lying in the field with her at Le Paradis, touched by the gentlest of breezes. She wasn't ready to begin a life without him.

Their new home was not much, but it was comfortable enough, and it was furnished with linens and kitchen equipment. After their quarters on the boat, it felt deluxe, private, and spacious.

Before leaving Paris, Henri had sent a few canvases to his New York gallery friend, Mr. Peterman. A couple had sold, providing enough income to sustain the Rosenswigs for a while. Mr. Peterman had offered to set them up in an apartment-hotel he owned in the theater district.

"Ah, an unencumbered modern life. How I love it!" said Sonia, the practical optimist. "Your Mr. Peterman is very generous, Henri. Is that typically American?"

"Mister Peterman can be very generous if you know how to handle him. And I do," Henri said.

"When can we meet him to thank him?" Sonia twirled around in the small kitchen.

"He's a very private person." Henri adjusted the cuff of his suit. "You can let me thank him for all of us."

Maurice's brows hovered low over dark eyes that moved from Henri to Sonia. "I don't understand why you're so excited. It's no Versailles."

She scoffed at him. "If circumstances had not forced us to leave our home on the rue La Boétie, I think you would have become blasé about our good fortune there. You would appreciate nothing and you would still find something to complain about."

"I'm not sure when we'll see the return of 'our good fortune,' as you call it, but I don't need to be separated from what I have to appreciate it." He searched for a comfortable spot on the rough-hewn brown sofa, and when he found none, he burst out, "My God, Sonia, you've no idea how I miss sitting in my red chair, surrounded by beauty and our Matisse."

"I know, Maurice, we all do. But for now, we mustn't dwell on it, or we'll never become situated here," she said.

"*C'est merveilleux!* Look! Broadway at night!" Henri's voice cracked with excitement that first night. Lili moved toward the window, but without much enthusiasm; she didn't want to dampen the elation gleaming in her brother's eyes.

"Still wobbling on those sea legs of yours, Lili?"

She stood next to him, looking out toward Broadway's blindingly bright lights on the theater marquees that flashed brilliantly most of the night. All she could think of was how they kept her from sleeping, and how her stomach had not yet settled. How could she ever feel his attraction to this city that looked to her dirty, too big and noisy, and quite charmless?

But Henri was impressed by it all. He and Sonia kept busy day and night getting the family settled in the new neighborhood, joining language classes, meeting people. Maurice went along, knowing he would be lost without them. Lili went, too, because she wanted to learn more English, but she saw no real reason to adjust to a situation that was only temporary.

Henri, on the other hand, was making new American connections by the minute. Mr. Peterman, he said, was introducing him around, helping him establish himself as an appraiser of modern art. Most evenings Henri went out, frequently dressed in the tuxedo Mr. Peterman had insisted he accept as a gift and wear when they attended the opera or fancy uptown clubs where he would introduce Henri to "the right crowd."

"My, you look so handsome," Sonia said one evening. "Maybe you'll find an American wife. It's the right time for that, you know. You could take her to live in Paris after the war."

An American wife for Henri? What a strange idea, Lili thought, expecting any minute that Maurice, seated next to her, would stop Sonia's badgering.

"Please, Maman!" Henri said sharply, and left the room. Her father's eyes narrowed as they followed him out.

The next day found Lili drawing lazily on the sofa when Henri rushed through, off to something. Maurice took one look at her and stopped him. "Henri, your sister is languishing here. Can't you please take her out with you? Show her some fun."

"Sure," said Henri, with his new American grin. "Tomorrow night I'm meeting some of the girls from the boat. You remember them, Lili, and they're always asking about you. We're going to a famous dance club. It's Polynesian-style. Come with us."

The last thing she wanted to do was dance, but she did feel curious to see what the fuss was all about.

"Come on, give it the old American try!" he said.

"Yes, go, Lili. Live a little," encouraged Sonia.

They were right. She'd been cooped up in the apartment, dreaming about the past. One look outside was enough to see that exciting things were going on.

The next night, crowds were queued up for blocks to get into the night-clubs that lined West Fifty-Second Street. Expressive faces bubbled with anticipation, but Lili recognized a familiar, frantic desperation behind the flirtatious smiles. "It's like Paris just before the Germans arrived, isn't it?" she whispered to Henri.

"Yes, it's because of the new peacetime draft. Now even the Americans are training for war. But tonight they will forget about all that."

Outside Club Samoa a sea of pulsing young bodies was dressed to the nines. Lili caught sight of the bright faces of the girls from the boat and felt a glimmer of belonging. Though she could barely tell them apart and wasn't quite sure of their names, they felt like old friends. They giggled when Henri embraced them all—in the French way, as he reminded them. "You girls are always having fun."

"Yes, we try to! It's the American way," one said, laughing. They hugged Lili, too, and another said, "You still look very French. We haven't rubbed off on you much."

"Ah, but there's hope for her yet." Henri lifted his eyes to heaven.

Inside, Lili was surprised at how densely the club was packed, like the streets of New York but more so. It was sophisticated, but in a different way than Paris. The bar was made of bamboo, and the atmosphere was strangely exotic. Trays of colored drinks whizzed by, and the whole club pulsed with the beat of jungle drums thrumming from a dance floor somewhere. There had been a time not so long ago when Lili would have been drawn to the energy of such a place.

A girl in a short-short skirt and a very deep bodice, carrying a basket of cigars and cigarettes, walked up to Henri, smiling coyly. He talked with her, glancing down from time to time, brushing against her while he chose and lit up one of her cigars. Irrationally, Lili felt annoyed that her brother's disreputable behavior had followed them to New York.

"Come on, Henri, let's get some booze," urged a pretty, gray-eyed blonde from the boat. "How about a cigarette, Lili?" she asked.

When Lili shook her head and said, "Thank you, but no," the girl's wide eyes opened even wider in disbelief. "Drinking and smoking are good for you, you know," she said in earnest.

The mere thought of mixing cigarettes with alcohol tonight in this place sent a sudden wave of nausea through Lili. She put her hand on her stomach and looked around for the *toilettes*. Certainly, she was not going to ask the tuxedoed waiter or one of those half-dressed girls her brother was toying with.

"Are you looking for the you-know-what? Let me come with you. I know where they are," the gray-eyed girl said. She took Lili by the hand and led her through the crowd. Lili heard bits of the conversations around them; the words came very fast and were barely audible over the band music and the clinking of glasses. She could pick up talk of war and new words that could be suggesting only flagrant behavior, and she felt an urgent need to get away from all of it.

In the room marked "Ladies," she sank into a green leather chair, facing a generous makeup mirror framed in bamboo, and felt a little better. The fronds of a large potted palm draped the mirror from above. "It's nice here," she said to her new friend, seated next to her.

"Swanky, isn't it? You seem like the kind of girl who belongs in swanky places like this. Or even swankier." Then the girl leaned forward in her rather too-short skirt, her exposed legs crossed at the knees. "Lili, may I ask you something in confidence?" she whispered seriously, sounding like a precocious child.

Lili was sure she was going to ask her about Henri, and she wanted to warn her against him before the poor girl embarrassed herself. But how should she put it?

"My brother, you know, he likes lots of girls. I'm sure he goes to all the clubs and plays the grand seducer with everyone."

"Oh! I wasn't sure if you knew!" Her friend leaned back in surprise for a minute, then came forward and, in her confidential way, arms crossed, holding her shoulders, gushed, "I suppose he hardly hides it. I heard it was the European way. Henri is so dashing; most of the girls here have crushes on him. Boys do, too. But high types like him go to clubs uptown for that kind of thing."

"What kind of thing?" said Lili, confused.

The girl bit her lower lip, then made a wretched face and shut her eyes. When they popped open, she said, "Just forget about all that . . . Do you like the club?"

"Oh, yes! It's like a movie here: Everyone is in a beautiful costume, trying to attract the most attention," said Lili, with a sweeping gesture toward the dance floor.

The girl giggled. "Well, New York is a competitive place. You could dress up to show yourself off even more. The American guys maybe don't appreciate au naturel like the French do. . . . Your mother, she's so stylish. You know what I mean, don't you?" She drew back and waited for Lili's reaction.

Lili lifted her face and looked into the mirror. Her cheeks were blotchy, and an unruly curl had escaped from her pulled-back chignon. She looked a mess, and mimed a pout at her reflection.

"Jeez, Lili, I'm sorry. I didn't mean it like that. You're absolutely beautiful. Anyone can see that."

"No, you're right. I look awful. I just haven't cared. I've felt not quite right for a very long time."

"Well, you certainly didn't seem too well during the voyage. What do you think it is?"

"My stomach hasn't felt settled since we stepped onto the *McKeesport*, and I'm tired, and I'm getting fat . . . though I haven't been eating much at all. But sometimes I'm hungry for days and eat all the time." As she heard her own words pour out this way, an explanation that was almost too shocking to consider hit her.

Her friend did not hesitate. "Honey," she said, leaning in closer and narrowing her eyes in confidence, "are you pregnant?"

"No. That is not possible," Lili said slowly.

"Isn't it? Didn't you have a sweetie back home in France?"

Lili thought back to Paul's bedroom the day of the air-raid drill, then to the last day they had spent together at Le Paradis, by the stream. That had been two and a half months before. Hadn't it been just after that when everything about her had changed?

When Lili told her mother, Sonia didn't ask questions—she didn't have to. She arranged a visit to a doctor the next day, and they went there together. Lili sat nervously on a fabric-covered table in his spacious office and looked into the doctor's gentle face. "You're far enough along," he said after the exam. "It looks like you'll be a mother in mid-March. Is the father here with you?" When Lili didn't respond, he glanced at her bare finger and asked in a low voice, "Do you want to keep the baby?"

"Yes, of course!" her mother answered indignantly.

Lili strained to imagine her immediate future with a child, but in the scenes that came to her, Paul was always there with them. Maybe he could make it to the States before the war was over; then they would stay until the fighting ended and the baby was old enough to travel back to France. He could intern in the office of this kind doctor.

Enough, she told herself. *Those thoughts are far-fetched and wishful.*

When they left the doctor's office, she was holding back tears, too confused to speak. Sonia squeezed her hand. "Darling, just be happy. There is nothing in this world that brings the joy of a new baby."

They followed a narrow side street that fell in permanent shade, where the pervasive stench of garbage rose from containers waiting too long for removal. A woman approached them hesitantly. She was very young and carried a lethargic infant in a tattered blue blanket in one arm. She held out her other hand. "Please, lady." Lili felt the girl's desperation as though it were her own and rummaged through her pocketbook, delivering all her coins into the girl's open palm, too aware that it would not go far. The girl muttered a thank-you and began searching for her next prospect.

Sonia stood by, shaking her head. "You should be thinking of yourself now, Lili. Your baby."

"I am doing exactly that, Maman."

Sonia reached into her pocket, retrieved a Sobranie cigarette, and lit it. After a long draw, she said, "Don't tell your father. Not yet." Lili knew neither of them wanted to discuss how shocked and disappointed Maurice would be in Lili's conduct with Paul, or how much further her predicament could destabilize him. "And there's no point in mentioning anything to Henri. That boy is so absorbed in his effort to establish himself here that he's hardly home with us anyway."

Lili had seen her brother become increasingly remote; he was away during the day and home late every night. But no matter how little he slept, he left early in the morning to check for mail at the Eighth Avenue post office. It seemed ages ago that he'd first written to Boris to send his canvases from France, enlisting the assistance of Claude Bessett. *Poor Henri*, Lili thought. *He returns every day with nothing, only to face Papa.*

Coincidentally, she and Sonia arrived home in the middle of a brewing storm.

"I don't understand it, Henri. Not a word of explanation from Boris? Not even a telegram from Claude?" Maurice's agitation reddened his face.

"I've told you, Papa. The French postal service is no longer reliable," Henri said soothingly. "Don't worry. The paintings will arrive,

Peterman will sell them in his gallery, and we'll have something more to live on."

"But what if there's a problem? If that doesn't happen soon, where will our money come from? How much longer can we hold out? We can't very well get along on nothing. And what if they never arrive? What will happen to us then?" By now he was shouting, his posture rigid with concern.

Henri's hands doubled into fists, and he pounded at the air with every word he shouted back. "I don't know, Papa! But if you leave me alone, I will figure out something."

"You had better, Mr. America," Maurice growled, then sank onto the sad brown couch. "Because you brought us here and we're counting on you. We have nowhere else to turn."

•14•

France, August,1940

Claude Bessett stood at the window of his art gallery on the rue La Boétie, pretending to examine his manicured hands. In reality, he was having a conversation with himself about whether to check up on Henri Rosenswig's gallery, as his friend had requested before he'd locked up and left Paris in the chaos of the June exodus. Henri had given Claude a key, which Claude had used the next day to remove the best of Henri's works to his own gallery for safekeeping. Then the Nazis had arrived and he'd dared not use the key again. That had been two months earlier.

The rue La Boétie has not been the same since, Claude thought wistfully as he looked down the empty, cheerless street. Since thousands of Parisians had fled the city, it felt almost lonely. Those who had remained preferred to stay indoors, now that the Germans were running things, and why not? It was altogether less interesting with so many galleries closed. Every day it seemed another one was declared abandoned and requisitioned by the Reich. So far, the Nazis had seized only Jewish art collections. *Thank God my own Galerie Bessett is free to carry on, at least for the moment; to be on good terms with the Nazis is essential for my survival.*

Claude's indecision made him wince. Henri was depending on him, would do the same for Claude if it were necessary. But should Claude risk everything to help an unfortunate colleague?

Claude pulled open the drawer to his desk where the key to Henri's gallery lay. He took it out and began flipping it from side to side in his palm, studying it. Then he sighed and put the key in his back pocket. He prayed that all would go well.

It was dusk; if he delayed any longer, it would be too dark to see indoors. He stepped outside as though preparing to lock up for the night. His eyes darted left, then right. With no one in sight, he strode boldly across La Boétie and down the block, slowing at the picture windows of the Galerie H. Rosenswig. Fortunately for Henri, the building was not boarded up; it had not been requisitioned. If it had been, Claude would have had every excuse to give up and go home.

He knew he could tell nothing more from outside; Henri had emptied the front gallery of artwork before his departure, to give the impression that his entire inventory had been removed. The paintings Claude was to check on would be stored in the far back stacks, along with Henri's gallery furniture. He pushed himself right up to the gallery entrance, hoping the wide door frame would partially conceal him from any eyes on the street. As he reached back for the key in his pocket, he had only one thought: *What I am doing is madness!*

He hesitated just long enough to feel a strong grip on his right upper arm twist his elbow back all the way to his shoulder, which was being wrenched, excruciatingly, from its socket.

"Halt, *sie!*"

The weight of a lead boot stomped on Claude's soft leather shoe with such force that he thought he might pass out.

"So! What have we here? A thief? Or is this your gallery?" A rough German voice spoke a French so mutilated that Claude could barely make out the meaning. The strong arm brought him around until he was face-to-face with a soldier in full Nazi uniform, his mouth twisted into a contemptuous smile.

"No . . . n-no," Claude stuttered, thinking how to protest. "It belonged to someone who disappeared. A Jew who said he was going to America. I just want to make sure that he's gone."

"I don't believe you. I think you were going to enter. Didn't I see a key fall from your hand?" The soldier lifted his boot off Claude's shoe and kicked Claude's foot aside, revealing the key underneath.

"You get it," commanded the German. Trembling, Claude bent down and picked it up. "Now you place it in the lock. Let's see if it works." Claude had trouble holding on to the key, and the German pushed his hand away impatiently to unlock the door himself. He grunted and in a single, violent motion used his heft to push the door wide open and shove Claude into the gallery. Then he shut the door behind them, blocking them both inside.

"Aha! Now I can easily see that you're trespassing, with intent to steal. Surely you know the rules: the Wehrmacht prohibits removal, alteration, or disposal of artworks without prior permission." The German uttered this as though reading an injunction. "I'm taking you in. Show me your papers."

Claude's teeth were clenched, and he couldn't breathe. He reached his hand inside his jacket to obey.

Then he heard himself say, "Look, let me make you a deal. I have money." Inwardly he groaned, knowing he was in for it.

To save his skin, Claude began paying off the German soldier, who came around every few days to collect. He fully expected the economic strain to become unbearable, but so far it hadn't been so bad; since the Germans had arrived in the neighborhood, Claude's business had exploded. He commented to his mistress, "All of Paris is for sale, as far as they're concerned, and they want to take it all back home with them to Germany. All the merchants are saying it's becoming a challenge to keep up with their insatiable demands for luxury goods, especially for art."

Galerie Bessett had always maintained a traditional German clientele, drawn by the older works that were the gallery's specialty. When dealing with this new breed of "connoisseur," Claude sometimes had to force himself to overlook their small vulgarities and often-negligible appreciation of French art. Of course they were not like the

French—how could they be? But they kept coming back for more, and he appreciated that.

"Fortunately for me," he mused while his mistress unpacked his newest custom shirts, "they seem to go for every Old Master German, Flemish, and Dutch work that I can get my hands on, regardless of the quality."

Hitler didn't allow modern or frivolous art—and certainly nothing by a Jewish artist—into his Reich; he labeled such works "degenerate." "The Führer's agents are scouting throughout France—indeed, all of conquered Europe—for the finest, most Aryan artworks to fill some giant *Führermuseum* that he's counting on opening after he wins this war." Hitler's selective taste in art was good news for dealers like Claude, because no Frenchman, even the greediest of dealers, would want every great French work to leave France. Claude was happy to provide them with Dutch skating scenes, rather than French paintings of bathers.

He had not been surprised when, shortly after the incident with the German soldier, Henri's gallery was requisitioned and the front space emptied of its art and turned into a men's shirting shop. He stopped to peek in through the window. Against a wall stood Henri's elegantly modern viewing couch, strewn with loose swatches of shirting cottons and dark wools. *I'm glad Henri isn't here to see this*, Claude had said to himself. Still, as a new address for fine tailoring, it looked promising. He went in and placed an order, just to give the place a try.

Henri had been a friend, a colleague, but it was every man for himself during these times. As Claude recalled it now, he had given Henri some assurances that he would look out for the Rosenswig art and antiques in Paris and in the countryside, but only because Henri had been rather insistent. Even at the time, Claude had thought it a difficult request. And look—he had done what he could to help Henri, and it had backfired.

Galerie Bessett, he further acknowledged, had begun benefiting from those clients who'd been disappointed to discover that Galerie H. Rosenswig no longer existed. Claude even made a special arrangement with the shirt shop to send those former Rosenswig clients down the street, where he did his best to serve them.

Then, almost unbelievably, Claude was handed an opportunity to supply the most important buyer in France. With no forewarning, a large and imperious German, wearing a heavily decorated uniform under a cape that he handled like a swashbuckler, entered the gallery with his formidable entourage. Claude recognized, unmistakably, Reichsmarschall Hermann Göring, the most powerful man in occupied France. He had reason to be frozen with fear but also to be jubilant.

Göring collected, it was said, even more art than Hitler. The latest joke among Paris gallery owners was that it was up to them to win the war by distracting the Reichsmarschall with round-the-clock showings of art so irresistible that he would simply forget about the war, call off the troops, and go back to Germany to hang his acquisitions in Carinhall, the gauche monstrosity of a country home where he indulged in excess. They laughed derisively, calling him "the grand amateur."

Claude wasn't laughing the day Göring and his team of "art experts" made their surprise visit to his gallery space. In poured the musclebound military guards, the huddle of Göring's advisors in long black trench coats, and the girth of the Reichsmarschall himself in his flowing cape. Claude gritted his teeth; he could not afford to appear weak or intimidated, though he still walked with a hobble and his shoulder was frozen stiff since his run-in with the German soldier.

Taking his instructions from Göring in German, one of them turned to Claude and demanded in French, "The Reichsmarschall will see everything you have here."

"Do you mean the paintings . . . of every period?" Claude wondered if he'd understood correctly.

"Everything. Every piece of art in the gallery . . . if you please," he said with a cold stare.

For the better part of the next hour, they ignored Claude, even as he directed his gallery assistant, a slight young man who laboriously pulled out every piece from the stacks, waited for the experts to discuss them in German, then replaced each one before taking out the next. Halfway through, the assistant was dripping with sweat. Göring peered closely at each painting but said nothing and seemed not to listen to the comments of his staff; he moved around the gallery as they discussed the works. Claude could see that in the end, Göring alone would decide.

After they had seen every last piece, Göring conferred briefly with his expert, who relayed his message to Claude. "You will reserve for the Reichsmarschall all the works in the front and back rooms."

"Of course." Claude knew better than to ask for how long, or how much.

They prepared to leave, but just before he stepped out the door, Göring turned back with a swirl of his cape and fixed his piercing blue eyes on Claude. He said, in perfect French, "Normally, I look for Renaissance painters and the Dutch school, but here in Paris I find I'm attracted to French art, especially the *romantiques*—the nudes. I'll even look at any modern pieces for the purpose of acquiring them to exchange for more appropriate subjects. You can arrange to have more nineteenth-century French art for me in a week's time?"

"Certainly, Reichsmarschall. After all, this is Paris," Claude assured him. Behind his genial smile, he was wondering how he could ever locate treasures enough to satisfy the voracious Göring.

As though it were the disappearing act of a magic show, with a final victorious swoosh of his cape, Göring was off. The last of his attendants, looking very tall in his hat and long black trench, informed Claude that a member of Göring's staff would contact him to "negotiate" the price. He offered a visiting card, imprinted with a swastika, which declared him "Curator of the Reichsmarschall's Art Collection." When Claude took it, the man bestowed a "Heil Hitler," as though in benediction, and clicked his heels together before his exit.

Claude collapsed into a chair, breath heaving, heart racing. As elated as he might be at the prospect of ongoing income in a time of war, especially when he was pressured by his financial obligations to the German soldier, his stronger emotion was a deep and growing fear. For more air, he loosened the collar of his new white shirt. *What if I fail to follow through?* He shuddered. *How can I keep these Nazi bastards off my back?*

I must have options. I could allow my distress over this to build up all week and kill me before the Reichsmarschall's return, or I could simply give up and tell the curator that since I probably couldn't come up with enough, I must forgo this opportunity to make a fortune and disappoint the most powerful man in France. Or I can use my knowledge of the art world and of human nature to transact something bigger than ever.

When he put his mind to it, it didn't take long for a decent scheme to come to him. This one was hovering above him like a fruit ripening on the bough, begging to be plucked. He had loaned Henri Rosenswig his truck to transport Henri's collection to safety at the château of the Assouline relatives Henri had spoken of with such secrecy. The whole of the rue La Boétie had guessed that Henri scouted for the owners of a fabulous collection, for which he procured only the finest paintings and objects of art. Claude had sold him some splendid Fragonard drawings that he'd been sure were destined for the phantom collection. Only when Henri, on the eve of his departure, had burdened him with the contact details for the château's caregiver had Claude put it together.

Early the next morning, he telephoned the Reichsmarschall's curator to say, "I've been thinking about the Reichsmarschall's needs, sir. I can recommend to him a very interesting collection, really two collections, stored together in quite a remote location."

Details? He could give some. "One collection is in situ at a château whose location I will reveal later. It contains . . . well, they, the family, have always been secretive about this, but I'm sure there are some Fragonards, and I thought immediately of the Reichsmarschall, as the work is so romantic. And there is much, much more."

Let's see, what had he heard? "There are many fabulous collections on the property, of both the decorative arts and beautiful old paintings and tapestries, all of them first-rate. The owner has fled, and was a Jew and a foreigner on top of that, so these masterpieces are up for the taking.

"Oh, yes, there is yet another collection stored there, full of modern pieces that are perfect for future exchanges for 'more suitable' art. It belonged to a Jewish dealer from the rue La Boétie who has fled France, disappeared."

Of course, the owner of Galerie Bessett would expect a commission—"that is, if the Reichsmarschall is still interested."

Later that morning, Claude and the Reichsmarschall's curator sat at the café La Coupole, not so far from the German embassy. Over two espressos and, for Claude, a shot of pastis to calm his nerves, they struck a deal. Claude assured the curator that only a tiny staff was left on the château premises—of this he was certain, because he was supposed to communicate with one of them regarding the safety of the collections. However, the assets of those who had fled France now belonged to the Reich. Though he wasn't sure of its exact value, this was "one of the great French collections," Claude said, leaning back confidently.

The curator listened quietly, eagerly. "Did this collection possibly belong to a Rothschild?"

"No, no. The head of this family is a comparable collector, but far more discreet." At that the curator rubbed his hands together. Claude Bessett was an expert salesman, and when the satisfied curator rose to leave, he had the location of a château, appropriately named "Le Paradis," written in blue pen on a fine piece of white stationery tucked inside his trench pocket. In return, Claude was to receive 10 percent of the value of both collections upon their retrieval and appraisal by the Reichsmarschall, and the opportunity to purchase at a fair price any pieces the Reichsmarschall deemed inappropriately modern or otherwise degenerate, or simply didn't want.

As he stood and watched the German depart, Claude breathed a heartfelt thank-you to Henri Rosenswig.

Forty-eight hours later, a four-truck German military convoy pulled out of Paris, heading south, the men aboard laughing and making crude jokes about what they might find at Le Paradis.

They were becoming known as Göring's Art Raiders, and while only their commander knew much, or even cared, about art, they appreciated the status their special assignment accorded them. But after they had driven around all day, attempting to navigate the country roads, their destination seemed as unattainable as the paradise it was named for.

When the eight disgruntled young men dressed in Luftwaffe uniforms finally leaped out from the backs of the pickups onto the entry drive that night, their boots landed hard on the pea gravel.

Boris, the cook and handyman, watched from the front window. He'd been expecting the Germans since Claude Bessett's call a few days before. He'd been up most of the previous night planning for their arrival, tossing and turning, while his wife, Annie, slept like an innocent baby at his side.

"What are you up to, Boris? I know it's something no good," she'd said to him early that morning, awakened by his restlessness. She'd guessed he had secrets; he'd never been open, even with her.

My God, they're big, he thought, watching the men jump from the trucks. They were young, like the French soldiers, but looked larger and tougher in their Luftwaffe uniforms. He tried to rationalize his sudden undercurrent of fear. Claude Bessett had worked out a fabulous deal for them both. Just show them the loot, Claude had said, and he would pay Boris off handsomely. Hopefully, Boris would never have to work again after feeding these Nazis and showing them around the place. Maybe he and Annie could even live here at Le Paradis for a long time, if the Assoulines didn't come back. If only Annie weren't so moralistic and so loyal to the family. When she found out, she would make him feel, well, like a traitor.

She would wake up, shocked and fearful, as soon as they came through the door. He turned to go upstairs, to warn her, to try to explain—

"Boris Lemoins!" came the shout from the terrace. One of the German soldiers banged on the door.

"Boris Lemoins!"

Boris was in shock as he watched his hand move toward the door latch, unlock it, and pull down on the lever. Entirely of its own volition, the hand opened the door to eight armed Nazis. He could imagine what they saw: a short, sturdy Frenchman in a white nightshirt hanging over rumpled pants, with unkempt graying hair, mouth agape, and glasses that reflected his widened eyes at twice their size.

"Are you Boris Lemoins?" the senior soldier asked in a booming voice, heavy with German vowels.

"Y-yes."

"Is the owner of this house Elizar Assouline?"

Boris nodded, his eyes and mouth frozen open. One of the Germans stepped forward and recited, "We are here under orders to secure the possessions of Elizar Assouline, who is no longer a citizen of France, and those possessions said to be left here by relatives of the aforesaid, who also are no longer citizens of France."

Behind Boris, Annie rushed down the stairs. Seeing the Nazi uniforms, her warm brown eyes tightened until they were the size and shape of small acorns. "Messieurs—what are you doing here? Get out of my house!" she demanded with sudden authority.

"Madame, do you know the whereabouts of Monsieur Elizar Assouline? We are here to reclaim the possessions of a Jew and a fugitive." The officer who appeared to be their boss addressed Annie, overlooking Boris.

"I do not, but this is his home. I am Madame Lemoins, and I am in charge while he is away temporarily."

"Madame, we were told that a Monsieur Boris Lemoins is in charge. In any case, I am Commander Stefan Schmidt, and I am in charge now, acting on behalf of Reichsmarschall Göring. We are authorized to take anything from these abandoned premises to Paris to be sold at auction, with proceeds going to the program to benefit the widows and orphans of France."

Annie sneered at that. Everyone had heard the talk of this so-called program. Like the rest of the French, she was skeptical that these soldiers were here to accomplish anything that might benefit France's widows and orphans. But how had they learned about Le Paradis? Until now, it had been a well-kept secret. Who could have tipped them off? She loved the Assouline family, though she knew that to Boris they were just rich Jews. Then it all came together: Boris's secretiveness, his recent phone calls, his restless nights, his talk of spending money they didn't have. She turned to him, furious.

He ignored her. "Annie, go to the kitchen and prepare something for our guests." He was in charge here, not Annie. He smoothed down his hair and regained his composure.

"Let's get started," said Commander Schmidt.

Though it was obvious that much had been removed, Schmidt told his men to work in the usual way, from the top floor down. Boris had imagined himself ushering them up the staircase, down the hallway past the gray blotches where the Assoulines had lifted their paintings off the walls for safekeeping, and through the top-floor bedrooms. But they tromped up the stairs ahead of him. When he arrived in the first bedroom, he was shocked to see that they had torn it apart, ransacked every dresser drawer, chest, and closet, and already moved on. Schmidt came through afterward, methodically scrutinizing every inch of every room. After they'd moved through, they brought up cartons to fill with leftover trinkets, some decorative items, and the leftover paintings. It took much of the day.

When they'd finished, the commander turned to Boris, feigning great disappointment. "Boris, little Boris, you know as well as I that we weren't sent here to pick up these knickknacks. We're waiting for you to show us where the important pieces are. I know they're here. We were told you were going to cooperate, that we had a deal. But you seem a little shy. Maybe it's time to get serious with you." His fingers tapped the Browning in the leather holster at his waist for emphasis.

"I will show you everything. It's hidden. Outside. And in the cellar." Boris tried to recall every secret hiding place Henri and Paul had planned so meticulously. The more goods he could deliver, the better his life would be.

"Sir, we need to eat first," implored the navigator.

Schmidt nodded. "Right. Where's our dinner, Boris?"

Annie came in. "It's ready for you. Potato-leek soup, eggs, a little chicken and bread—that's all we have. It's not like before the war . . . not at all."

"How about the wine?" said Schmidt. "We all appreciate a good red."

"We have no wine here. The owner is allergic to alcohol," Annie lied. She wanted at all costs to prevent their going to the wine cellar and discovering what was hidden there.

Schmidt laughed. "Madame Lemoins, don't try to fool us—the place is surrounded by vineyards. We want your best. Boris, which way to the cellar? Who's coming with me?"

Annie didn't know how to stop him. Her acorn-brown eyes pleaded with Boris. He avoided her and went for his lantern to lead them downstairs. Boris himself had nailed the cellar door tightly shut, under the direction of the Assoulines. The men lost no time kicking it in. They seemed pleased by the number of bottles visible in room after room, grabbing them up and speaking about them in German.

But this wasn't everything Schmidt had in mind. He wrapped one large hand around the back of Boris's neck and rested the other hand on his holster.

"Now, now, little Boris, as long as we're here, I want to see the stuff we came for. Where, exactly, are the great works of art we are here to pick up?" He tightened his grip on Boris's neck. "You don't want to disappoint the Reichsmarschall, do you? Show me, *now!*" Schmidt raised his voice and tapped at his gun insidiously.

Boris heard his own heart beat fast and loud. He could think of a very special painting to show them.

His trembling finger pointed to a dingy corner. "That one, back there, behind the bottles. That one was of great value to the family." The men helped Boris remove certain bottles, and carefully he reached through the dark, empty spaces they left to lift what appeared to be an old oilcloth, revealing shades of red and white that shone intriguingly through the shadows.

"Well, well, what have we here?" said Schmidt. "Remove it so I can take a look."

The men maneuvered a large painting over the top of the wine shelves and laid it flat on the ground. The gray cloth covered it entirely.

"It doesn't look like much from here. Show us what you've got, Boris." Schmidt looked on keenly while he pressed Boris's neck in such a way that Boris understood he was to kneel on the stone floor of the wine cave while he pulled off the cloth.

"Aha. A portrait of a woman. A beautiful woman." Schmidt stroked his chin. "The colors, the shapes . . . lovely. It's a Matisse, is it not? Yes, even a signature, there." He pointed to a lyrical scrawl in the lower right.

Boris was fixated on the face of Madame Rosenswig, who seemed to be looking right at him, as though she were there with him in the cellar, judging him. Not only was she beautiful, but she had always been kind. What would she think of him now?

"I hope this is only a start, little Boris, because this painting is modern, therefore degenerate. The Reichsmarschall won't keep it for himself. Its value will be in trade. You need to find us older pieces. Don't you have some Renaissance or medieval works stashed around here somewhere?"

Boris cowered, still kneeling. He didn't know much about art, but he would show them everything. No point in holding back now.

When he located a suite of thirty Rembrandt etchings hidden nearby, Schmidt was pleased. Boris received a friendly whack on the back that almost knocked him over. "*Ach!* So you have something for the Reichsmarschall after all. Good. And how much more like this?"

"M-m-much, much more. Many pieces like this, and some modern, and furniture and decorations. In every room down here. I can show you."

"Good—then let's get our liquor and eat now, men. You will show us after. Everything." Schmidt bared a mouthful of white teeth in a broad smile and pushed Boris up to the dining room. The men followed, each toting several choice bottles.

Boris was thankful that Annie was nowhere to be seen.

"I'm pleased with you," the boss said. "Sit down here next to me, at the head of the table." Boris had never sat in this room before. Even with the family away, Annie had never allowed it. Again came an amiable whack that pushed him into a gold damask chair. *We should have hidden these*, he thought in disgust, forgetting for a moment whose side he was on.

Wine was running freely, and someone poured from the bottle into Boris's crystal goblet. He didn't want to drink. He was ill at ease. As often as he'd imagined himself master of this house, he was not comfortable like this. He felt sick to his stomach.

"To Boris!" shouted one soldier, grinning, and they all lifted their glasses to him.

"Come on, Boris, we're toasting you. Drink," came a voice from down the table. They were looking at him. He had no choice. As he raised the glass to his lips, they laughed and hooted, "Heil Hitler!" They filled his glass a second time, then a third, then again.

Boris did not enjoy the attention. He was not enjoying himself at all. He tried to focus, but the room had become blurry, so he pushed his glasses up closer to his eyes, but that didn't help. He wasn't used to drinking this much. He looked around the table at the oversize boy-soldiers, boisterous and jerking in every direction as they barked at one another in guttural tones. The scene was jarring: behind the men in uniform behaving badly, a delicate scene of an Indian garden was hand-painted on the wallpaper. He cringed at the sight of red wine stains on the white damask cloth. Everything seemed terribly wrong.

"Don't let my men frighten you," Schmidt said calmly, as he poured Boris another glass of the Assoulines' finest Bordeaux. "Boris, tell me about the family who lived here."

Boris was rattled by the way Schmidt talked about them as if in the past, then grilled him on the Assouline collections: specific pieces that might be of the most interest, and their value. Boris did not know very much. It was obvious that Schmidt understood quite a bit about art and antiques.

Then Schmidt asked about the business arrangement between Boris and the Galerie Bessett. How had it happened that they had come so obligingly to offer the Assouline collections? Feeling more than a little tipsy, and trying to show that he was not unsympathetic to the occupiers, Boris said, "Everyone is entitled to make a profit someday, and today it's my turn. I've never liked the family very much. They seem so . . . different. Not like us Europeans. I have no difficulties in turning in their private treasures for the common good. But don't tell my wife," he added quickly. What Boris was actually thinking was that the beautiful works assembled by Monsieur Assouline belonged here at Le Paradis, not in the hands of these brutes.

The worst was yet to come. While a few of the men went back to the trucks for extra lanterns and a supply of paper and cartons to use as packing materials, Schmidt led the way downstairs, pulling Boris upright by the back of his shirt whenever Boris swayed a little. Schmidt seemed to remember the secret passage to the wine cave even better than Boris did, but it was Boris who pointed to the hiding places throughout the warren of spaces.

He watched with unanticipated regret as Schmidt uncovered and admired the Assoulines' and Henri's treasures, then carefully repacked them and carried them out in cartons for delivery to their new owner. When he located the Fragonards, Schmidt said, "These are the pieces we were told about. But everything here—everything—is remarkable. It's shocking to me that no one was aware of what these people had here. You may end up a rich man, little Boris."

The day before, this last comment would have left Boris gloating, overjoyed, but today he was emotionally numb as he watched the young Nazis file past him, carting out masterful canvases and tapestries and collections from so many civilizations, brought together by the discerning eye of Eli Assouline.

"That's all; we're done," a soldier reported at last to Schmidt.

The trucks were loaded and ready to go. Boris stood in the driveway, depleted. "Wait, there's one more coming," someone shouted from the château. Two men balanced between them a large painting, too big to wrap completely; it was the portrait of Madame Rosenswig. Boris was caught in an overwhelming moment of remorse. Would he ever see her again? Overcoming a wave of nostalgia, he hoped not. He could never face any of them after this.

The soldiers left as abruptly as they'd arrived. After raiding the wine cellar one more time, then the pantry, they climbed onto their packed vehicles and were gone. Boris wandered through the house, now truly empty, looking for Annie, until he found himself in the unlit foyer. The grand chandelier had been taken, and it was dusk. He shivered but reminded himself that he was soon to be rich, perhaps even the master of Le Paradis, or what was left of it.

Annie stepped out of the shadows onto the landing above him.

"Annie, is that you?"

She said nothing. Then she unleashed a voice of cold fury that he'd never before heard: "You fool! Get out of my sight. You've always been a Nazi sympathizer. But to do this when Monsieur Assouline was so good to us? You're the worst kind of traitor!"

"I did it for us," he pleaded. "So we could survive the war and come out on top. The Assoulines would have lost it all anyway." He began to climb the stairs toward her, to hold her, but her arms folded tightly across her chest and her eyes hardened. She backed away with such rage that he dared not approach.

"You did it for you, you money-grubbing bastard. Leave! Leave and never come back here. I am no longer your wife. I want nothing to do with you or your money, ever. I never want to see you again."

Boris didn't try to defend himself. He knew Annie was right about him. It was finished for him at Le Paradis. He felt he was in the eye of a hurricane that had twirled him 180 degrees and out the door to the back terrace. He walked toward the pond, which had become muddy and foul smelling since the gardeners' departure. He felt wretchedly sick. He leaned over the water and vomited into it, again and again, until he was completely empty. On impulse, he threw in the house key. He had nowhere to go. He stood there in the gloom and cold, watching the water make never-ending circles, feeling more miserable than he had ever in his life. Briefly, he considered ending it then and there, in the water somehow. But in the final analysis, such as it was, he decided there was only one thing to do: He would visit Claude Bessett in Paris and claim his money.

•15•

Paris, The Following Day

The Jeu de Paume was a serene pavilion set in the northwest corner of the Tuileries Garden, opposite the Louvre, in the center of Paris. Napoleon had built it to house tennis courts, and its high white walls had served most recently as an impressionist museum. But when the Nazis arrived in Paris and began seizing private Jewish collections, the initial storage rooms in the nearby German embassy were soon filled to overflowing. Urgently, four hundred cases of work were moved to the Jeu de Paume, which then became the official repository and sorting center for all the art that the Nazis confiscated in France.

On this very early morning, its gravel paths and park-like surroundings were tranquil and still under the shadow of the moon. But indoors the museum was a hive of activity. In just a few hours, Reichsmarschall Hermann Göring was to arrive for a private viewing of the latest confiscations from recently "abandoned" collections belonging to French Jews.

Late the night before, four trucks had pulled into the delivery dock, stacked high with an extraordinary cache of artwork. Luftwaffe soldiers jumped out and began to unload while the officer in charge, Commander Stefan Schmidt, looked on, stomping his boots to awaken his circulation and explaining to a museum guard, "What a haul. It came from the middle of nowhere, watched over by a frightened little

French elf. You should have seen him. And who has ever heard of this collection? No one." He sniffed and shook his head.

A full-time team of German art experts had taken over museum operations earlier that month and expelled the entire French staff, except for one. The German team came outside, anxious to see the latest acquisitions, but Schmidt shooed them away while his men hauled in and dumped pretty much everything in the first room of the museum.

Rose Valland was the lone French person among them. Alert for the clatter of heavy boots on the stone floor that announced every new delivery, she'd overheard Schmidt's intriguing description of the newly arrived "unknown" collection and had managed to stay unobtrusively, almost invisibly, nearby.

Officially, she was not yet a curator in the French museum system. With degrees in art history from Beaux Arts, the École du Louvre, and the Sorbonne, she had been a committed, unpaid "volunteer" at the Jeu de Paume when the Nazis took over, and Jacques Jaujard, the director of the French National Museums, had called her into his office to ask her to remain at the museum, ostensibly to maintain the building. Her real mission, he made very clear, was to spy on the Germans and keep a secret record, for France, of the stolen art that came into the museum, where it was from and where it went. If and when the Germans lost the war, France would look to her records to help restore the art to its original owners.

When Schmidt and his men were set to go, Rose was there to hear him turn back to warn the museum staff, "The Reichsmarschall is particularly anxious to view your top selections first thing tomorrow morning. Better snap to it."

She was sure the Germans would be up most of the night, scrambling to inventory the new arrivals and set up for Reichsmarschall Göring's visit, and she wanted to be with them, to look over their shoulders. She conceded that if they had any positive attributes at all it was their astonishing degree of due diligence; when they catalogued their acquisitions, it was as though they were trying to cover up what they lacked in background. She had watched them slave over detailed handwritten inventories of every item that entered the repository, giving a full description, measurements, and a photo of each piece. Next, they would record the name of the family whose collection it had come from. Later, they would add the destination of every piece leaving the Jeu de Paume. They were never so trusting as to let her take part in their inventory process, but she'd come up with her own list of trivial tasks, excuses, really, that allowed her to hang around and observe. In her own inconspicuous way, she'd managed to learn their routine.

At night she would be the one to stay and lock up, rifling through the trash for notes and carbon copies left over from the methodical German cataloging. When the others had left, she would sneak out with the photo negatives the Germans took of each item and make copies of them, returning the originals by the next day. She worked with the painstaking thoroughness that she had developed as an only child left to play by herself. Certainly they had no inkling that she was keeping a diary of everything that took place in the Jeu de Paume. If they had, she would have been shot.

Tonight I'll stay and reorganize bookshelves, and do whatever I must to learn the identity of these new arrivals, she thought, approaching a harried German curator who was already examining the back of a canvas he'd just set up on a long table in the middle of the gallery. In French, she offered to make coffee for the late-night crew, at the same time positioning herself to be able to look at the canvas, if he didn't move. From past observation she'd learned that confiscated paintings arriving at the museum were routinely stamped on the back of the canvas with the initials of the original collector and assigned a number.

Her eyes shifted, subtly seeking the identifying initials from the "unknown collection," but she had not focused on it clearly before the curator turned to her to say, "*Oui*, mademoiselle. We'll all need coffee tonight," and waited for her to back away.

She blinked, trying to think of another excuse, another opportunity. "And for how many, sir?" She knew how idiotic that sounded.

"The usual, of course," he snapped, turning back to his work.

In the few seconds that followed, she pretended to adjust her glasses while stepping to the left, in full view of the initials.

Without a second glance, she scuttled away to the museum kitchen, trying to place them: *A. E.* It didn't match any of the names of the great French collectors she was familiar with. Then an alarm sounded in her head. Elizar Assouline—was that not the name her friend Henri Rosenswig sometimes mentioned? When Henri and his family had left Paris months before, it had been to join the Assoulines, Rose had assumed. Henri had intimated to her on several occasions that his uncle Eli was a first-quality collector.

She had little time to wonder. The German curators were asking her, in French that grated on her ears, for background information on some of the newly arrived pieces by French artists.

"Don't waste your eyes on these," a German curator sniggered to his colleague as they shuffled past, carrying two small, bright cubist works that looked to Rose like a couple of early Légers. If not asked outright, Rose always kept her opinions to herself. She was, in fact, so discreet on this point that they really had no idea how well she understood their German.

In a spacious suite at the nearby Hôtel Ritz, which had recently become a lavish barracks for top German military, Hermann Göring woke from the dream he had almost every night. He kept his eyes tightly shut to hold on to the vision. He was back in Sweden, 1920, a down-and-out pilot on his last skids. Then he saw her for the first time: Carin, descending the staircase at Rockelstad Castle. He remembered her best as she had been at that moment—an elegant, auburn-haired vision in an ermine-trimmed white dress. When her blue-green eyes shone down on him, he met her gaze and was knocked nearly unconscious. She responded with a warm, almost beckoning smile. He wanted her then and would never stop wanting her. But her weak heart had deteriorated at the same unstoppable rate as his rise within the Nazi Party, and now he was Reichsmarschall and she was gone.

It took maximum effort to force a deep breath, push off his sleeping mask, and open his eyes. He heaved himself upright, his green silk pajamas in disarray, and took a long look around the room to bring himself back to reality. Paris, France. If only she could be here with him now. Though his life had moved rapidly forward since her death, not a day passed when he didn't mourn her. When she had shared with him her love of art, she had told him that he would appreciate the beauty of this city, and how right she had been. Sometimes in Paris he could almost forget the burdens of running a war. What distractions it offered! Everything he needed to fill his Carinhall was here. This morning a shopping trip to the Jeu de Paume was planned, and he felt particularly invigorated. On his first trip to that extraordinary repository, he had chosen no fewer than twenty-seven pieces to send to Carinhall, some of them masterpieces.

Today he would wear his street clothes, though they fit a little more tightly than they once had around his middle, thanks to irresistible French cuisine. He threw on an overcoat cut wide enough to button around his new girth and so long that it brushed his ankles as he walked. He had begun, of necessity, to carry a cane, and today he donned a soft-brimmed hat. He was not going to be bogged down with military costume this morning. How he looked forward to visiting the museum as a private collector. He'd already received word that an interesting new group of works had arrived late the night before.

Paris was a heavenly emporium for the rich. Given Göring's tastes, he thought it a good thing that he was one of them . . . and the highest-ranking officer in Europe, next to the commanding Führer, of course. When it came to ferreting out the best of the best, he could rely on the support of the French police, the German armed forces, and his own curatorial staff and art agents. His private guards and trains were there to take his acquisitions back home to Carinhall. It was as though everything was collected just for him. His only real rival in this effort was Hitler, who had terrible taste, in Göring's opinion. Göring planned to be the first to preview whatever was brought in, so he could earmark his favorites for himself before Hitler's men could put the Führer's stamp on them. Hitler collected for his *Führermuseum,* but Göring was building what he hoped would be the biggest and finest private art collection in Europe, one that he might one day leave to Germany, one that could outshine even Hitler's museum.

The Jeu de Paume had been set up just as he had requested, like the poshest of art galleries, with confiscated Oriental carpets and antiques placed to complement the art, and champagne served before the viewing. From the moment he began his tour, he was completely seduced by the unsurpassed quality of the collection—one such as he had not seen before, extensive but personal, guided by an eye that required nothing less than exquisite beauty. Touring through the first rooms with his art historians and military attendants, Göring was well aware of showing too much excitement and had to control himself to appear nonchalant. When a Courbet landscape was pointed out to him, he nearly choked on his champagne. By the time they'd gone through it all, for his personal collection Göring had chosen the Courbet, three Bouchers, two Cranachs, four Fragonards, an assortment of other masterworks, and several exquisite carpets.

Elated, he turned to the officer in charge. "This certainly didn't take long. What more do you have for me?"

The officer at his side cleared his throat briefly and answered reluctantly. "We do have some side galleries full of degenerate art. It has a high value, good for trading purposes. But that is perhaps not what you would care to see, sir. In fact, we call it the Room of Martyrs."

"Since I'm here, I may as well see it all."

Rose Valland had not been invited to join the Göring tour that morning, so she did what was expected of her: She kept busy, as usual, watering the potted palms and slipping quietly from room to room.

"Madame Valland," called out Göring's chief curator, a tall, rigidly polite man who spoke proper French with a heavy German accent, "I'm unfamiliar with the collection that arrived last night. What can you tell me about its collectors?"

So, she thought, *provenance remains important to these "connoisseurs."*

Even under the outrageous circumstances the Germans had inflicted on the collectors, they relied on their victims' good taste for validation. She turned to walk into the annex where they'd gathered. The four men were there together—the officer, the curator, the French policeman, and Göring in the middle. She had not been this close to him during his first visit to the Jeu de Paume.

Here she was with public enemy number one. Until he had appeared on the scene, she had assumed the greatest threat to French art would be Hitler's bombs, and the second threat Hitler's collecting. But no. This one man could undo centuries of French culture simply by dismantling it. He seemed to have at least some background in what he was looking at (unlike what she'd heard about Hitler), and he was focused entirely on the art. No doubt it was he who had made the inquiries about provenance. No one moved as they waited for her response. The group looked to her like a single, ominous sculpture in marble, with every head turned in her direction—a fascist monument. A shiver ran through her.

Determined to remain calm, she looked through them and answered with her usual directness, "I'm afraid I can't tell you anything. Because they never lived in Paris, and the dealers I know here never worked with them directly, if at all, I have no knowledge of exactly what they have or where it was acquired."

Göring stepped forward. "Do you mean to tell me that not one dealer or curator has any information about this collection . . . or if there is yet more elsewhere?"

She stiffened at the intensity of his steel-blue eyes, set in a wide, white forehead shadowed under the brim of his hat, but answered boldly, "That's right. No one in Paris has ever spoken to me about the extent of their collections. One must assume that no one has seen them." She was thankful that she had never pressed Henri about his cousins' acquisitions. He had once told her of his uncle's superstitious nature and how fear of the evil eye seemed to dictate his lifestyle. They had laughed about it then, but she had understood from that how it would be an invasion of their privacy to ask more.

Göring's eyes bored into her, as though he expected to frighten out information. She braced herself. But he turned to his entourage, smiling jovially, and said, "Whatever they had is theirs no more. What a shame to abandon such a collection!"

Rose's shoulders collapsed with relief when he diverted his attention. She wanted desperately to flee, but she needed to be with them when Göring made his selections from what belonged to her friend's family, to remember, to later make notes, and to one day return every piece to them, if such a thing were possible.

Göring indicated he was ready to view the rest, and her mind raced, looking for any excuse to accompany them. "I could walk through with you and survey the collection," she offered. "Perhaps something more will come to mind as I see the work here. When it arrived last night, we were so busy preparing for your visit this morning that I haven't seen everything yet. But I did recognize many of the modern artists. I'm sure I could be of help." Göring nodded at her absently and was off, the others rushing to keep up. Rose followed behind.

When they entered the first wing, a chaotic display of "degenerate" modern art, she heard him gasp with wonder. Paintings were propped everywhere—hung against the walls and placed on viewing stands along exhibition tables in the middle of the room. Large abstract sculptures flanked either side of the main doors.

"Reichsmarschall, I'm so sorry to expose you to this pathetic lot," an officer entering behind them said feebly.

Ignoring him, Göring came to a halt. Rose watched him slowly rotate his head around the room as his gaze moved from top to bottom like a typewriter. Was he calculating what they would be worth on the open market or in trade for art more in keeping with the Nazi standard?

"No, no, it's quite all right. It's better that you separate the unsuitable pieces from the rest. Most are far too modern. Some, I can see, are by Jewish artists. We can't have any of that in the Führer's museum," Göring said, with no interruption in the movement of his head.

Nevertheless, thought Rose, *it is impressive.* She recognized Picasso,

Pissarro, Braque, Giacometti, and Matisse, and she couldn't help but think that if this were a real museum show, the critics would go wild over such a selection. Some she'd already seen in the Paris galleries she visited regularly to keep up with the modern-art scene, as she believed a curator must. A few she remembered from the homes of collectors who had been so kind as to invite her.

Leaning discreetly against a far wall was a startlingly familiar face. Rose recognized the Matisse portrait of Henri Rosenswig's mother that she'd seen in Henri's parents' apartment when she'd been invited to dinner there the year before.

Furtively, out of the corner of her eye, she studied the portrait of the redheaded woman in a white dress. This particular confiscation she felt as deeply as a personal affront, and she struggled to conceal her outrage. She remembered Madame Rosenswig as warm and vivacious, and recalled Henri's story about how he'd managed to talk Matisse into having his mother sit for her birthday portrait, and how excited she'd been. Where was Madame Rosenswig now? And how had this portrait gotten mixed in with what was here today? Of course—Henri must have sent his family's private works, along with his gallery inventory, to the home of his relatives. Rose feared particularly for the beautiful portrait of Madame Rosenswig, for she'd seen that the Nazis' typical, odious treatment of portraits of Jews was to slash the painted canvases out of their frames and burn them.

"I think we could use some of these pieces for exchange purposes," boomed the Reichsmarschall's voice, interrupting her thoughts.

"Allow me to recommend a few that would command a great deal in the Paris market, sir. They're mad for these moderns, you know," said the chief curator, anxious to be helpful. "I would suggest the Degas ballerinas and the Matisse portrait," he said, pointing at Madame Rosenswig. "They'd do well for us."

Rose watched Göring with disbelief. He had turned to look at the portrait of Madame Rosenswig. The red of the hair, the whiteness of the dress, the sea blue of the eyes were painted in an expressive modern manner that should not appeal to a Nazi. But he couldn't take his eyes off her; he stumbled, barely catching himself on the cane he clenched with knuckles turned white. From the glass in his other hand spilled what was left of his champagne.

Someone pulled a wide, carved chair up for him. He fell into it wordlessly, laying the cane to rest across his lap as though to bar any intrusions. Deep in concentration, he seemed to trace with his eyes the outline of her face and body. "Carin, I am with you again," Rose thought she heard him whisper.

Göring's face was pale when he looked up from where he sat to Rose and asked, "Who is this?"

"This is a portrait of . . . a woman." Rose did her best to discourage his interest, adding, "It was painted by Matisse but is not one of his best works, only something done quickly for a friend. You see how the bright color overpowers the features."

Göring didn't appear to hear her. His gaze was locked on the portrait. He blinked and strained oddly, covering one eye, then the other, as though trying to see the woman from all angles. Then he was mumbling again in soft German, "Carin, it's you. In your white dress, descending the staircase at Rockelstad."

Rose hardly knew what to make of this crazed man and his behavior. She could tell that his staff, standing by uncomfortably, had no idea what was going on.

At last he spoke aloud, his tone again imperious. "I'll take this one. Have it put with the others to be sent to Carinhall. Put it in my private bedroom at Carinhall, not the one I share with my new wife." No one present dared point out that, as a modern piece, it didn't meet the Nazi standard for entering Germany, especially as Göring followed up immediately with, "It will go on my private train."

Rose was thrown off balance. She had never expected to hear this. Now how could she protect Madame Rosenswig's portrait? She listened while they discussed an appropriate description in German and watched them write on the back of the canvas: *Porträt einer Frau in Weiß*. Portrait of a Woman in White. They stamped the initials "H. G." beneath, to indicate it would be part of Göring's personal collection.

In Parisian art circles it was rumored that Carinhall was an ungainly château, continually growing and swelling with gifts and collections that had no common thread except vainglory. It was whispered to be a fitting personal monument from Göring to himself. After what she had just seen and heard, Rose could piece together why he had chosen the portrait. The thought of it hanging in his bedroom was sickening. She swore she would never divulge that to Henri. She hoped only that someday the portrait could be restored to Sonia Rosenswig.

By late that night, the portrait was loaded in a tightly packed car on Göring's private train, shrieking its way into Germany, destination Carinhall, where it would become a portrait of the Reichsmarschall's beloved Carin Göring.

•16•

Paris, One Week Later

Boris had never found Paris to his liking. It was too busy and too grimy, and there were too many foreigners for his taste. And now the German soldiers, too. The food in Paris had always been good, though he expected that this time there would be less of it. Nevertheless, with the fortune he would soon have in his pocket, he had confidence that the great meals would find him.

Turning onto the rue La Boétie, he glanced down the street nervously, looking for Galerie Claude Bessett. He had never been here before, and it made him a bit uncomfortable—to be surrounded by art again reminded him of the Assoulines. He fought to suppress a flood of acid in his stomach.

This part of town wasn't as drab and empty as where he was staying, a hotel in a forsaken quartier that seemed to attract those with drawn faces who had nowhere else to go. He pulled himself up taller. This would be the last time he would have to stay in that kind of a place, he told himself, as he spied the door of the gallery. He would walk in empty-handed but walk out with a fortune. Maybe this would be *his* street one day. He caught his reflection in the window. Yes, his clothes were worn and dirty, and maybe he did look a little haggard from the road, but so what? He had helped immeasurably with the Nazis' confiscations at Le Paradis; he was someone of influence now.

He rang the buzzer. A man emerged from an inner office, immaculately dressed, his hair trimmed perfectly around the ears, his shoes shining. When the man caught sight of Boris, his eyebrows rose in disapproval. Nevertheless, he opened the door. Boris had thought they would be expecting him.

"It's Boris Lemoins. Here to see Monsieur Claude Bessett. We have some business together. . . . We're partners."

"I am Claude Bessett." The man exhaled and held the door open slightly with both hands, effectively blocking the entry. He looked Boris up and down, taking in his soiled and tattered pant cuffs, muddied shoes, and gray hair, kept too long, then drew a long breath in through his nose, as though registering an unpleasant odor. "So, you are Boris Lemoins, caretaker for the relations of the family Rosenswig?"

"Yes, sir, for the Assouline family, lately of Le Paradis."

With a nod, Claude Bessett allowed him in and led him into a back office, where he motioned for Boris to be seated, though he himself remained standing behind the desk.

"I gather it is not expected that the family will return to Le Paradis?"

"N-no, I hope not," Boris stammered. In the ensuing silence, he understood that Claude was waiting for further explanation.

"I've heard some things," said Boris, feeling himself deflate, actually shrink, in Claude's presence.

"Tell me what you've heard," Claude prompted, drawing a finger across one thin eyebrow.

Boris grew agitated and blinked several times before answering. "For one thing, the son, Paul, he was drafted into the army, then deserted. A traitor. In the village they told me he was reported by his unit as picked up and shot by the Germans. He was their only child. He won't be coming back." He bit his upper lip and looked up at Claude, who showed no reaction.

"Ah. And what of these other—Assoulines, did you say?"

"Yes, Monsieur and Madame. They fled to Constantinople, where Monsieur was born. Monsieur told me he might never return to Le Paradis and that I should safeguard the property and wait to hear from him. He said his son would take care of things if he decided to stay in Turkey. But now his son is dead, so there's no one."

Claude looked thoughtful. "Who is at Le Paradis now? Is there anyone there who knows about the confiscations?"

"Only my wife, Annie, is there. I mean, she was my wife, but no more. She's the only one who saw what happened."

Claude nodded as though in sympathy. After a moment, "Then is there no one else who knows about the confiscations? Think, now. This is important."

"No. Nobody but us."

Claude walked to the back wall and opened a small safe, then stuffed a paltry handful of German-occupation francs into Boris's palm. "This should get you by for now," he said. "We've been paid with modern-art pieces from the Rosenswig gallery, and those sorry things are languishing in my back room, just taking up space. But who wants to argue with the Nazis, eh? Over time I can sell them and give you your share. But for now those funds are frozen."

Once Boris had fumbled his way out the front door, Claude walked back to his office and cleared his desk, pushing aside a stack of telegrams from New York to make room for a fresh piece of stationery with the gallery's name emblazoned across the top in bold black ink. Opening a side drawer, he chose from among several elegant pens. Then he made himself comfortable in his chair and began to write.

It's a dirty, dirty business, but a profitable one, thought Claude as he sealed the letter. He had to hurry to prepare for this afternoon's meeting with some new German clients. What Hitler and Göring hadn't yet claimed was bound to be swooped up by other smart collectors, who'd descended on Paris to shop a market in such upheaval that the cream rose to the top. Some of the best privately held pieces were available for purchase; indeed, it was a buyer's market for now, and those savvy enough to shop always paid in cash, to avoid any record of their transactions.

Claude liked doing business that way, too. He would get a good price for the older works, but his hope, his future, his greatest stroke of luck and genius, lay in his stockroom, now home to Henri's modern masters. One day the war would be over, and then Claude planned to sell these extremely valuable modern pieces, either in a liberated France or in America. Even now the French were paying ultrahigh prices for the canvases of Matisse, Pissarro, and Picasso.

For the second time, he whispered a devout thank-you to his friend Henri Rosenswig, whom he hoped never to see again.

•17•

New York, September 1940

Every morning Lili sat at the small kitchen table and wrote to Paul. Her letters, full of news about her dreams for the two of them and their baby, were stacked high in a box underneath her bed in blank envelopes, waiting for an address. She was pouring her heart onto the paper when Henri returned from his daily trip to the post office, holding the usual short stack of local mail. Flipping through, he discovered a thin envelope, postmarked Paris.

"It's from Claude," he shouted, tearing it open.

Maurice heard him and rushed into the tiny kitchen. Lili looked up eagerly as Henri silently skimmed the first sentences. Then his face went white.

"At last! What does he say, Henri?" asked Maurice.

Henri read aloud, slowly, his voice hollow and unbelieving:

September 1, 1940.
Dear Henri,
I have received your telegrams and write to tell you of the sorry state of affairs here in France, in particular those affecting your family. I have just met with your man Boris Lemoins, up from the Assouline property, and feel confident that he has given me a full report of the following very unfortunate events.

First, I must tell you that the Galerie H. Rosenswig is no more. It has been taken over by a gentlemen's shirting and tailoring shop. Everything belonging to you, as well as your father's antiques, has been emptied from the building, including from the apartment and the downstairs storage. It happened overnight. The Germans came through and closed down the Jewish-owned galleries on the street, confiscating their inventories. Yours was the first. I'm sorry, but there was nothing I could do. I have it on the best authority that all they collect, they send directly to Germany.

Secondly, according to Boris Lemoins, a troop of German soldiers raided the Assouline residence Le Paradis, loaded everything of value onto their trucks, including what was stored in the outbuildings, and drove away. As Monsieur Lemoins himself has fled, we must assume that there is nothing left that can be of interest or use except the buildings themselves.

By now Henri was shaking. He held up the letter and, waving it, began shouting, "It's *gone*! Gone, gone, gone! Everything in Paris, taken! The gallery, the apartment, the antiques. All of it! And they got to Le Paradis, too, those damned Nazis. They took it all."

Sonia ran into the kitchen. "Henri, what are you saying? It can't be."

"Henri, I don't believe you. Let me see that," Maurice demanded, attempting to grab the thin sheet from Henri's upraised hand.

Henri fended him off and turned his back on them to continue reading to himself. He glanced at Lili. "There's more. Claude says Boris told him that Paul left his regiment. Escaped."

"Oh my God! Lili!" cried Sonia.

He turned to face them, his body rigid. Avoiding Lili's eyes, he read in a monotone:

I deeply, deeply regret what I now have to tell you. Boris has learned that the Assouline son (I think there is only one) was drafted into the army, but then deserted and was found and shot by German soldiers.

When Henri looked up at her, there were tears on his cheeks. "Paul is dead, Lili."

"No! You're lying!" Lili's hands covered her ears, as when they were children, and she waited for him to tell her so.

But Henri turned away from her, the letter falling from his hand. "Damn them. Those Nazis. Damn them."

For the next long minute, the four Rosenswigs were immobilized in the heavy air of the cramped kitchen, their breathing the only sound as each worked to absorb the devastating news. Lili gulped audibly with every breath, fighting against Henri's words, struggling for air.

"Lili!" Sonia shrieked, just as Lili felt her eyes roll closed and she slumped to the floor. She saw her mother's arms shoot out to catch her, but it was too late.

When her eyes fluttered open again, Henri was gathering her up. "I'm taking you to your room, Lili. It's best for you to sleep now," he said tenderly.

"But the baby!" Sonia's fingers flew to her cheeks. "We must be careful of the baby!"

Henri looked up at her. "My God. Not that, too."

"*Baby*? What baby? What are you saying?" At the look of abject horror on her father's face, Lili shut her eyes and the world went dark once more.

While Lili slept, Sonia had no choice but to spell out her condition to Lili's unbelieving father. Stonily, Maurice shut himself in their bedroom. Henri kissed his mother gently, gathered his coat, and went out. Alone in the kitchen, Sonia picked Claude's letter up off the floor and read it to the end:

My dear friend Henri, I grieve for you all. I only hope that you find that America is truly a new world, and that you and your family are able to remake your lives. When I think how lucky you are to have escaped! I do, in that respect, envy you. Paris is a

German city now. I only wonder what future horrors we have to look forward to here.

Please convey my deepest sympathy to your parents and sister. I will certainly report to you anything more of pertinence that I should hear.

Your faithful friend,
Claude Bessett

She crumpled the pages in her fist and began to sob.

A heavy pall fell over the Rosenswig household. When Lili awoke, she felt barely alive. Her father was sitting on the edge of her bed.

When she looked up at him, her face felt swollen; she realized she'd been crying in her sleep. "Papa? Is it true?"

He reached out and stroked her hair. "I don't know what to say that can help you." Gray curls fell onto the creases of his forehead. He looked so much older now, almost frail. Then he covered his face with his hands and Lili writhed in shame.

She reached out to take his hands so she could look at him. "I didn't mean to disgrace you on top of everything else. I'm sorry, Papa."

His dark eyes were like shallow pools looking back at her. "It's my fault. I didn't let you and Paul marry when you had the chance. Your baby would have had a father." He blinked away tears. "No one must know that your child was conceived out of wedlock. The story will be that the father died in the war. That's all."

Sonia had slipped quietly into the room. "There is another solution, you know. Lili doesn't have to give birth."

Maurice hoisted himself to standing. "That is out of the question! We are still a family of some dignity." And he walked out.

Lili turned her face to the wall. "Papa is right, Maman. I'm going to have Paul's baby."

That night Henri returned home and was surprised to find Maurice on the sofa, waiting up for him. He said wearily, "Papa, I'm too exhausted to think anymore. After a day like today . . . Can it wait until tomorrow?"

Maurice stood and shook his head. "I need to talk to you about your sister. Your mother is counting on you to find Lili a suitable husband. The sooner the better."

Henri brushed a hand through his hair. "Lili is in a real fix. But I'll see what I can do. I'll ask Peterman. He knows everyone."

Maurice's expression lifted; his eyes were riveted on Henri. "Does he? Then ask him to find a nice girl for you. It's time you settled down, too."

Henri released a long breath of air. "I'm afraid that's not going to happen."

"And why not? I thought you liked the girls here." Maurice had pulled back slightly, and the pads of his fingers pushed into his thighs.

Henri met his father's eyes. "I do like girls. But not enough to marry one. I'm . . . different. You must know that about me by now. You can stop waiting for me to marry."

Maurice looked at him, seeming to refuse comprehension.

"Papa, I prefer boys."

His father looked away to hide his sickened expression. After a minute of silence, Henri turned and left for his room.

The air in the small apartment quivered with tension all the next day. While Maurice felt himself to be crumbling from the inside out and Henri seemed a volcano on the verge of eruption, Lili lay in her bed as her mother nervously entered and exited the bedroom, chattering about the baby.

"It's too much! I'm not sure I can survive all this," Maurice cried out suddenly, collapsing onto the sofa.

Sonia came in and then, seeing him, put her hands her hips. "Of course you can. We're facing it together. Everything will turn out fine. You'll see."

"How can you be so sure? The loss of Paul, and what it's doing to our Lili—we can never change that," he said darkly.

"No. But Lili will pull through. I feel certain that she and her baby have a beautiful life ahead."

"I don't know. My God, I wish we could go back to Paris, to our lives as they were," he moaned. He spit his next words through the grim line of his lips. "We never can. When I think of those filthy Nazis creeping into our home! They have your portrait, Sonia." His eyes narrowed. "I'm certain they're admiring you at this very moment. I can see them leering."

"Don't be ridiculous," she said. "Those are just things, possessions, props. I am here. Our lives and memories are with us. We will rebuild."

"You don't understand. The rue La Boétie is all I know. Everything I've built for our family was there. And now it's gone. Maybe you can rebuild, but it's too late for me. I'm lost without it."

Before she could form a response, Henri walked in on them.

"Dammit, Henri! It's all your fault," Maurice lashed out.

"What exactly is my fault?" Henri asked.

"Everything that went wrong! Leaving France, losing our fortune. We should have stayed in France—in the free zone, with our inventory—until the war was over, then taken it all back with us and resumed our lives. But you insisted we leave everything behind to come here, uprooting us all in your madness. It wasn't enough that you were crazy for America. You had to drag us all here with you!"

Henri turned deep red, and his temples pulsed with indignation. "Papa! How can you blame me after all I've done for this family? But, of course, you don't understand what I do. You couldn't take it if you did. Don't you think I'd like a life of my own? Unfortunately, that's not possible for me. You need me to plan for and protect all of us. Because, frankly, you're not capable!"

With that withering epithet, Henri turned away from them and fled the apartment. The door slammed behind him.

He did not return that night, nor had he the next when Sonia sat down on Lili's bed with a sad smile. "Poor Maman," said Lili. "Henri has left you to care for two emotional invalids. I'm not much help, am I? I'll try to be better."

"All right, then. Since you're determined to have the baby, this is what we must do." As Sonia laid out their next steps, Lili remained curled up, facing the wall, but her eyes were wide open and she heard every word her mother said.

"Lili, I understand that inside you are mourning—we all are. But on the outside we must go on. It's the only way. And in this case, we do not have the luxury of time.

"Since you were a little girl, you've always been stubborn but practical. I see only one decent solution here: Henri must find you an appropriate husband. There's no time for discussion about this. It simply has to be done—for the baby's sake. The longer we dilly-dally, the fewer your prospects."

"No, Maman! I can't . . . I won't!" Lili already had other plans for herself and the baby. She was sure she could raise the child alone. Sonia would help her. "I can never be with anyone but Paul."

"That's not right, Lili. Not right for the child or for you. Paul would want his child to have a father."

Lili turned to her in a pleading silence, but she couldn't argue with that. Paul always did the right thing. It *was* what he would want.

She tried to think of herself as Lili the Brave. No matter that she wanted to be alone to mourn, to feel closer to Paul. She was beginning to show, if only a little. A small round was building under her hips, but she was no longer feeling queasy. She had Paul's baby to plan for. If that was really what Paul would want for them, where was Henri?

Late that afternoon Henri returned, hanging his coat in the closet and loosening his tie as nonchalantly as if he'd never left them. Maurice stood by the door, waiting for Sonia to finish her seemingly endless hugging.

"Welcome back, Henri," Maurice said, laying a forgiving hand on his shoulder. He retired to his sofa, and Henri followed him, while Sonia stayed away and nodded to Lili to step outside with her. Henri settled in an armchair across from his father, seemingly as determined as Maurice to move beyond their recent ugly encounter.

"We need you here, Henri."

"I know that, Papa."

"Let's try to forget about what happened between us. Your mother was very worried; where have you been staying?"

"I was at Mr. Peterman's."

"Peterman's?" Maurice raised a brow. "You've never brought him around. Does he have a wife, a family, children?"

"He does not. He's a private man, Papa, and I . . . " Henri trailed off, sitting back in the chair and crossing one ankle over the other knee, then uncrossing it. Maurice met his gaze and sensed a distance there—a sadness, as though they'd become strangers.

"He does quite a lot for you, doesn't he?"

"He does a lot for us all, Papa."

"He must like you very much."

"He does." Henri nodded. "In fact, he's promised to back me in a gallery here after the war. It's likely I'll . . . I've decided I'll stay in New York and not return to Paris."

Maurice felt his forehead contract with pain for a moment. "I'm sorry to hear that, though I can't say that I'm terribly surprised. I don't think there's anything anyone could do that would surprise me now," he said dryly. "But let's not tell your mother quite yet."

"Of course not." Henri hesitated. "You were right about one thing, Papa: I *was* too afraid to risk staying in France. The Nazis are as tough on . . . a man like me . . . as they are on any Jew. They would have found me out one way or another, and I would have been sent away wearing a pink star next to the yellow. What good would I have been to you then? We're better off here, with the help of Mr. Peterman."

Maurice shut his eyes and gathered his breath. "Explain to me . . . You and Peterman have a business relationship. He sells your paintings, and we live on that. What more does he do for us, Henri?"

"Oh, Papa. He arranged for us to reach America, but the few of my paintings that he had, he sold long ago. More never arrived, and we know now they never will. He loans us what we need to live on, because he believes in me. After the war, with my expertise, we'll deal in French art here, together."

"But you can't pay him back with paintings that have been taken. Have you told him?"

"Don't worry. We've worked out an arrangement. He'll continue to support us."

Maurice grimaced. "An arrangement, with a man, to support us? Do I understand you correctly? Oh, Henri, what have we done to you!" he wailed.

"Papa,"—Henri leaned forward, reaching across the space to grasp his father's arm—"listen to me. Without Mr. Peterman's generosity, we would have nothing. Think about it. Nowhere decent to live, no food on the table, no clothes for Lili to court in. We have no choice. Need I go on?"

"Stop! I've heard enough." Maurice lumbered to his feet; beads of sweat had formed on his face. He turned away, then turned back, his voice strangled. "Promise me . . . promise me you will never, *ever* tell your mother or your sister."

Outwardly, Henri and Maurice settled into much the same relationship they'd held before, and Sonia, who watched Maurice closely, convinced herself that whatever had passed between them had been resolved. To her great relief, it didn't take long before Henri had netted a prospect for Lili. His name was Max Kahn. He came twice a year to New York on business, and Peterman had met him through mutual friends who were gallery clients. According to Peterman, Max Kahn had impeccable personal credentials and no wife. After meeting him casually in the gallery, Henri gave the go-ahead. Peterman whispered in Kahn's ear that Henri had an eligible and beautiful sister from France. Kahn said he wanted to meet her.

"He's perfect," Henri said summarily to Sonia when he told her the news. "He owns a clothing store in San Francisco and is in New York to look for fresh designs. He was hoping to find more French merchandise here, but it's difficult because of the war. I think he would appreciate returning home to California with a French wife. Since he goes back in two weeks, let's do whatever we must to make sure he decides on our Lili."

"San Francisco!" Sonia said shrilly. "We would never want Lili and her baby so far from us. What were you thinking?"

"That you would want to go there, too, of course."

"There's simply no stopping you and your mother, is there?" Maurice said, shaking his head in dismay. "I want to be left out of this scheming entirely, until it comes down to a final decision."

Henri turned his back to leave and gave them a flip of his wrist indicating that no matter how distasteful, he had done his part. Now it was up to Lili.

"But what do I say? How do you know he will like me?" Lili asked.

He looked over his shoulder and said, "Tell him anything but the truth. He's coming here to meet you tomorrow night. Don't worry—if you look your best, he'll like you. So, Lili . . . look sharp!" he added in English.

Sonia fussed over Lili all the next day. She had given a great deal of thought to how her daughter should present herself, because while outwardly Lili was going along with their plan, inside, Sonia knew, she was all resistance, believing it too soon to think of another man.

"We'll make you look particularly French, because you certainly don't look American. I doubt he wants that anyway—there are plenty of American girls around here for him," Sonia said. With great care she applied a little rouge to Lili's lips, arranged the natural arch of her brows, and fashioned her hair into smooth, glossy waves that fell just past her shoulders. She'd splurged at a sale and bought Lili a chic dress in an unusual rust-colored silk that fit gently over her recent curves. "At least now you have a few," she pointed out.

Lili knew she should feel grateful, but what was required of her now was all insincerity and acting. Hair, makeup, costume were all in place; she'd memorized her lines. But how to infuse them with feeling?

An actress should feel emotionally prepared for the role, and she did not. Henri did his best to let her know that she looked "tip-top," a compliment he'd never before conceded; it was meant to bolster her confidence, but it didn't. When the door ringer sounded, her heart sank into her stomach. Henri answered, and Lili heard a pleasant, deep-voiced exchange. Then he led their guest into the salon, where Sonia had artfully arranged Lili next to the fireplace mantel.

"Ladies, may I present to you Mr. Max Kahn. My mother, Sonia Rosenswig. And my sister, Liliane."

He was probably ten years older than she was, and nicely dressed for an American, Lili observed dispassionately. He was broad shouldered, like Henri, with a strong build and dark, wavy hair, combed back. His deep brown eyes were kind, and he swung his arms as he walked into the room in a manner that was not quite gruff but to Lili seemed definitely American. Why this surprised her, she wasn't sure, unless maybe she was still hoping for Paul. Her throat tightened. Could she ever accept that he was gone?

Max Kahn extended his large hand. "It's a pleasure," he said warmly. She almost expected him to brush a kiss over her hand, but instead he held it briefly and scanned her face. He seemed nice enough, but she couldn't return his direct look. She tried to make amends by asking, "Mr. Kahn, what is your given name? Is it Maxim? Is your family French?" She couldn't help but hope.

"I'm afraid not. It's Charles Maxwell, an American name," he answered with a wide, healthy smile, his eyes crinkling at the outer corners. "My mother named me. Her family was from Russia. They got out early. They didn't get along with the Tsar."

"That was smart," Lili said. The conversation was not quite as awkward as she had expected. Henri and Sonia spoke easily with their guest, while Lili listened, for the most part, not quite distancing herself. When it was time for him to go, Henri accompanied him to the door.

"Well, what did you think?" he asked when he came back into the room.

"I found him to be lovely," said Sonia, a little too eagerly for Lili. "He appears to be mature, responsible, and, I believe, quite well off. What about you, Lili?"

"He seemed . . . fine. What should I think?" she answered curtly, turning away.

"Well, I like him. He's solid," Henri said thoughtfully, "and that's what Lili needs. But most important, he likes her. Did you see how he was looking at you, Lili? He thinks you're very beautiful. He asked if he could invite you to dinner. I told him it was acceptable to me but I could promise nothing on your behalf. I'd be surprised if you didn't hear from him tomorrow."

Sonia smiled and hummed to herself, almost gaily. Henri looked relieved, then said, "And Lili, try to flirt a little." She wanted to snap back at him, but she was numb.

For the next two weeks, Max Kahn arrived at the apartment almost every evening, bringing flowers or chocolates or champagne, and once an amusing little wind-up dog that barked, and one day an elegant hat for Lili. After an appropriate visit with her parents and Henri, he would take her to dinner or to a show; twice they went to Charlie Chaplin films, silent ones, which she adored and where she didn't have to worry about understanding the English. Despite herself, she was beginning to more than tolerate Max Kahn's company. He was not unlikable. She could admit to herself that he was interesting and independent, that he spoke well and had a sense of humor and an easy smile. He handled himself like a gentleman throughout their dates, though he seemed unable to entirely hide his attraction to her. Lili even allowed herself to think he might make a good father. He had been engaged to marry once, years ago, he told her, but it hadn't ended well, and now, he said, he was thankful.

Lili revealed nothing about her own past and was quietly grateful that he was considerate enough not to ask. Henri had underestimated her; she had not stooped to blatant flirting, and yet Max Kahn seemed properly smitten.

On the night before Max was to leave, Maurice, Sonia, and Henri were out to an early dinner. Max arrived, as usual, but stopped inside the entry. "Are they gone?" he asked, his brown eyes searching her face. Lili nodded. He held her hand between his, as he had when they had first met, but he didn't let go this time. She felt more relaxed with him now and could feel the warmth of his palms. His fingers were thick and tanned, and a sprinkling of wiry dark hairs covered the back of his hand. In every way he seemed to her a grown man: calmer than Henri, more adaptable than her father, and perfectly capable. She had come to like and even admire him. He was nothing like Paul, but she didn't allow herself to dwell on that.

"Lili, you must know I care for you . . . very much. Certainly, we don't know each other well. You are a mystery to me, an intriguing mystery. But I trust you, and I want to be with you, and I've been waiting for this feeling for a long time. I've tried to present myself to you as honestly as I can, so you could get to know me. I'm a simple man. I know my mind, and I'm ready to marry you. Could you take a leap of faith and say yes to an engagement?" He squeezed her hand, and she could hear his deep breath quicken in the silence that followed.

Her head began to spin. A proposal was what they'd supposedly been working toward, but she wasn't ready to face the consequences. As though he felt her hesitation, he moved in closer and leaned down until their heads touched, and she felt his breath when he whispered in her ear, "Lili, I'm crazy about you. Marry me."

When she didn't respond, he stepped back and regained his formality. "A word from you, and I'll go back to California tomorrow a man content. But before I leave, I need to know that you'll have me, that I can count on you, and that when you're ready, you'll come home with me as my wife."

She could feel the baby pushing inside her even as he spoke. She was a fraud, and she hated herself for what she was about to do. *Tell him anything but the truth.* Henri's words of warning played again in her head. She wanted to be as honest with Max as he was with her, with the exception of this desperate cover-up, that she carried the child of another man, whom she still loved. With great care, she chose her words.

"Yes, I agree that I don't know you extremely well, Max, but I trust you, too, and I like you very much. Since I am not . . . in love, I will tell you that if I had to choose from among all the men in New York to marry, I would choose the one whom I liked best and who would care for and protect me, and one day my children. And it would be you. Could you marry me knowing that?" She felt her cheeks flush and looked away, realizing she now belonged to a class of women whom she'd scoffed at in her past innocence.

His hand squeezed tighter. "Does this, then, mean yes?"

Lili could barely breathe, so stifled was she with the guilt of her deception. She thought of the snuffbox incident at Le Paradis, when her lies had only caused her more trouble. Taking her hesitation to mean acquiescence, Max tilted her chin up gently with his thumb and kissed her fully on the mouth.

It was entirely wrong to let it happen this way. She could not continue with this fiction, and Paul would not have wanted her to. Ashamed of herself, she abruptly pulled away to stop Max from going further.

"I understand," he said, and dropped her hand.

"No, Max. You don't understand," she said firmly. "There's something more I need to tell you. There was a man in France. He's gone now, and I'm carrying his child. If I marry you, I would go with you to California and you would become the father of my baby. But you would have to promise me that you would never, ever bring this up again, never ask me about it. Is that really what you want?"

The shock on his face was devastating, even more than she'd been prepared for. "I had no idea," he said coldly, taking a step back. "You lied to me; you led me on." He stared at her, his dark eyes growing darker.

"Well, Max Kahn, now you have it. Your Lili is not so lily white after all," she said, relieved to think that now he would withdraw his offer, and that would be the end of it. There was an uncomfortable silence, and she turned away. She did not want him to look at her. "I think you should go now," she said. Then she shut her eyes and tried to breathe, listening for the sound of his footsteps to the door.

When none came, she looked back. He was watching her, scrutinizing her. She felt sure he was condemning her. She wanted to melt, to disappear entirely. He had every right to be angry, but when he finally spoke, it was without malice.

"Let me see if I understand you correctly. You're telling me that you've been lying to me all along. But you don't apologize. No, instead you demand that I lie, too. That shouldn't be too difficult, because I don't know the truth, and I'm not allowed to ask questions, ever, or the deal's off. All I'm to know is that you loved someone else and you're having his baby, whom I'm to raise and pretend to be the father of. Do I have it right so far? Or do you have further conditions for me?"

How ridiculous I must have sounded, she thought, and covered her face in embarrassment. *If I didn't feel like such a fool, I might laugh at myself.* She looked up warily at Max, whose eyes crinkled slightly at the corners, as though he were about to smile and make one of his jokes. But he did not.

"Well, mademoiselle, it seems that you need me even more than I need you. Now that you've come clean with me, how would you advise me?"

When she didn't answer, he let his arms fall and stepped toward her. In a low voice he said, "Could you ever love me?"

"Maybe. Yes," she whispered.

A look of hopeless despair crossed his face. "Oh, Lili, you will always be a mystery to me. I'm sure of that. I've never met a woman like you—even knowing, maybe especially knowing, what I do now. You're so different from the others. Despite all of it, I can't let you go. I'm in love with you, and I want to marry you."

"Are you certain?"

He nodded slowly, his eyes fixed on hers. "But the child must never be told. It must be our child, my child."

"This child *will* be ours."

"So, then when, Lili? When will you marry me?"

Anguish twisted her heart. What about Paul? Shouldn't she be allowed a period of mourning? How was she to turn her back on their story and never speak of him again? But there was no time now for these questions. She had no choice but to move forward.

"I think . . . as soon as possible. When could you come back to New York? Maybe you could even delay your return for a few days and we could be married this week, before you go. Then we could go to California together," she suggested bravely.

His eyes widened again, and he broke into a smile. "I'm sure that could be arranged."

Sonia was ecstatic at the news. Apparently Max had spoken to Maurice about his intentions earlier that day, so they had expected it.

Late that night, Maurice knocked on Lili's bedroom door and asked if this was her own decision. "I just want to be certain that you were not coerced by your mother and Henri. They have no right," he said, almost angrily.

She wanted to assure him but knew she could not entirely. Instead she embraced him and gave him a measured and steady response.

"Papa, I have no choice. If it must be, I think Max Kahn will do. I'm fond of him as a person, and I think he will be a good father to the child." But her resolve faltered. She bit her lip and asked helplessly, "Am I doing the right thing?"

He stared back at her for a full minute, brooding, then sighed deeply. "Honestly, Lili, I'm not sure. I'm not sure about anything anymore. But, under the circumstances, I think you're making a good choice. He appears to be a fine man, and I think he'll make you a good husband and, yes, be a good father to the child. I wish you every happiness together. You must know how very sorry I am that you have to decide under such pressure. I wish that everything was going as we had planned for you . . . for all of us. But it's too late for that now."

Sonia worked quickly. Two days later, Max and Lili stood side by side before a rabbi in a small Reform synagogue on the Upper West Side, with only her family in attendance. It was an expedient occasion, and accordingly Max was dressed in a business suit and Lili wore a subdued, tailored day dress in navy and the hat Max had given her. "And this, to commemorate our three-day engagement," he said, teasing, as he slipped a diamond ring on her finger.

As much as she had come to value his sense of humor, on this occasion it only heightened Lili's sense of loss. It should have been Paul, and the emerald ring.

Max had arranged for a postceremony lunch at an elaborately decorated restaurant that claimed to serve "authentic" French cuisine. While the waiter poured a bottle of their best champagne—French, but not Veuve—Maurice silently reviewed the menu. His skeptical expression said there was nothing terribly French about it, but Max didn't seem to notice. He was in a fine mood, talking about San Francisco and how Lili would enjoy living there; more than once he pressed her thigh gently under the table.

They were to leave for California the following morning, and in the early spring her parents planned to join them there. That would be just before the baby was expected, as they were all aware, though they never spoke of it. Presumably, that would give the newlyweds time to get to know each other and to find an apartment for Sonia and Maurice. Henri would stay in New York to open a gallery with the backing of Mr. Peterman, and later, he promised, he would expand with a branch in San Francisco.

Sonia and Henri looked relieved and happy, gaily laughing and joking with Max. Lili did her best to play along with their mood, but she was distracted and noticed that Maurice, too, was quiet.

"Are you tired, Papa?" she asked.

Sonia answered for him: "Of course. And he's been telling me that he's going to find a job to relieve Henri of pressure. Can you imagine? He's exhausted already."

By the time coffee was served, Maurice was complaining of chest pains.

"Oh, Maurice, indigestion again?" said Sonia. "You can lie down when we get home, I promise. I'll wait on you hand and foot. After all, our children are raised. I'll have no one but you to take care of until we move near Lili and Max," she said.

Lili did not even try to imagine her future. It took every bit of her concentration just to go along with the plan. It was hard for her to believe that she was a bride. She was dreading her first night with Max. For her, it could only be a disaster. While the others talked, she listened to the voice in her head that reminded her of what was to be.

Tonight I will sleep with my husband. Not Paul, as it should have been, but a man whom I hardly know. Tomorrow I will leave my family for the very first time to cross a foreign country and make a home with him and have a baby that isn't his.

After the celebratory wedding lunch, Lili and Max said their final good-byes to her family on the busy sidewalk outside the restaurant. Max watched with her until they were out of sight. Her eyes were damp. When they turned the corner, she was all too aware that she was completely dependent on him now. She owed him everything.

She tried to think only of that when she slid half-naked into their bed in the honeymoon suite he'd booked for them before their early-morning flight west. She looked away when he climbed in next to her, his olive skin against her pale white. He pulled her into his arms and, lifting her face to his, smiled his warm, crinkly-eyed smile. He looked so happy that she could almost forget herself. His touch was gentle. He was a man in love, and she envied him that.

She was only twenty-one, but she felt much, much older.

•18•

Near Saint-Étienne, France,
October 1940

Inside the prop plane it was deafeningly loud, and the air oppressively stuffy. Paul felt the familiar rise of acid in his chest, along with the thrill of adrenaline.

He counted ten of them onboard, parachutes strapped to their backs, each face as nervous and excited as the next. The small craft was so loaded with gear that there was no place to sit. He squatted, leaning against his parachute pack. Before takeoff he'd double-checked that his kit bag contained the essential tools for a doctor. He never asked about the others, knowing the bulging bags of the Resistance fighters held the stuff of sabotage.

Up front someone was demonstrating with slow, exaggerated motions how to strap the bag to the pant leg. The propeller drowned out the man's voice, but Paul could read his moving lips. He heard his own heart pounding in anticipation. By now the air inside the plane was almost too thin to take in, and he breathed heavily. Beads of perspiration had formed on the face of the man next to him; impulsively, Paul reached out to clap him on the shoulder and with a reassuring smile mouthed the words "Don't worry. It'll be fine." The plane was roaring, and a red light beamed on and off in time to the siren.

"The jump light—it's on!" Someone near to him pointed and shouted. Paul ran through the instructions he'd memorized a dozen jumps before: *Jump, pull the cord, and let your legs fold.* Common sense told him it shouldn't be that simple, but in his experience it always was. The side door opened, and the first man dropped. The next in line, with the sweaty face, braced himself at the door; he turned to nod tightly toward Paul and squeezed his eyes shut, then jumped.

The siren sounded, and the red light flashed; Paul was up next. He forced himself to look down at the moving treetops and sodden green below until the dizziness had passed, and with a little smile and a deep breath he pushed out, opened his mouth wide, and delivered a deep, liberating shout of exuberance. In the four months since he had been separated from Lili, the jumps were a welcome liberation, his sole source of joy.

On a bright Sunday afternoon the previous June, the Leron parents, their four children, and the family dog had taken a picnic down to the river. The German shepherd had run ahead, barking excitedly. The children had arrived first and seen what appeared to be a village fisherman lying on the ground, his red beret fallen beside him. He had been barely conscious, and the children had thought he might even be dead. Their parents had come running after them.

Later, Paul told them that just before he had passed out, ill and exhausted, he had heard a dog bark and strange voices from far away. He had closed his eyes, thinking they were Nazi soldiers and his end had come. Hearing that, the youngest child laughed aloud and hugged her dog.

Dr. Leron, Nurse Leron, and their many children were always anxious to put their skills in the medical arts to good use. They willingly took Paul in, caring for him as one of their own. Under their watch, he began to heal. Nurse Leron started by hand-feeding him liquids. Then she placed a tray and helped arrange his pillow so he could sit and eat comfortably. She smelled good; he thought she was calm and beautiful, and a natural nurse. When she was surrounded by her family, her great capacity to love and nurture flourished. He knew it would be the same with Lili.

In his pocket, the Lerons found a family photograph. The children were excited to prop it up on Paul's bedside table, hoping that when he saw it, it would remind him of something nice. But he shared only minimal personal information with them—solely that he'd had a medical education.

"You and the doctor have been so good to me. You saved my life," he said to Nurse Leron.

"It was fate that brought you to us. My husband is hoping that you will stay on to help us. "I told him I thought you might have other plans. Perhaps with the young lady in your photograph." She picked up and studied the photo. "She's very pretty. And you are quite the romantic."

"How did you know? Did I say something in my sleep?"

"No, no," she said, laughing. "But look how near you are standing together, and, see, your hands are touching."

She passed the photo to Paul, and he looked at it for a long time. She was right. He'd never before noticed that his fingers seemed to entwine with Lili's in the folds of her skirt.

"Besides, it's all you had with you. I knew it must be important," Nurse Leron said.

He was breathing through open lips, still staring at the photo, at Lili. He spoke slowly: "I think it's kept me from going crazy during this whole ordeal. When I look at it, I know I'm not making up my memories."

His finger passed lightly over Lili's face. "You're a good detective, Madame Leron. The young lady is my fiancée. She's all I want in life. Unfortunately, this war has gotten in our way. But it's only a small setback in the grand scheme of things. As soon as all this is over, I'm going to find her and marry her. She's waiting for me somewhere in America. Her name is Lili."

During the first meal he was revived enough to take at their table, Paul looked around at the Lerons' pale and serious faces and brunette heads.

He appreciated this large, close, industrious family that so resembled him that he could be taken for one of them. He wanted to trust them, to relax his guard, but it was too soon for that. Under the terms of the armistice, Jews were to report their identities to the Germans. On top of that, Paul was a deserter, and deserters were maligned everywhere. He shuddered at the horrific consequences his presence could bring to these kind people, especially all those little ones.

That night, Dr. Leron came into Paul's room and shut the door behind him. Paul saw his fatigue when he took off his glasses and wiped his tired eyes. When he'd put them back, he turned to Paul.

"Now that you've almost recovered, it's time you tell me more about yourself."

Paul hardly knew how to respond. He dared not tell the truth, and he wasn't physically strong enough yet to move on.

Doctor Leron cocked his head, studying him, then said, "Then let me tell you what I think. I can recognize men like you. I think you are a Jew and a deserter."

He has a family to protect! thought Paul. *I must flee somehow, tonight. What if he turns me in? I might make it as far as the border, and from there to Lisbon. Somehow I'll get a boat to America, and then I'll find Lili, wherever she is.* A wave of fatigue passed through him. None of this would be easy; it seemed so only because he wanted it so.

Dr. Leron was watching closely for his reaction, sizing him up. When Paul finally slumped with discouragement, he said, "Don't worry, you don't have to tell me. I understand the risks." He lowered his voice. "I work with the Resistance."

"The Resistance? They're here?"

"Oh, yes. They operate in all the nearby villages. They intercept supplies going to German troops, disrupt their communications, do anything they can to make life difficult for the Nazis."

"You?" Paul looked at the gentle man.

"No, no. Not like you think. My wife and I treat the villagers by day, but at night we work wherever we're needed to tend the Resistance wounded. That's why I have these dark circles under my eyes, which

I hope my glasses hide. And that's why my poor wife looks so drawn. We don't have time to sleep. We are asking you to help us. You know medicine, and doctors are few. You strike me as an idealist. One who could dedicate himself to our cause."

"You are right about me. I did belong to such a group, in Paris," said Paul, with the deep relief that comes with honesty. The doctor's earnest face and words ignited the patriotic spirit that Paul had felt among his comrades in the Catacombs; it surged through him. "But I have a fiancée in America. I must go to her."

"You're lucky. Your fiancée is safe. But it's unlikely you could make it to her now; it's too late to get out."

Paul's heavy brows knit together, and he looked away, thinking of his obligations as a Jew, a medic, and a Frenchman. How much he could help here.

The doctor saw him hesitating, and he knew what to say. "Son, fulfill your duty to France. Prove that you're not a deserter. Stay to help us, and after the war reunite with your fiancée and bring up your children in a free world that you helped to save."

That night, Paul sent a telegram to Boris and Annie Lemoins at the post office closest to Le Paradis.

I am safe. Let my parents and the family know.
Tell Lili that I love her and will come to her after the war, and to write me.
Where can I write her?
Send to me c/o Leron, Poste Restante, Saint-Étienne
P. A.

To protect his identity, they called him Dr. Bachelier, after the aspiring do-good knights of the Middle Ages. As he resembled the Leron family in his dark and somber good looks and in his medical calling, he was introduced as a distant relative from Paris. Paul had the daytime responsibilities of a village doctor: treating appendicitis and broken limbs, attending births, and standing by to ease the pain of death. But at the odd hour he was called to the outskirts of town.

Most everything exciting happened after midnight, when a car or motorcycle or bicycle pulled up to the Leron house and a clod of dirt would bang against his window. A moment later Paul would bound down the stairs, medical bag in hand, and, with no words to the driver, be transported to an open field or a hidden shed to treat a serious mishap, such as a delirious youth, screaming in pain, gushing blood, a leg missing from the knee down. Paul became familiar with the smell of blood in the dark.

Dr. Leron went with him in those early days, as an advisor. "It's not so different from any hospital emergency," he told Paul. "Just more violent." Paul had heard the rumors that the local Resistance fighters were not at all cautious in their tactics. They blew up bridges, derailed trains, cut telephone lines, and committed other acts of sabotage, even the poisoning of German food supplies. They were ruthless with their prisoners, preferring to dispose of them, sometimes quite cruelly, rather than take them hostage. Knowing that he might disapprove of their methods, Dr. Bachelier preferred never to be told exactly what had happened.

This schedule kept Paul indoors during the daytime. Madame Leron felt it was safer for him that way. He did insist on going himself, very early in the morning, to check for mail at *poste restante*, the general delivery, in Saint-Étienne. He was bright-eyed and eager when he started his long walks to the town, even when he'd had no time to sleep after his nighttime operations. But there was never anything for him at the post, and he came back tired and discouraged time after time. He talked about making his way to Paris or to Le Paradis, to find out for himself what he could.

"Ridiculous! Go into the occupied zone? Are you trying to get yourself killed? Better to save yourself for the young lady," the doctor told him.

So Paul continued his trips to Saint-Étienne and wrote weekly to Le Paradis, always the same message. In addition, he wrote to his father's lawyer in Constantinople and to Henri's gallerist friend Claude Bessett in Paris. No word came back to him.

"Nothing yet," he would report to the Lerons, trying not to let on how worried he was.

"It's the war. Everything's disrupted," said Madame Leron.

A few weeks into Paul's work with Dr. Leron, the doctor came to him with a special request. "The British are loaning us an aircraft to drop some of our men near a German encampment. Things will be rough. They asked to have a medic onboard with them . . . just in case. I'm too old to parachute. Would you want to take it on?"

He lifted off his glasses frames and peered at Paul with warm brown eyes that seemed to float above deep gray shadows of fatigue. Paul looked at the older man who had treated him like his own son. He risked his life daily, even with a family to care for and the threat of Natzweiler-Struthof, the Nazi camp for apprehended members of the French Resistance. To Paul he epitomized selfless generosity and goodwill, the same qualities Paul aspired to possess.

"I can't say no to you. When do I leave?"

This was his thirteenth jump.

It was a beautiful, clear late afternoon. As he looked down into a landscape that reminded him of the Garden of Eden, he became lost in his thoughts. Too soon he was landing, his left knee twisting beneath him in an agonizingly unnatural position. When he tried to roll off his knee, to relieve it a little, he found he couldn't. It was all he could do to lie there and pray for help, his eyes following the few divers left in the skies, like great white birds that he hoped would swoop down gracefully to save him. He waited, but none did. His eyes closed.

Much later, when he came to, he held his eyes tightly shut. The air smelled of familiar nighttime fragrances. Was he at Le Paradis? "Lili?" he whispered. There was no answer. He opened his eyes to a sky the color of dark ink, with the darker outline of two broad, leafy trees looming above him. The moon, a half sliver, dangled between them.

An excruciating pain in his leg reminded him why he was lying alone at night in a nameless field. Dear God, what was he to do now? He reached into his pocket and touched the photograph to assure himself it was still there. From a distance, he thought he heard someone call his name. It was a male voice, definitely not Lili's. He took in just enough air to call back feebly, "I'm here. Here."

The man's voice came again, but now he heard it clearly. *"Achtung!"*

A light beamed high through the tree branches, and he heard more male voices communicating in gruff German. Paul made the quick decision to try to live. Bracing himself on his left elbow, he managed to roll onto his belly, forcing himself to deny the searing pain in his leg. He could not cry out. It took all his willpower to lift his torso, badly bruised from the fall, in order to use both elbows and his good knee to propel himself forward through the dirt, dragging his left leg behind. He saw bushes to hide in just ahead. He wanted to live to be with Lili, to go home.

The German spotlight was sweeping the ground just inches behind his extended, lifeless foot when he reached the bushes, pulling and gathering his parachute into a lump with him. In a final, violent move, he heaved himself under the thick, thorny branches and buried his face in the dirt, then lay completely still. The words *"vive la France"* rang in his head, as though to mock him. Again, he passed out.

When he awoke, it was almost midday. He heard a male voice speaking in French; someone was trying to turn Paul over onto his back. Pain shot through his leg, and he cried out.

"Hey! I'm a farmer, not a doctor," the man said. "If you'd been awake to yell like that when the Germans were having their party here, they would have found you for sure. The rest of your gang got out of here right away. Good thing for you they sent me back to find you." The man cleaned the dirt from Paul's mouth before pouring water from a canteen into it. Paul felt a little better, held his arm out to the man, and mumbled a barely audible *merci*.

Days later, he was recuperating in his bed in the Leron household, his left leg elevated in a partial cast. He held the wrinkled photograph in both hands, studying it. At times he thought about his parents in Constantinople or the Rosenswigs in America, but mostly he saw and considered only Lili.

Madame Leron appeared at his door. "And how is the doctor today?" In her arms was a tray arranged with his breakfast—a croissant, café au lait, and a boiled egg—and a small nosegay.

"I'll be much happier when this knee is good again. But I *am* awfully well treated . . . for a complete failure," he answered with a wry smile.

"Don't worry. We'll make sure you're back at it soon. Do you know how much they count on you around here? You're a local hero. They call you the Drop-in Doctor."

"A hero? I hope not." Paul looked away ruefully. "That's exactly what my fiancée was afraid of."

"Well, you've found the right calling. And the right girl." She nodded at the picture in his hands.

"Yes, I'm sure of that. And I will find her," he said, indicating with his chin a stack of papers piled on his bedside table.

"Your telegrams? So many."

"Mmm. And letters. They pile up when I don't know where to send them. The complete breakdown in communication is another casualty of war I hadn't counted on."

When Madame Leron had left the room, Paul kissed Lili's image, then pressed it tight onto his chest and wondered how much longer he would have to wait for this madness to be over.

•19•

San Francisco, November 1940

"Shut your eyes, Lili," said Max, as he carried her across the threshold of a white townhouse with ornamental moldings.

"Now you may open them." From the back of the house she saw wide-open views of the bay, an ever-changing gray-blue palette of sky, water, and fog. It felt almost like Europe, but not like home. She was four and a half months pregnant, and Paul was gone.

At least San Francisco was not New York, thank goodness. Lili could already see it was far more civilized, cleaner, calmer, more manageable, and not always trying to outdo itself.

What Henri had understood to be a dress shop turned out to be a small but important department store that took up a corner downtown. Max's paternal grandfather, who had come from Germany, had once run a dry-goods operation in the same spot. The business had evolved to employ members of the Kahn family, and now Max was at the helm. He had only his brother, who had long ago settled in Hollywood as a writer, and a couple of older, retired cousins, also living in Southern California.

Lili had landed in a fine situation for her baby, but too often she caught herself allowing her thoughts to return to Paris and to Paul. It was not that Max made the early days of their marriage difficult. She saw as clearly as everyone that he was a good, caring man who wanted

197

her to be happy. As she had hoped, he appeared to be relaxed in and satisfied with their life together. The last thing she wanted was for him to know the extent of it—that she would catch herself sometimes living a second life, in her head, with Paul.

Max worked long days, before, during, and after store hours. In the early days when he left for the store, Lili took out her sketchbooks and drew scenes of her life in Paris, and with Paul, to lose herself in memories. When she heard Max's key in the lock at the end of the day, she hid them.

"Tell me, what did you do today, Lili?" he asked one evening when he came home.

"Oh, this and that."

His arms circled her from behind, and he nuzzled around her neck. "This is a wonderful city. I wish you would get out more." She couldn't see his face, but she heard his consternation. He was always pushing her to get involved.

"My friends are all waiting to meet my new wife. What shall we tell them?"

"Why don't you explain that you met her quite recently, that she's expecting a baby soon, and that her English is terrible?" She said it jokingly, but deep down she was afraid of causing him embarrassment.

"Don't worry about the baby part. I've said that we started seeing each other early last summer but that I kept it a secret."

"Wait until they see me." She patted the small bulge of her tummy. "They'll know I'm a loose woman, but they'll think it's because of you, because you are irresistible."

"That's the spirit. I like the way you put things in English," he said, obviously pleased. "But if words fail you, you still have your old friends."

"What old friends?"

"Well, me, for one," he said, as though she needed reminding. "And your sketchbooks. You still design in them, don't you? Your concepts were good, from the little you showed me in New York. I'd like to see you go somewhere with that someday."

"Would you really? I'd like that, but would you want your wife to work?" She had assumed he had her father's conservative attitude.

"Lili, I'll do whatever it takes to make you happy." His eyes lingered on hers, inviting her to affirm her happiness, but when she said nothing, he went on: "But first, my dear, you have a baby to bring up."

Sonia and Maurice had never been open with Max about their knowledge that their grandchild was not his. "How insulting that would be," Lili had warned them at first. Now that their daughter was legitimately married, they could openly reveal their happiness at the prospect of a grandchild. Sonia was already making plans for their move to San Francisco.

"Your father and I are tired of New York. There is nothing at all to keep us here now that you will need us to help with the baby," she called Lili to say.

"Nothing? What about Henri, Maman?" She worried that her father couldn't take another move.

Lili heard a crackling on the line, and with a voice full of hurt, Sonia said, "Lili, he moved out on Tuesday. He says it's time that he lives his own life, away from us, and your father agrees with him. Papa says we're much better off near you, where I can be useful. And that with Henri's busy, important social schedule and his business successes, you know, we would see him only once or twice a week." Her voice lowered to a whisper. "Things are not the same between your father and Henri. Something has happened, but they won't tell me. And life in New York is too difficult for your father, especially after what he's been through. He goes out every day to look for work. I've told him it's ridiculous at his age; he should let Henri take care of those things, but he insists. I must take him away from here."

Max's brother in Hollywood called regularly and kept them abreast of the newest films, and on Saturday nights Lili and Max often escaped to dinner and a movie. The local movie house was a Hollywood version of an Egyptian temple, with murals of Alexandria and hammered-copper relief work shining under a brilliant sky-blue ceiling, and the glamorous staging of the day showed the best in costume design. Lili's English had improved to the point where she could read through the newspapers, but the cinema and newsreels were still her fastest link to the outside world.

One evening they went to see *Lady Be Good*, a musical with songs by Gershwin, Lili's favorite American composer. First came the newsreel. These all began the same way: An authoritative American male voice would begin to report what was happening in Europe, and would then be temporarily drowned out by the roar of prop planes and the whizbang of dropping torpedoes. Rarely did they show any actual damage, but Lili didn't want to see any of that anyway. *On with my musical*, she thought.

Across the screen flashed a panoramic, bird's-eye view of Paris. Suddenly, Lili's eyes were following the camera down familiar streets, all the way to the Eiffel Tower. She hated what it showed her. Above the tower, a huge flag with a big swastika was blowing in the wind. The reality was too shocking. Next, Hitler's train arrived at the Paris station. Then Hitler himself appeared, posing like a legitimate hero.

When Max noticed her gripping the sides of her seat, he said, "We can leave right now." But she couldn't tear herself away.

The eye of the camera settled on German soldiers, absurdly visible on the main streets of occupied Paris, walking among the French as though they belonged there. Astonished, Lili tracked it into her neighborhood, right down the rue La Boétie. The lens crossed in front of the Rosenswig home and Henri's gallery. How things had changed! The sidewalks were empty, and a well-dressed mannequin stood in the window of Henri's gallery, under a sign that read *"Lucquot Chemisier."* What Claude had written was true. Galerie H. Rosenswig was now a men's shirting and tailoring shop. Outraged, Lili started to explain it out loud to Max, and already couldn't wait to get home to call Henri and tell her mother what she had seen, when she was transfixed by the next short segment.

A group of young Frenchmen flashed on the screen. They were full of bravado and, said the newscaster, determined to defy the Germans. "The Resistance movement is making some inroads," he said, "though soldiers like these have been caught by German troops and shot without question."

She thought of Paul and her stomach churned.

In the musical that followed was a new song, "The Last Time I Saw Paris." "I will never go back," she told Max as they left the theater. The life that she remembered, that she had clung to, had disappeared and could never return. She did not want to challenge the beautiful memories of her youth, nor to desecrate them. Yet she did not want to lose them, either. She understood that she could not proceed at all if she allowed herself to regret.

But that night the newsreel ignited horrifying dreams she had never allowed herself to imagine. She heard gunshots and awoke in a sudden sweat, her heart pounding. In a panic, she forced herself to sit up and open her eyes, only to see Paul at the foot of the bed. Paul, shot in the head, the face, the chest—red blood everywhere.

Max wiped her face with a cool cloth, pushing the damp strands of hair from her warm forehead. "It's just a nightmare. Can you tell me about it?"

She shook her head.

"Lili, I understand that you have your secrets, and I've promised to respect that. But why you keep them from me, I don't know." He rolled over in frustration.

The next morning, she called her mother. She bit her lower lip as she spoke. "Sometimes it is so difficult for me. I try to live here in the present, with Max. But I feel such guilt. I cannot just turn my back on Paul. He's always with me. He should be here with me when our baby is born."

"But he can't be," Sonia said cautiously.

"I know that, and I am trying, Maman, but I'm not doing very well. If I seem terribly happy, it's because I'm putting on an act."

"Lili, no one can live two lives at once. I can see what it's doing to you already, and it will not make you happy. Paul will always be with you, but now you are Max's wife, and you must succeed in that for the baby's sake, if not your own. Max is good to you, isn't he?"

"Yes. But I am afraid for Max that with Paul's baby, he will feel Paul's presence in our home. He's so hurt already by my history with the baby's father. And he knows nothing, really, about it."

"You haven't explained to him about Paul?" Sonia said.

Lili lowered her head. "I can't. It would only undermine him more."

"That's wrong, Lili. You owe that to Max, at least. Paul is a part of you. He can and should keep his place in your memory, but he must be in balance with the rest of your life, or you will not succeed. And that would be a shame for everyone."

Balance. Lili's mind circled around the word. It stirred something in the past, and she was back in the studio of Monsieur Matisse. She heard his words again clearly, as he had explained it then: "The entire arrangement of the picture is expressive. The place occupied by the figures, the empty spaces around them, the proportions—everything has its share. Everything must balance, always."

She understood what Matisse had shared with her that day; that she had the ability to space and balance her memories to create equilibrium for herself. She would paint a fluid picture in her mind of her life, from memories past and present, a changing picture that would maintain that balance.

One day Max put his hand on her bulging belly and gave a sudden little laugh. "It's a kick, Lili! The baby is kicking!" Surprised as she was, she watched him nearly burst with joy and pride. That moment freed her to begin to make peace with her past. She understood that Max accepted their circumstances and would be a dedicated father, and that Paul would approve of him to raise his child. Paul lived, still, in the most private room of her memories, but she was determined to make the best of the turn of events in her life, and to make a triumph of her choices. When she had chosen to bet on Max's reliable nature, she had been drawn in by his sense of humor. Had she recognized then, intuitively, what she saw now: that he had an equally strong sense of self? Over time, she hoped, she would be capable of giving him her deep and abiding love.

On March 7, Miriam Paulette Kahn was born. They called her Mimi. From the moment she arrived, she became not just the center of their world, but Lili's entire world. So mesmerizing was she, with her hazel eyes and shock of black hair, her long, defined fingers and fair skin, that, it seemed to Lili, even strangers couldn't take their eyes off her. When the nurse held the baby up for Lili's first look, she saw Paul.

She watched Max follow with delight Mimi's untiring facial contortions. *What a tiny thing to be the source of such joy*, she marveled. The three of them burrowed in, and in his new role as a devoted father, Max moved closer to Lili's heart.

Soon after, encouraged by Henri and his reliable monthly check, Maurice and Sonia moved from New York and settled into a small apartment on a street nearby. As Sonia had hoped, Maurice was distracted enough by the baby to put off looking for work, and most days he stopped by Lili's alone, just to visit the newborn.

"It's true what your mother says, that nothing else brings the joy of a baby," he whispered to Lili as the two of them peeked into the crib where Mimi slept.

"Yes. Sometimes I even forget that there's a war going on in Europe," she said.

"Not I. I think every day about going back. But I'm not sure I can wait that long." He put his arm around his daughter and led her out of the baby's room. "I worried so about you in New York, Lili. I never believed then that things could turn out this well for you, and now you have little Mimi, and a fine husband in Max. You've found your peace with all that's happened to us—especially to you. You are able to make the best of things. I doubt I ever will."

Behind his smiles and coos for the baby, Lili recognized the drawn face and slumped comportment that had aged her father dramatically since their family had left France. But she could never bring up those

SUSAN WINKLER

troubling changes with her mother, nor the frequent bouts of "indigestion" he suffered from. She answered him now with a hug.

"It's Henri who concerns me. I try not to judge that boy, but, my God, I think of what he's become and it nearly kills me," Maurice said bitterly. "A parent never stops worrying about his children. You will see."

A few weeks later, the phone rang at dawn. "Papa won't wake up. You must come!" Sonia shrieked over the line. By the time Max got them to her parents', he'd arranged for an ambulance, too, but it was too late.

Swallowing tears, Sonia explained how she had gone to bed that night before Maurice, and when she'd woken early, he had been still reclining in the armchair in their tiny living room.

"His eyes were closed. I think he was imagining himself in our old salon in Paris, sitting in the red chair, looking at the Matisse portrait he loved so dearly. He was happy there, and change has been so difficult for him. I should never have encouraged him to come as far as America. If we had stayed hidden in France, perhaps among others who'd also lost everything but who believed that the tide would turn, that we would all go back to our homes and things would be the same as before . . . maybe he could have withstood. I should have known."

"I won't let you blame yourself," Max told her. "You heard the doctor. It was a heart attack, a medical problem caused by any number of physical issues."

"No, Max," said Lili, wiping her eyes with the back of her hand and huddling next to her mother. "I'm at fault, too. Papa felt beaten that horrible day when Claude's letter arrived. Then he learned I was pregnant. Even his daughter let him down."

Henri came out for the funeral, three days later. Under fog and dark clouds, he shoveled the first dirt onto the lowered coffin, and when they heard the irrevocable thud of earth landing on the wooden casket, Henri turned to them with a look so full of pain that Lili wondered if he could ever heal.

"I still can't believe he's gone," said Henri afterward, back at Sonia's.

He hid his face in the crook of his arm and cried out, "Oh, God. It's all my fault. It's because of me he lost everything. I was a disappointment to him in so many ways. I killed him!" He dissolved into convulsive weeping.

Sonia reached out and stroked his head, saying, "Papa always loved you, Henri. That never changed."

Their only consolation was Mimi. Henri had never seen her and was to leave for New York in two days. He relaxed while playing with her at Lili's but seemed easily distracted by his own thoughts. "The last thing Papa would have wanted was to be buried in America, and now he's here forever because of me," he said to Sonia right before his departure. "I told him I wasn't planning on returning to live in France, and who knows about you, Maman? I doubt you'll leave Papa and Lili and the baby after the war."

Henri's taxi pulled up outside. After their final good-byes, he picked up his luggage at the door and Lili saw the regret and emotion so visible on him the past days suddenly vanished, replaced by a determination so intense it was almost palpable. Then he said, "Papa was counting on me to keep our things safe, and I failed him. But I will get them back. I swear I will get it all back for him. His Matisse portrait will hang again in your salon, Maman, wherever that may be. I promise you that."

When Mimi was nine months old, Max came home from his doctor with sad news.

"I was seventeen when I had a serious case of the mumps, a child's disease. I was too old to handle it as easily as a younger person, and there were complications." He looked at the floor, and when he looked up again, there were tears in his eyes. "Lili, I'm not able to father a child. I'm sterile. Mimi is our blessing."

They had recently started planning for a large family, but now it was not to be. As Lili's role as full-time devoted mother prematurely wound down, she cherished every moment with Mimi, but during nap times, she turned to her sketchbooks to ward off her encroaching feelings of sadness and loss and to thrust herself back into the adult world of fashion design.

One evening she sat down with Max and showed him her drawings. "I've been thinking, Max, with Paris occupied by the Germans, and the French couture houses shut down, there's an opportunity for American fashion to shine. American women who can afford it have always bought French clothing. They say it's a minor casualty of war to be without."

"You're right about that. At the store we have to rely on American fashion houses exclusively now. They're scrambling to come up with fresh designs made especially for the American woman. It's a real challenge for them."

"Exactly! This could be the beginning of a strong new industry. An American industry. And I would like to be part of it. Max, I want to design useful, practical clothing." By now she was bursting with excitement.

Max nodded thoughtfully. "I understand your desire to work at something. And you do have natural talent. But I don't want Mimi to suffer because of it. It's too early yet." He put his hand on hers, reluctant to deny her. "Eventually, when Mimi is in school, if you had your own label, ours to sell exclusively . . . it could work. Yes, I'm all for it."

He surprised her that week with a pile of books that he heaped onto her dressing table, volumes devoted to fashions by some of her favorite Parisian designers: Schiaparelli, Vionnet, Chanel.

"You can begin by looking at these," he said. "If you go through with this, to make it worth your time and mine, and Mimi's, it must be done well. I won't accept anything less." It was a tremendous challenge, yet Lili had a renewed sense of exhilaration. From the store Max brought home prewar fashion reports from Paris and Rome and the newest magazines from New York. When the time came, it would be Lili's job to create the ideas and patterns and choose the fabrics; Max would arrange the production.

Soon after that, in December 1941, Pearl Harbor was bombed, America was at war, and Lili was hurled back into the strawberry bedroom at Le Paradis on the eve of their final departure, that nightmare of fear and confusion. She was pursued by war. Her America was no true safe haven, and she felt afraid for Mimi. While others shed stalwart tears and then turned to prepare for the demands to come, her eyes were dry, but her mind could not focus. She took little Mimi everywhere with her and kept her next to their bed at night. *And what if Max is called up?* she thought frantically. Mimi could not lose two fathers.

By now even America had heard too many stories, once thought rumors, of the fates of those Jews who could not escape the Nazis. Lili's guilt over having been one of the lucky few to have slipped out of Europe early was surfacing—that and the inaccessible part of her past that she kept from Max.

While the war dragged on, Mimi started preschool and Lili claimed a desk in Max's offices. Few women were shopping, so Lili transformed the store's display windows into an homage to women in the war effort: Mannequins sported practical wartime work attire to reflect the large number of Bay Area women who helped in the shipyards. Since yardage and materials were limited, designs compensated by keeping to a narrow silhouette with square, military-like shoulders and short skirts, and boxy shoes that accommodated longer working hours. The new clothes were not terribly flattering, but Lili was inspired by the way they combined the stylish with the practical, and she began sketching ideas for her first official collection.

Her work allowed her to focus and to forget, and she had a reason to work like mad. She had become—almost—a modern American wife.

Part III: Liberation

•20•

France, August 1944

Upon the liberation of France, Paul rejoiced with the Leron family in Saint-Étienne, knowing that all of France was celebrating with them. The Lerons wanted Paul to stay on longer, perhaps to settle there. There were plenty of wounded to attend to, and after four years together, the children had forgotten that Paul was not really their cousin from Paris after all. When old Dr. Leron told his neighbors that the young doctor must return to his practice in Paris, the whole town said, "Why so soon?"

Paul, too, felt a certain familial attachment. The last night at the dinner table, six pairs of brown eyes looked at him regretfully and six dark heads bowed in prayer.

"For the continued safety of Paul Assouline, known to us as Dr. Bachelier, who has set an example of selflessness for France and for all of us in the humble family Leron," Dr. Leron prayed, his eyes squeezed shut.

Paul's face grew red. "Please, don't say that—it's not true," he protested. "I had no choice. It was all I could do. I followed your example, Doctor."

Dr. Leron looked at him fondly from behind his eyeglasses. "No. I could see when you first came to us that you had made that choice for yourself long before arriving here. And I know you will continue on that path."

The next morning, Paul left for Paris to pick up the threads of his life, beginning with the one that would lead him to back to Lili. All of France seemed to expect that the national wave of gaiety would engulf its people. But, like many, Paul found it difficult to shrug off the heavy mantle of his wartime experiences and was more somber than he had been before them. Yet he knew things would be different when he found Lili and they could make a life together.

He passed near the region of Le Paradis but had earlier decided he did not want to take time for even a quick detour to check on things there. Whatever had happened at his home since he'd left (and he shuddered to imagine the possibilities) could wait. All he could think of was getting to the Paris gallery of Henri's friend Claude Bessett. Henri had said that Bessett had promised to watch over the Rosenswig interests. If Lili's family had kept in touch with anyone during the wartime disruptions, if anyone could reach them, it would be Bessett.

When he arrived in Paris, the city was in an ecstatic state of disarray. Parisians were by turns gleeful and distraught, depending on whether, at that moment, they were celebrating the departure of the Germans or were scrambling to provide their families with food, fuel, and other basics still in scarce supply. He shuddered to see the apprehensive faces of men and women waiting in lines outside the Red Cross office for displaced persons; notices with pictures of the missing were pinned to the sides of buildings and on posts that had so recently held signs in German. When he passed by a synagogue where dozens were swarming in to wait for some information about loved ones who had been taken, he stopped to rest and to absorb the full extent of the tragedy. He breathed a prayer for them, then thanked God that he had made it through the war and that his family had gotten out in time.

He went first to inquire about his old rooms near the medical school. The concierge's wife came to the door. The features of her wizened face gathered together in a tight squint; then, obviously not recognizing him, she pulled down her reading glasses.

"*C'est moi*," he said, patting his chest with one hand and pointing upstairs to his flat with the other. When she smiled through a newly missing tooth and nodded vigorously, Paul took it to mean he was welcome back. Then she pointed to his leg and frowned, saying something in Portuguese. He had forgotten that he'd wrapped his bad knee for the journey, and, looking down, he saw that his bandage over his pant leg had become a filthy rag. He smiled back at her and said, "The war." Shaking her head in sympathy, she went to get him his room key.

He glanced around the flat; the little that remained was as he had left it. There was the desk that had been emptied but was too heavy to be easily removed. And there was his bed, where he'd been with Lili, a memory he'd revisited a thousand times since. The space itself had never been much, but he felt comforted thinking that here, at least, time had stood still. He had looked forward to unburdening himself of the cumbersome leather knapsack that held his few possessions, and he dropped it on the desk. Now, to make it to the Galerie Claude Bessett before it closed for the day. On the way out, he caught sight of his reflection in the mirror and was startled to see, in the familiar light, how his face had become rough and lined. He'd been away for four years, he had to remind himself; it would be foolish not to expect some change.

Paul had never been to the gallery or met Bessett, but he remembered it was located somewhere near the Rosenswig home on the rue La Boétie. He felt like a stranger, even as he passed familiar landmarks. When he came to the space that had been Henri's gallery, beneath the Rosenswig residence, he stopped cold at the sign above the door: "*Lucquot Chemisier.*" A shirting shop—how Lili's family would hate to see it. But he didn't want to think about that now. He hurried past and asked a woman on the street for directions to the Galerie Bessett.

Yes, it was just a few steps farther down. She eyed him warily and added, "They have remained open these past years. Not every gallery has been allowed that luxury." He knew better than to consider her meaning.

He arrived just as a "Closed" sign—"*Fermé*"—was being hung in the window. Paul knocked loudly. The man inside glanced up, then turned away and made ready to leave for the day, ignoring Paul, who watched him through the pane adjust his necktie and straighten his suit. *Judging from his proprietary manner, this must be Claude Bessett. Once he steps outside, he'll have no choice but to acknowledge me.*

Bessett opened the door. "We're closed for the day. We'll be open again tomorrow," he said curtly, turning and fitting his key into the lock. "Excuse me," said Bessett. "Let me pass." Paul did not stand aside for him.

"My name is Paul Assouline. I am a cousin to Henri Rosenswig. I'm looking for the family . . . my family."

He saw that Claude Bessett's hand began to shake and that he was suddenly having trouble with the key in the lock.

"Did you not receive my telegrams?" Paul persisted.

Claude turned to face Paul and cleared his throat; he was stone-faced. "Let's see. Assouline—I believe I received a telegram once from an Assouline. I was told the Rosenswigs had left for America and that the Assouline son was dead," he said calmly.

"Dead?" Paul shook his head. "No. And do you know their address in America or how to contact them?"

Claude glanced down the street, as though anxious to end this conversation. "Not really. Henri is in New York somewhere. Our correspondence has been difficult with the disruptions, as I'm sure you understand. When I hear from them again, I will gladly let them know that you're trying to reach them. I could pass on your address," he said quickly. "I'm sure you've seen Henri's former gallery?"

Paul nodded. He'd been hoping for much more than this from Bessett.

"The Nazis took everything, of course, from the household and the antiques shop, and, I was told, from the family's country home."

Paul suppressed a cry of shock. He had feared for Le Paradis and its treasures but had never imagined this.

Claude continued, "Hopefully they'll get it back some day. I've advised Henri to stay in New York. Things are terrible here and will be for a long time. Anyway, they seem to be settled in America."

"Any news about . . . his sister?"

Claude tilted his head. "I believe his mother and sister are living in San Francisco."

"San Francisco?" Paul repeated.

"Henri wrote me that his sister is married there and has a child. Their mother moved to be with her when her own husband died."

Every bit of life drained from Paul's cheeks, until they were ashen.

"I'm so sorry. He was your uncle, of course," Claude said, misinterpreting Paul's anguish. "So . . . you are the son of Elizar Assouline—the only son?"

Paul barely nodded. Claude became solemn. "Then I have to give you some very sad news. I've saved the newspaper clipping."

He went inside to find it, whatever it was, while Paul stood outside the gallery and felt a deep pain begin in his stomach and rise to his chest. How was it possible that Lili could be married to someone else? And the mother of another man's child?

Claude returned, pressing a news article into Paul's hand. Paul hardly paid attention. *What is this?* he thought, catching the headline. *So, a boat of refugees was torpedoed during the war. It happens.*

"Read it," urged Claude. Paul did, but it didn't register, even when he came to the names of the passengers, including Elizar Assouline and his wife, Jeanne. "I'm afraid it's your parents, on the boat from Lisbon to Turkey. Everyone was lost. . . . Bad luck. . . . My heartfelt condolences."

When he left Claude's, Paul's stomach was heaving and his breath came sporadically. Nothing had prepared him for this devastation. He went back to his tiny room, but as soon as he arrived there, he turned and went out again. He could not be still, and he did not want to be alone. He wandered the streets of Paris aimlessly and found himself just before dawn in the Luxembourg Gardens, where he and Lili used to walk. His dark hair had fallen into his face, and wet drops ran down his cheekbones onto his unshaven chin.

In total exhaustion, he threw himself onto a park bench and buried his face in his shirtsleeve, sobbing bitterly for his parents, for Lili, and again for his parents and for Lili. When his tears stopped coming, he was consumed by Lili's betrayal, and he tried to banish her from his thoughts, but she would not go.

Lili, you had no right to do this to us! I told you I would find you, and I trusted you to wait for me. Did I leave you so lonely, or did you love me so little, that you let another man take you and keep you?

Slowly, he lifted his face and wiped it dry with his sleeve. *I should have come after you. I should have said no to Saint-Étienne. I should never have let you go.*

He began making plans to win back Lili's affections, but the more he thought about it, the more foolish it seemed. She had a husband and a child. It would be wrong of him to go after her. She had made her choice, as impossible as it was for him to believe that she had chosen someone else.

She must have believed I wasn't coming back, he told himself. *She must have.*

In the ensuing months, he moved like a zombie through his daily life. It helped somewhat to have a routine, so he rose at dawn every morning to brew a coffee bitter enough to remind him he was alive. When it was still dark, he reported to a nearby hospital that was set up with minimal supplies to treat the most serious cases of the war wounded, those injured or ill who had been unable to get appropriate medical attention during the occupation. He chose to go by his Resistance name, Paul Bachelier, and continue as a medical assistant without his degree. The schools hadn't started up again anyway.

Every day at the hospital, he was expected to repair the pain of others. If he felt anything at all, it was hopelessness. He returned to his barren quarters late at night and fell bone tired onto his bed. Often he didn't bother to undress. He didn't dream. He had no thoughts about his life. What was there to think about? He was a man with no future, no past, no family, no life, a stranger to himself.

The constant ache in his knee was the only reminder that he still had a body. One day he looked in his mirror and noticed that his abundant black hair was turning prematurely gray. The protective amulet of the evil eye that dangled over his bare chest disgusted him now. "You are worthless," he grumbled bitterly. But he didn't take it off.

For months he sustained this meager day-to-day existence, until the numbness in his soul began to thaw slightly and he was able to think of his parents. His father would have wanted him to return to Le Paradis to check on things there, to take charge of the Assouline accounts in Swiss banks he'd had the foresight to establish, to speak to the lawyers and make the necessary decisions. Those responsibilities fell on Paul, and he had to rally to carry them out.

Paul arrived at Le Paradis late on a winter's day. He'd been offered a ride most of the way with a sympathetic farmer from the village; then he had continued on foot. He shoved his hands, raw and cold without gloves, into the pockets of his too-thin coat and carefully chose his steps over the frost-covered ground. The trees, absent their leaves, were like leggy spiders, and no houselights greeted him. Even from a distance, the property looked barren. He'd been forewarned in town that the Germans had been there several times and had gone through absolutely everything, so that not so much as a lampshade was left. When the German soldiers had been billeted in the village, several of the officers had stayed at Le Paradis. Paul wasn't surprised at that. In fact, he had expected it, as he had come recently to always expect the worst.

The farmer had told him that shortly after the Germans had come through for the first confiscations, the cook, Boris, had left. And since there was nothing that needed keeping up on a daily basis at Le Paradis, Annie had gone to the South to seek the protection and companionship of her family for the duration of the war.

Paul had been hoping that Annie, at least, would be there to greet him. But he didn't really expect her to come back. He had never felt so alone. Putting forth a tremendous effort to remain stoic, he trudged through each of the unfamiliarly empty rooms before turning to inspect the outbuildings. By the end, he felt exhausted from pushing away his memories.

No matter how much he suppressed the past, though, one memory persisted. There was an emerald ring in a black walnut box buried under the plane tree where he'd lain with Lili. He did not want to go there—he did not want to unearth emotions that now seemed tragic—but he must. Sonia's ring, Lili's intended wedding ring, had been meant to bring luck and happiness. Could he leave it buried underground? It no longer belonged to him and Lili. Not knowing why, with dogged steps he walked back to the toolshed, where a few rusty pieces had been left.

The ground was frozen under the plane tree and was at first impossible to penetrate. After attempting a dozen sharp blows with a blunt spade, he'd moved only a few centimeters of soil. He bowed down over his good knee. His fingers stiff and icy white, he pounded the spade into the dirt again and again and again, until it hit wood. He eased the dirt around the wooden object until he could push it up and out with the spade. Taking his coat hem, he wiped the old watch box clean. With grim anticipation, he started to lift the latch. But he could not bring himself to open it. It would remind him only of his sadness. He stowed the box in his pocket and tried to forget about it.

His knee ached like mad. As he walked back to the house, he allowed himself to stop and sit on the stone surround overlooking the pond. He did not want to regret—that would only sink him deeper into his depression, and he feared succumbing. He had seen enough during the war to recognize that he desperately needed something meaningful to grasp onto in order to stay afloat.

Staring into the lifeless pond, he understood that to move forward with his life, he must accept what had happened. He must force himself to remember.

A childhood memory sneaked in. He was a young boy playing sailboats with his cousins on a sunny day. Wading in the pond in warm water that reached almost to his knees, he heard his mother call them inside for lunch. Lili was with him, as was Henri. They were happy.

Paul reached into his coat to assure himself that the photo was in his pocket. He felt the presence of his parents, and it came to him then, as though they were whispering in his ear, that maybe he could restore Le Paradis to the family museum it had once been, if he could locate enough of its missing furniture and art.

He would dedicate himself to honoring the memory of his parents by finding their lost pieces and opening for public viewing a restored Le Paradis. There were rumors that headway was being made in a vast effort to track down all that the Nazis had looted.

"Yes, that's it!" he said aloud, and his hands clapped together with the first excitement he'd felt in months. Then a flood of thoughts tumbled forth, surprising him. *Through this project, perhaps I can cure myself. First I must accept that I will never live here with Lili, that I must let go in order to rebuild. If I dedicate myself to bringing back the cosseted and refined world that my parents created, it could help heal the loss of my family and even propel me into a new life.*

With newfound resolve, he patted the photo in his pocket and whispered, "Maman, Papa, *merci.*"

•21•

Carinhall, Germany, March 1945

Hermann Göring had been awake much of the night, listening for bombs. With a damp palm, he pushed off his sleeping mask and blinked his eyes open. Through the midmorning light, he surveyed the opulence surrounding him. All night he'd been tormented by disturbing visions of victorious Russians taking over and inhabiting Carinhall, and that was more than he could endure, even after it was emptied of his collections.

Reality provoked in him an angry despair. "Cilla! Cilla!" he shouted.

In rushed his gray-headed maid, anxiously wiping her hands on her white apron. "Good morning, sir. Did you sleep well?"

"I did not. Get me my medicine," he replied curtly.

Cilla obeyed, as she always did. She had never let down Reichsmarschall Göring, though his doctor had made her promise to be very, very stingy with his morphine. The war was not going well for Germany, and he'd been asking far too often for the mind-numbing doses. He'd been frequently upset these past weeks since his second wife and their little girl had been sent to southern Germany for safety. Hardly anyone visited him. And the men in uniforms who did visit were not as deferential to him as they had once been.

Göring lifted his eyes, darkly shadowed from lack of sleep, to the portrait that hung on the wall directly across from his bed, where he could look upon it just before falling asleep and first thing when he awoke. He always found sustenance in its image, seeing Carin as she had been the night they had met at Rockelstad. Her smile, her laughing green-blue eyes, her auburn hair set off against the white dress— she was there to listen to his concerns and to keep him company. How had Matisse captured her beauty so perfectly, never having seen her?

Of late, though, she ignored him. She no longer spoke to him in his dreams, as she once had, and she seemed to look at him with disapproval, just when he wanted her sympathy.

"*Ach!* Carin." He put his head in his hands and rubbed his eyes with his palms. "With the Russians and the Americans closing in on us, and my Luftwaffe planes grounded for lack of fuel, Hitler blames me for everything. He shouts at me, Carin, in front of everyone, and I know that when my back is turned, they have their fun with me."

Cilla walked into the room, carrying a silver platter on which she balanced a Dresden china plate and pillbox, a crystal water pitcher, and an etched glass. Watching from his bed, he felt the rush that always came with the anticipation of his doses. His heavy eyelids popped open as the flaccid white flesh of his arm reached out involuntarily and his eager hand grasped the pillbox in the thick pads of his fingers.

All at once he stopped himself, looked uncomfortably at the portrait, then turned his back to the image of Carin before he swallowed the pills.

He ordered Cilla out and moved to his dressing table, which was covered with his collection of spray bottles and potions. Already he was feeling better.

Hitler had called him a corrupt drug addict, but what did anyone know of his tribulations? And why couldn't Hitler, who pretended to know so much, see that they were losing the war? The Führer was the real lunatic.

"If I can't protect Germany, at least I can try to protect my own property," Göring said to Carin as he made his daily preparations. No barber would come today, and there was no valet to help him dress. As soon as the residents of Berlin had heard Allied bombs dropping around the city, all but Göring's most devoted staff had begged to leave. Göring had called on his Luftwaffe paratroopers to come protect Carinhall, but when Hitler had found out, he had been furious and ordered the troops straight back to Berlin.

Göring knew it was the kiss of death for Carinhall and that he must prepare. He couldn't stomach the thought of the Russians arriving to inhabit his home and get their hands on his precious collections, which had been crammed floor to ceiling: 1,375 paintings, 250 sculptures, 108 tapestries, 75 stained-glass windows, and 175 objets d'art.

For weeks since, he'd been supervising the packing and loading of these items onto trucks and his four personal speed trains, to be transported and hidden in various secret locations.

One gigantic shipment had been unloaded in a mountain village shelter until it could hold no more. A grocer who lived nearby claimed sympathy and had agreed to take in the excess. Another shipment, the one that contained the most valuable paintings, was stored in an old mine shaft in Altaussee, Austria.

"My beautiful things, scattered from here to the hinterlands. But my man in charge tells me he's keeping a good record of the location of every carload," Göring lamented to Carin, in a voice that had become cracked and dry.

This morning he would send out the final carloads, filled with his favorite, very best pieces, the few he couldn't bear to have out of his sight. Last to be packed up would be the portrait of Carin. It and several other paintings, all masterworks from France, would be sent by truck to Berchtesgaden, where his fellow top Nazis would all retreat. There, he would be reunited with his second wife, Emmy, and their daughter, and with those favorite works of art.

He stood by to watch while the portrait was finally removed from his bedroom wall and placed with great care onto the truck convoy. Then he turned and walked solemnly toward Carin's tomb on the wooded banks of Lake Wuckersee. The air chilled on his final descent into the crypt, where he was to have been buried beside Carin in their pewter sarcophagus. It would not be his eternal resting place after all.

He leaned all his weight against the cold metal wherein she lay, rubbing it, lost in thought. There was nothing more he could explain to her, and so he left.

Late in the afternoon, he sat next to his driver in a limousine bound for Berlin. Cilla held his medicine cabinet tightly closed in the backseat. He was not looking forward to the stop in Berlin, where he was to visit Hitler in his bunker and celebrate the Führer's birthday. What a charade that would be! Afterward, he would join his family in their remote haven, where he planned to occupy his time by checking on things and verifying inventories of evacuated art against the running lists his manager had kept. Then it would be wise to think about his future. Perhaps he could extend some appropriate gestures of friendship and goodwill to Eisenhower and Churchill.

As they drove away from Carinhall, he felt in his bones every familiar curve in the road, recognized the shades of green on every tree leaf and just where the colors of the first blossoms of spring would appear beneath them. He knew he would never see them again. They drove far into the countryside, away from Lake Wuckersee, and he did not look back. His steel-blue gaze stared ahead, unflinchingly, to his future.

Unbeknownst to Hitler, he had managed to keep a small squadron of Luftwaffe demolition experts on hand and had instructed them to wire his beloved Carinhall to be blown to bits when the Red Army approached. It was inevitable—he could not give the Russians his home.

Not long afterward, the demolition squad set off twenty tons of explosives in and around the grounds. When the Red Army arrived, they found nothing but stone and ashes. As Göring had intended, all structures collapsed into rubble, even Carin's crypt.

Of the four trucks Göring sent out on his final day at Carinhall, one was lost en route; it was the truck that held his favorite paintings from France—notably, *Portrait of a Woman in White*.

It was reported that one of the trucks from Carinhall broke down in a small village and fell prey to looting by hordes of greedy villagers, who fought like dogs to take home bits of the rich Göring heritage. Looting was an unfortunate casualty of war that Göring well understood, but this was a case his men were not anxious to explain to their Reichsmarschall.

Unable to stave off the villagers, the hapless driver and guard began serving the fine wines stored onboard as a distraction. It worked, but only temporarily. Within the hour, all was lost: the bottled wines, the paintings, the furniture, and heavy loads of carpets.

Those who stopped to drink hardly noticed while a father and son loaded a gilt-framed portrait onto their donkey cart and ambled away into the hills. And no one heard the older man say to the younger, "She's a beautiful woman. And your mother will be pleased to have this painting hang in our humble home."

•22•

San Francisco, August 1945-1955

One day the sun rose and the long war was over. The harbor and city overflowed with returning American servicemen. Lili felt as if the entire world shared in her excitement. She dressed four-year-old Mimi in red, white, and blue, explaining that it represented the flags of both her heritages, and, joyfully, she and Max walked with Mimi between them to Union Square, where they could view the celebrations in the streets from the safety of Max's office.

Mimi, thrilled with it all, chattered away in both French and English, happy to be part of the exuberant crowd. Laughing, she broke from Lili's grip to point to a handsome young soldier reuniting with his girl in a passionate kiss. As Max smiled in appreciation of his daughter, Lili saw him look to her to share the moment; instead, she felt her face transform with a sharp pang of remorse. Paul should have come home, too. She had been lucky enough to survive the war, but she felt a hundred years older.

She saw Paul now in her mind's eye as she'd seen him last, surrounded by boy soldiers at the French border, shoving a picture into his coat pocket. He hadn't been able to take his eyes off her. She hoped he'd found comfort in that photograph. If she had kept it, she certainly would, even now.

She let her mind conjure the family as it had been the day Henri took the picture, everyone squeezed together, tight and close, Paul's hand in hers. If only she could be, just once, with Paul and their daughter. She could not put an end to the images in her head of the three of them as a family. Even now that the war was over, it did nothing to heal her wound.

She sensed that Max was still watching her, but when Lili finally turned back, once again smiling, to her husband and daughter, he frowned and looked away.

One morning Henri called from New York, very excited, to say that he was in touch with Rose Valland. She had written to thank them again for their part in the evacuation of the Louvre and to report that right after the liberation, the *Winged Victory* had been returned to the museum, along with the other evacuees. All of France, Henri said, was learning about Rose Valland's bravery at the Jeu de Paume.

"They say she was in grave danger, but her secret record keeping is now proving invaluable in the French effort to track down the thousands of missing artworks. Now Rose is helping to recover art stolen by the Nazis, as a member of France's new Commission for Art Recuperation. She said she will help us, and she already has special information about our case! I'm going to read to you from her letter."

Lili and Sonia huddled together by the phone, in anticipation of marvelous news.

Henri read,

I personally witnessed works from your Paris gallery, and Assouline art treasures and antiques from Le Paradis, as well as the beautiful portrait of your mother painted by Henri Matisse, brought to the Jeu de Paume as Nazi confiscations. Fortunately, I was able to keep a record of much of what came in that day and where it was destined, including photographs of many pieces.

Hearing this last, Sonia clapped her hands with glee. Lili held her breath for what Henri would reveal next.

I hesitate to report to you that a fair number of pieces, including the Matisse portrait, were personally chosen by Hermann Göring to be sent to Carinhall, his home in Germany. Others were traded on the art market, but we haven't yet been able to track them further.

I was able to visit the ruins of Carinhall with my colleagues just after the war, and the grounds were littered with eighteenth-century statues knocked off their pedestals by the explosions and broken. We even saw a pathetic plaster cast of our Victory at Samothrace, after the true Victory had already been reinstalled in the Louvre. I can report that nothing of value is left there. I did find a few of the lesser confiscated works on my list, but yours have vanished without a trace.

Officially, all of the Rosenswig-Assouline collection remains missing and possibly destroyed."

"Impossible! My portrait in the home of that monster!" Sonia said.

"And what about the rest?" Lili asked, her heart beginning to sink.

"I haven't finished yet. Listen," said Henri.

So many, many pieces are missing from France. My office is buried under a deluge of claims, and the machinery for restituting those pieces is not yet running as smoothly as we'd like. But the game is far from over. We are only at the beginning. It's much too early to give up hope. At any time something extraordinary might unexpectedly appear.

Yours, Rose Valland.

As the two women remained silent, Henri sounded rankled.

"I want you both to know that I'm not going to give up. I swear that I will find Maman's portrait and much, much more, and I am prepared to fight to get it all back. That is what Papa would want, and he would expect me to succeed, even if you do not!" he said, before slamming down the receiver.

Soon after that conversation, Henri put into motion the reclamation and the eventual sale of the Rosenswig home on the rue La Boétie. He also began the lengthy process of filing claims for his gallery art and, separately, for *Portrait of a Woman in White*, for the estate of Maurice Rosenswig.

Henri had remained in New York, where his new gallery business was booming. He had remade himself there, playing the role of the charming, well-connected Parisian art dealer to his every advantage. New Yorkers commented that he seemed so very French, but his mother and sister accused him of having become terribly American, or, rather, "so New York."

"Won't you ever move back to France, Henri? Don't you miss our old Paris? I do," Lili asked him one day.

"I'm a bit like you, Lili. Paris is over for me. My life there wouldn't be the same; it doesn't exist anymore. When I travel to Paris for business, I'm always looking over my shoulder. The war may be over, but the Nazis still rule. I'm used to my life here, to my . . . freedoms. My men's club there is closed permanently, you know." He knew she understood what he was referring to, though they always skirted the subject. Paris was no longer so tolerant of men who liked men, but New York was.

Not even Sonia seemed to expect him to fulfill his promise to move to California. "Life here is too slow for you," she sighed.

On the rare occasions Henri did visit San Francisco, he was an attentive uncle for a few days, wheeling and dealing with the local galleries, then grew fidgety enough that they would send him home.

On the first visit he brought a girl with him, as a foil to present to Sonia, but his impatience with the girl eventually reduced her to tears. She seemed to adore him in her own innocent way, but in the end Henri wore her out emotionally, to the disappointment of Sonia, who had been hopeful that a marriage might come from it.

Once, when Lili asked him about Mr. Peterman, Henri shrugged and said, "He backed me in the business, but we're not as close as we once were. Father never did approve of him."

It was 1955. A decade had flown by. Lili hadn't minded working from home during Mimi's childhood, taking occasional appointments in her office at Max's department store. She had worked hard for over ten years, and her collections had grown strong; the design world had begun to take notice. Her name was mentioned in fashion magazines, and Max was sending her pieces out to specialty shops around the country. When American *Vogue* did a small spread on her collection, they wrote about Liliane Kahn, a success that could happen only in America.

Shortly after that, French *Vogue* called. They wanted to send a reporter and photographer from Paris to interview her for a story on her life and on the way she personified French fashion influence in America.

"You know the French, Max," she explained modestly. "They don't like to lose out to the new American fashions. They have to publish a story that puts French fashion back on top. It's a rivalry, don't you see? I'm their pawn." Still, Lili was tremendously satisfied to receive this acknowledgment from the French press—it was a reward for her professional and personal successes, and the maturity and confidence with which they had endowed her. She thought about her father and how proud he would have been.

The day the crew from French *Vogue* arrived, no one was as excited as fourteen-year-old Mimi.

From the moment the dashing Parisian photographer, who could not have been older than twenty-two, stepped into their home, Lili saw her daughter blossom. Mimi's hazel eyes fluttered, and she flipped back her light brown curls with the insouciance of a professional model while she conversed with him in French, asking endless questions about the camera he lugged over his shoulder. Lili didn't know which fascinated Mimi more: Julien—as he introduced himself—or his complex camera.

Lili, Max, and Sonia were equally amused and embarrassed to observe this sort of behavior for the first time, and Sonia did her best to subdue her granddaughter. In the end, Max promised that Mimi could be in a photo but insisted that she be pictured only at a distance, if at all, and left unnamed, so she would not be recognizable to the magazine's readers.

Julien was setting up for some outdoor photographs to showcase the American home. He sent Mimi to the far edge of the garden, where she would be intentionally lost in the glare of sharp sunlight reflecting off the bay. "Julien, Julien!" she called for his attention. "How about like this?" she said, striking a pose, one hand on her hip, the other fluffing her hair. Julien laughed.

Lili and Max were watching all this from the house. Max had his hand on Lili's shoulder.

"Is this her first big crush?" he asked.

"Yes, I think so," said Lili cautiously. "But Julien is not a little boy. He's a grown man, and so professional."

A moment passed before Max spoke, his voice casual. "They say a girl never gets over her first love, don't they? Especially if he's a hero in her eyes."

Lili heard the weight in his voice when he added, "I didn't believe that when I married you. . . . But since then, I do."

"Max! You can't believe it still!" Both men had found their places in her heart long ago. She and Max had never discussed it, but it shocked her that he didn't recognize how strong her feelings for him had grown. She turned to face him.

"I've always known you'd never love me as much as you loved him." His brown eyes looked into hers, and with a sad, almost amused smile, he said, "Don't let it worry you. I've stopped waiting for it."

"But, Max, I do love you. I do," she said, surprising herself with the sudden depth of her emotion. "I can't imagine my life without you."

"Is that true, Lili?" He held both her shoulders, and his eyes locked onto hers so she couldn't flinch or look away. It was unnecessary—she didn't want to be evasive; she wanted him to understand that she had changed.

"When you asked me if I could ever love you and I said yes, I'm not sure I believed it myself. But I know now that I do. I love you, Max."

She kissed him and took his hands in hers. "Now, come, let's go get our daughter."

"May we begin now?" The *Vogue* reporter, a chic and compact blonde, pulled off a pair of dark-framed glasses and placed them in her purse. She spoke in French, hinting to Max that he should leave.

Sonia offered to stay outside to supervise Mimi and the photos; the interview with Lili would take place indoors.

"Aha. A Belle Époque salon. Very nice," the reporter said, casting an approving eye over the living room, furnished with French antiques.

"Yes. They say that one always ends up back at one's beginnings, don't they?" Lili answered thoughtfully.

"That's good. In the magazine we want to emphasize your roots, your way of thinking. Your Frenchness."

Perhaps because the interview was being conducted in French, Lili was already seeing herself again in a French context, one that began to unearth not just memories, but emotions from her past.

"Your husband is American, is he not?"

"Yes, entirely."

"So, has he been much of an influence on your designs? I understand that he is important on the retail side of fashion. And what about your daughter? Would you say she takes after her French mother or her American father?"

"My husband has always let me be what I am. He has never tried to sway me to any American point of view. I suppose one could say that he values me for the ways in which I'm different." Lili looked out the window. The photography session was over. Julien was leaning down, his face brushing just above Mimi's hand—a formal French good-bye, just as she used to play at as a child in France, with Paul. She had never told Mimi about him. Would she ever?

"And, Madame Kahn, just one more question. From where do you get your inspiration?"

Lili turned back to the reporter and said softly, "I invent nothing that's truly new. I follow a formula of simple elegance that is the French tradition: a harmony of shape and color—proportion, the same as you would find in any tableau of Henri Matisse. Everything must balance, always. Just as in life."

Lili's daily life had become a safe and busy triumvirate of work, family, and memories, but she always made time to attend the museum shows with Sonia. San Francisco was a city that loved its modern art, and the San Francisco Museum of Modern Art was dedicated solely to work from the twentieth century. Lili looked forward to the newest exhibit more than she had any other. It was entitled "Paris *Moderne*: A View from the Galleries" and billed as "a showing of modernist work on loan from a variety of Paris galleries." Despite her decision never to return to Paris, she was always eager to learn about what was happening there, and European-American cultural exchanges were becoming all the rage.

Henri had written that he'd heard much about this exhibit and that it was not to be missed, that he envied her going, and that he expected a full report right after Lili and Sonia's visit.

On opening day, Lili and Sonia prepared to be at the museum first thing. It was cool and foggy as they walked through the garden that led to the matched pair of beaux-arts buildings facing city hall. Today the fog enveloped Lili and lifted her out of the present. Sonia was so excited that she walked briskly and a little ahead, her gloved hand pulling closed the camel-hair coat Lili had designed for her that wrapped around her slender figure. A hat, also of Lili's creation, balanced on Sonia's graying head.

"What do you think—will there be something from the old galleries? And what about the artists? Do you expect our old friends, like Monsieur Matisse, or someone remarkably new and different?" They pushed through the gold-tipped iron gates and then the doors of the War Memorial that housed the museum.

"For me, no painter could match Monsieur Matisse, and no American artist ever approached the talent of those who showed their works on the rue La Boétie when we lived there, Maman."

Lili picked up a brochure at the entrance and perused it while Sonia fumbled in her purse for her new reading glasses. The list of works on display was extensive. A large number of Paris galleries had loaned pieces, many of which Lili recognized from before the war.

"Look at this, Maman. I see that Galerie Claude Bessett has some pieces here. I didn't think he would ever move into modern works."

"Oh, Claude would do anything to improve his business affairs. I never really cared for him. I always wondered why Henri did."

"I think for Henri he was just an expedient friend," Lili said. "It would have been too much trouble if they hadn't gotten along. You know how Henri leaves every door open."

Sonia sighed. "Your brother can be too trusting."

When they entered the exhibit, the first room was already crowded. Lili wanted to take her time so she wouldn't miss anything. She recognized every artist and moved slowly from one picture to the next, stopping to take each one in. Sonia was less patient, and when she moved ahead of the first wave of visitors to view the next rooms at her own pace, Lili was happy to be left to her reveries. The rush of familiar images took her back to the rue La Boétie. It was a gentle way to revisit the past without having to go there.

She stopped in front of a Matisse portrait of a woman, not as beautiful as the one of Maman, but painted during the same period. Old Monsieur Matisse, famous as far away as San Francisco. A young man stood next to Lili, looking at the same portrait. She wanted to tell him that Matisse had come to her house, that he had painted a picture of her mother, that she had been in his studio before the war. But she didn't. She thought about the portrait that had been lost. To have even the photograph of that painting, with all of them in it, as happy as they had been then, would be wonderful.

"Are you okay, miss?" It was the young man next to her. She looked at him through a blur and realized that she was crying.

The next minute, Sonia returned. Her eyes were a roiling deep sea of murky gray, and her jaw was stiff when she tried to speak. She motioned with her head toward the door and led Lili out of the gallery.

"What is it, Maman?" she whispered.

Once they were outside, Sonia shut her eyes, put a gloved hand to her face, and breathed deeply. But when her eyes opened, they were still dark and stormy.

"You won't believe it! They're displaying a picture here that used to hang in Henri's gallery! You remember the Dufy watercolor that he kept in his office, of the horses in the Bois de Boulogne? It's the same. It's here—on loan from Galerie Claude Bessett! Oh, that lowlife Claude."

"And what a fool he is to have sent it here! Henri will be able to prove that the Dufy is his, and it will not be returned to Claude," said Lili, recalling the records Rose had kept, and about something Henri had told her: that many French art galleries had lied after the war about dealing in stolen Jewish art, then collaborated to protect each other. To his credit, Henri had persevered in his effort to track down the Rosenswigs' lost works and had reclaimed a few of his own pieces, which he'd come across in American galleries and auction houses, and others, with the help of Rose and the commission. But he was deeply frustrated by the dead ends in his quest for the Matisse.

Sonia was already lighting a cigarette. "And then what about the rest? Where are our antiques? And where is my portrait?"

They rushed home to call Henri. On the phone, Sonia explained it to him in fast-spoken, outraged French: "If Claude has this piece from your gallery, then he has more. Henri, you must do something!"

The next day, Henri got on a plane to Paris to confront Claude, armed with copies of photographic images and lists that Rose had sent him after the war. They heard from him again a week later.

"I think I always knew that Claude was capable of treachery; I just prayed I would never have to see it," he told them from New York. "At first Claude denied everything. The coward! He said he bought the Dufy from an established dealer, and it came with a complete and irreproachable provenance. I threatened to bring charges against him, not just for the Dufy but for all that was lost at Le Paradis: my inventory, as well as the Assouline collections. He as much as admitted all by begging me to drop charges in exchange for giving me my Dufy! I refused. He didn't know that I'd already arranged for its legal return to me in New York after the San Francisco show.

"Here's where it takes a bad turn. Then it came out that Claude had sold all the modern pieces from my gallery to dealers in Switzerland, just after the Swiss five-year statute of limitations for art restitution had expired. I might have to buy back every damned piece!

"I'm going to press charges against him in France, if it takes both of our lifetimes to get to the bottom of it. I told him he helped ruin Papa and that I would do whatever it takes to get back my art and Maman's portrait."

Part IV: Restitution

•23•

Switzerland, 1955-1963

Heavy snow was falling in the Appenzell Alps near the Swiss–German border when Paul Assouline, his black Renault covered in white, pulled up in front of a familiar bric-a-brac shop. He climbed out and wrapped his blue scarf more tightly, tucked it into his overcoat, and headed indoors. Inside the entry, he stopped to brush wet flakes from his hair and stomp the snow from his shoes while his trained eyes scanned the premises, seeking a familiar family object.

"Monsieur Bachelier, is it you, out on such a day?" the proprietor greeted him.

"You know me. I'm always looking," Paul smiled.

"Sometimes I think it's you who keeps this business interesting, monsieur. Most visitors here want only a souvenir, an Alpine cowbell to take home with them. But you recognize what is special. You should visit us more often," said the proprietor. It was known in the trade that Paul Bachelier, a Frenchman living in Geneva, owned a fine-antiques and Old Masters gallery in the medieval ramparts, and that he spent most weekends traveling in his car, attending auctions and flea markets, visiting dealers, and stopping in at antiques shops along the way, always engaging in friendly conversation. He was a good customer; he always paid in cash and had his acquisitions sent to his warehouse in Geneva, but he revealed nothing about himself.

He'd named his gallery "*Au Temps Perdu*," after Proust's *In Search of Lost Time.*

"So, do you have anything special for me today?" Paul asked.

"Yes, I just might." The proprietor thought for a moment, then walked to a carved case filled with small objects behind a glass front. Opening it, he said, "I've never seen a more beautiful box than this one that came to me recently. Very special."

Paul came closer to examine what the proprietor held out to him. A Japanese snuffbox. It shimmered. A painted swan floated under a cherry blossom tree—exquisite. His heart beat faster. He had to be sure it was the same. He took it and turned it upside down to see that the reversed initials *A. E.* were printed there. Yes, it had belonged to his father, Elizar Assouline, before the Nazis had taken it. His heart leaped quietly, and he remembered how important this particular box had been to his father, how Eli had come to depend on it for his hashish. Slowly, Paul twirled the delicate box in his fingers, allowing his mind to return with both joy and melancholy to his father's study at Le Paradis, and the day when Lili had tipped it open and fainted from smelling its contents came back to him. When he had found her on the floor, he had known even then that he loved her.

Now thirty-nine years old, he recalled the day he had visited desolate Le Paradis after the war and was reminded of the despair he had felt upon seeing it. After that trip, he had had the estate boarded up, had returned to Paris, and, following seemingly endless meetings with his father's lawyers and bankers, had put in order what was left of the Assouline family's affairs. His father had been wise in his financial dealings and had left Paul with the resources to proceed with his plan to restore Le Paradis, which Paul grew to think of as an empty tomb, waiting to be opened and brought back to life.

As there was nothing left for him in Paris, Paul had chosen to begin his undertaking in Geneva, the crossroads for lost art, where he was well situated to track down and restore his family's collections. Swiss dealers and collectors had taken advantage of their country's wartime neutrality and secrecy in banking to do business with both the Reich and the Allies during the war, and were now known to sell and exchange plundered art from that time.

Under the dark clouds of his early years in Switzerland, when damp brown leaves fell on the gray cobblestones of the Old Town, Paul grew accustomed to depression and relied on his work as a dealer of beautiful, high-quality objects to buffer him. Quietly and discreetly, he spent his days, weeks, years, in the gallery, seeking traces of the Assouline collections. No one, except perhaps a curator or two at Sotheby's Geneva office, had any idea how passionate he was about finding certain pieces of art and antiques. The quest gave purpose to his life, but many works remained missing.

When the frustrations and false starts of tracking down the Assouline collections threatened to overwhelm him, he could rely on his greatest source of satisfaction: One day each week, he closed the shop to volunteer as Dr. Bachelier, training medics being sent to disaster sites by the International Red Cross.

Well into middle age, Paul remained handsome, even with silver-gray hair and a slight limp that required him to use a cane. He was also a confirmed bachelor, so no one was more surprised than Paul himself when, in 1963, he suddenly realized that he had been seeing Claire regularly for almost a year.

Sylvan, a married man and Paul's closest friend, had introduced Paul to Claire at a soiree in Sylvan's home that he had plotted exactly for that purpose.

"You're a fool if you don't marry her. She's perfect for you," Sylvan had told him, both then and since.

Claire was originally French, and high up at the World Health Organization. When Paul asked her why she had never married, she replied, "My family had been taken to the camps, and I was emotionally absent for so long after that. Bad timing, I guess. Just like you." Paul understood her, and he liked their similarities and felt at ease in her calm and gentle presence. Since they had begun seeing each other, he had a new twinkle in his eye.

Sylvan is right about her, thought Paul one night, lying next to Claire in bed. *At last I can be free of the disappointments of my past. It's time.* He asked her to marry him, and when she said yes, it was with such love and warmth that it kindled in him a strong sense of alliance. He remembered the feeling he'd had jumping from a prop plane in a parachute, waiting to experience the world anew.

He also knew it was time to let go of Le Paradis, and three weeks later he was on the verge of completing its sale to an American family. Though he'd had no desire to live in France since the war, over time he'd fully rescued Le Paradis from near dilapidation and continued to maintain the property once he had restored it. It deserved a family who would take care of it and reestablish the active household it had once been.

Paul's warehouse had been slowly filling with art and furniture that had been taken from the Assoulines, and, though a sprinkling of important pieces had turned up over the years (a pair of rare Chinese vases, a Savonnerie carpet made originally for Versailles, a Rembrandt drawing), he was discouraged that he hadn't recovered enough to reopen Le Paradis as a memorial to his parents. Despite his long endeavors, he didn't begin to recover his sense of family until he met the American couple one afternoon at his attorney's office for the purpose of signing the closing papers of sale.

When he arrived, the American couple was already waiting for him, and Paul prepared to speak English. The woman stood slender and pale near her businesslike husband, chattering excitedly and whispering something about a "decorating budget." This was a term he'd heard from time to time in his gallery, always from Americans. The concept was silly, he thought. But he felt kindly toward this attractive young woman and her good intentions. She seemed overjoyed with the idea of living in France.

The lawyer, a reserved man who spoke with the staccato *tick-tock* of an old clock, had represented Paul for many years. His forearm thrust out like a minute hand to make the introductions to the current owner. "Monsieur Bachelier."

The woman, Mrs. Hardy, looked confused. "But I thought we were buying the Assouline property." The lawyer, unsure how to proceed, cleared his throat and looked at Paul to give the go-ahead before he explained that Monsieur Assouline and Monsieur Bachelier were one and the same.

"Oh, thank goodness," she said. "It would be so disappointing to learn that it wasn't the famous Assouline property after all, the one we've heard so much about."

Her comment threw Paul, who hadn't heard anyone mention the Assouline family since he'd left France. "But, Madame Hardy," he said, "where did you hear of the Assoulines and Le Paradis? What do you know of the family?"

Mrs. Hardy looked at her husband, who offered simply, "We're clients of Henri Rosenswig's gallery in New York."

Paul felt his knee begin to give way, and he leaned heavily on his cane.

"That's right. Henri told me once of an Assouline family home called Le Paradis that the Germans completely swept through during the war," the woman continued. "His descriptions of family life there were so beautiful, and the end so tragic, I simply couldn't forget it. Now that we're looking for property in France, to stumble upon it like this, it is just amazing."

"You know . . . Henri?" Paul dipped deep into a well in his chest to be able to say his cousin's name.

"Why, yes. Everyone who has an interest in French modern art knows Henri. He's one of the most important modern dealers in New York, you know," she said.

Of course he would be, Paul said to himself. "Has he said anything about . . . his family?"

"Well, he once told me that the family who were left in Europe didn't survive the war. But his mother and sister are on the West Coast. He goes to San Francisco a lot to visit them. His sister is a well-known clothing designer. I read about her from time to time in the fashion magazines. She has a line she started years ago for her husband's department store. Oh! And I once met his niece in New York. A darling girl. Henri is very proud of her, the first generation of his family to be born in America."

In a daze, Paul signed the closing papers. "Selling must be very emotional for you, Monsieur Assouline," said Mrs. Hardy.

"No. No, it really isn't. It's time," Paul said, before excusing himself politely and bolting from the lawyer's office to be at the library before closing time.

He spent the first minutes at the card catalog, looking for articles about Lili Rosenswig. It seemed useless. Then he remembered: Her name would have changed. He found something under 'Liliane, fashion,' in an old French *Vogue*, dated 1955. The article was long. Some of the pages had been ripped out, probably for pictures of the clothing collection. There was no picture of Lili. But wait. There was the home of Liliane Kahn—could it be his Lili? And, from a distance, a young girl on the verge of becoming a teenager. She had Lili's size and shape at that age. The photo was black and white, and he couldn't make out the details of the girl's face, but her hair's soft waves and her wide smile reminded Paul of his mother.

Could it be possible . . . our child?

Paul felt electrified and unsettled. He called Claire with a last-minute excuse. "Not tonight, but we'll see each other tomorrow. I'll explain to you then. I'm afraid I can't go into it until I understand it myself."

He spent the evening home alone, nursing a cognac and pacing his apartment and thinking. Eventually, that wore out his knee, so he installed himself on the leather sofa, cradling another drink.

He became aware that he had been, for the most part, successful in avoiding his past, preferring to focus on the race to find bits and pieces of his parents' collections. But the events of this afternoon had caught him off guard. *Naturally, they would be living their lives, Henri, Lili, and Auntie Sonia. Were they living with the misinformation that I had not made it through the war, as the American woman had suggested? That could make sense. Otherwise, they would have found me.*

Did I purposely make myself obscure by changing my name and moving to Switzerland?

He stood again to pace and take a hard look at his own motives. *Perhaps I took on the new identity to distance myself from Lili, and by default from them all. What a fool I've been!*

He convinced himself that the Rosenswigs had no way of knowing he had survived the war and was living in Switzerland. Would Lili have made the choices she had if she hadn't believed him lost? How could he tell them that he'd been alive all this time and not searched for them? Sooner or later, the Hardys would tell Henri that they had bought Le Paradis from Paul Assouline.

Then he realized that none of his speculation even mattered. In its place rose an overpowering desire to reunite with them, and maybe even to meet the girl he suspected was his daughter. He tried to imagine seeing Lili again but did not know where to begin. Yet not letting it happen, denying himself that chance, would be impossible now. He must see her.

That night, Paul didn't sleep. He lay awake in his bed, his eyes wide open in the darkness. His restless fingers alternately soothed his bad knee and rubbed his old amulet of the evil eye. He spent the night recalling his past, before the war, when he was Paul Assouline. It all burst forth so clearly, as though he were watching a film. He followed scenes of himself as a child living with his parents at Le Paradis, of his young cousins and his visits to Paris, of his long days at medical school. Then the memories stopped. When they took up again, the scenes that followed were dramatically slowed down. In near-excruciating detail, he relived every aspect of his life with Lili, of their secrets together and their dreams for their future. His eyelids shut tightly to allow him to experience every bit of emotion. As he lifted his hand from his knee to wipe his cheek, he admitted to himself that Lili was his true war injury, and that the lingering wound had not healed.

The next morning in his gallery, Paul hung up the phone, scarcely believing what he'd heard. A longtime associate, Mademoiselle

Molyneux, had called from Sotheby's and urgently requested that he come to her office "right away, if possible . . . I may have something of interest. It cannot be discussed by phone. And bring the photo."

For years Mademoiselle Molyneux, along with her predecessors at the auction house, had tried to be of help in Paul's search for the art looted from Le Paradis. Today he detected an excitement in her voice that he couldn't remember ever having heard before.

In his desk drawer the old photo, its edges worn, lay in a velvet pouch. He slid it securely into his vest pocket. Then he placed his hat on his head just so and grabbed his cane on the way out, suddenly exhilarated.

He headed down the winding, cobbled street that was the main artery through the Old Town, to the Quai du Mont-Blanc. At the foot of the ramparts, he stopped just long enough to breathe, taking in the view of the snowcapped Mont Blanc, backdrop to the landmark fountain that gushed high into the sky from the middle of Lake Geneva.

The doorman who pushed open the auspicious bronze doors at Sotheby's welcomed him. At the desk, Paul nodded to the receptionist, who hurried him to the third floor, where Mademoiselle Molyneux was waiting.

Paul saw an unaccustomed glimmer in her steady blue eyes. She was almost smiling. "Monsieur Bachelier, I'm glad you could come right away. The London office was hoping to include the piece I spoke of on the phone in next week's auction of important modern paintings. I've been able to hold them off since it came in yesterday. I think that, at last, this may be something that you've been looking for."

He tried to ignore his pounding heart, steeling himself against disappointment.

"Follow me," she said. Keys in hand, she led him to the rear office annex. The few times he had been invited into this secret chamber, he had been struck by its relative emptiness yet also by its disorder. It was a holding room for orphans of the art world, those pieces of unknown or dubious provenance. Until they were categorized and their value proven, they were treated like changelings.

Today was no different. He noticed a few heavy gilt chairs with tattered upholstery, obviously a set, strewn about the room; several small canvases were leaning against them. Propped against the far wall was an imposingly large piece, partially draped in a plain cloth.

It was this one that Mademoiselle Molyneux indicated with a jangle of raised keys. She stopped so he could give it his full attention. He felt himself tremble as she lifted off the cloth, revealing markings on the backside of the canvas. She allowed him a moment to register them. Surely he would have at least some knowledge of their meaning.

"See, here—it is stamped 'A. E. 806,' initials you might recognize as indicating it came from the collection taken from the residence of Assouline, Elizar." She searched his face for a reaction before continuing. He nodded slowly.

"And here is a description: '*Porträt einer Frau in Weiß.*' German for *Portrait of a Woman in White.*"

At that Paul removed his hat and moved in closer to read it for himself, his brows pulling together as he peered through his reading glasses, aware that Mademoiselle Molyneux was watching him with curiosity. He knew his own origins were as mysterious to her as those of every piece in the room.

"Down here is another stamp." She pointed. "'H. G.'" She looked up at him. "For Hermann Göring."

Paul's mouth opened involuntarily. He knew exactly what that meant.

"Monsieur? Are you all right?"

"I think so," he whispered.

"So, let's have a look at it, shall we?" She dragged the painting, heavy in its ornate frame, roundabout for his full-frontal viewing. "Well, what do you think?" she asked when she had slid it into place and it rested once more against the wall. "Does she look familiar?"

Paul's eyes widened in astonishment, then fell, turning soft and moist. He was gazing into the face of his aunt, Sonia Rosenswig, just as he'd done that day so long ago when the painting had been presented in his cousins' salon on the rue La Boétie.

Without a word, he pulled a velvet pouch from his vest pocket and brought out the photo of the portrait, surrounded by his family, all together and smiling. Mademoiselle Molyneux simply nodded, understanding that at long last she had found for him something he valued.

He stood contemplating. Then he asked her, quietly, if she would help him. Could she somehow discreetly fix things for him so he could purchase the portrait right away, avoiding public auction? He wanted it today or tomorrow, if possible, in a no-strings arrangement that didn't involve the usual legal complications of restoring a piece of art to its rightful owner, even with his excellent documentation. He wanted nothing to do with lawsuits. He would purchase it up front from the seller, before it hit the market, he said, and give it back to its rightful owners, the Rosenswig family.

She was silent for a few moments, then smiled gently. "For a good Sotheby's customer such as you, Monsieur Bachelier, I could possibly manage it. I will try."

The next morning when Paul walked into his gallery, the phone was ringing. He picked it up and heard the voice of Mademoiselle Molyneux, unusually warm. "It's done. The painting is yours as soon as your bank makes the transfer."

"Excellent," he said, and released a breath he hadn't known he'd been holding. "But, could you tell me, who is the present owner? I mean, who brought you the painting? In other words, whom am I purchasing it from?"

Her tone changed back to that of her familiar professional self. "As you know, Monsieur Bachelier, this is a special situation. Normally, once we have accepted a lot item for a sale, we are obliged to offer it as an auction item. Because of our long-term association with you as a client, and because the seller's ownership and right to sell may be in question, we will oversee this transaction as a favor to you both. Frankly, we want to help you and we will take our commission, but we fully expect that no one on the outside will ever hear of this. It would not reflect well on you, or on us, or on the seller. For that reason,

Sotheby's cannot release the name of the seller or give the seller your name. It's the only way to avoid future legal issues. I am sorry."

Paul listened. He understood the trade-off. "In other words, I will never have the opportunity to ask the seller where he got the portrait or what more he knows of its history?"

"No, I'm afraid not."

He felt almost cheated. "And you, Mademoiselle Molyneux? Will you not tell me the story?"

She hesitated; then he thought he heard her cup her hand over the receiver. Her voice was hushed. "Monsieur, I do know this: It came from a family who has had it since the war. The seller said that he and his recently deceased father found it in a truck wreck in northern Germany at the time of the Russian invasion. It has been hanging 'peacefully and anonymously'—those were his words—on the wall of his parents' farmhouse ever since. For the longest time, they didn't know what they had, only that they had become very attached to their beautiful portrait. Later on, when the seller moved to Berlin to study, he recognized the name Matisse in a museum and learned the value. But even then, his parents did not want to let her go. And now he's free to sell. I think that you are the lucky one, monsieur."

The timing is perfect, Paul thought. *I can approach Henri with the portrait as an offering, and that will surely open the door to something. But how should I begin?* He didn't like the idea of making initial contact by phone after all these years. The conversation would be too abrupt, too strained, too unpredictable. There would be too many questions he wasn't sure how to answer.

He began to feel horribly guilty for what he was sure they would deem his outright neglect. As he took an unflinching look at his behavior over all these years, he knew there was no use in trying to come up with a justification for it, because it was inexcusable.

How could I? And why? he asked himself. *Was it because I'd lost Lili and I believed she'd rejected me?* He shuddered to think back to his desolate state at the time. *I accepted that fate, as absurd as it seems today, and I've been spending the rest of my life trying to live with it.*

Paul was not happy with what he wrote to Henri: an uncomfortably formal letter in which he explained that he had just recently learned of his cousins' whereabouts, that he was living in Geneva and had come across the Matisse portrait of Aunt Sonia, and that he had purchased it and would like to offer it to his aunt. But it would have to do. He sealed the envelope and addressed it to Gallery Henri Rosenswig, an address on Madison Avenue, New York City, America. As he wrote it out in his flourished Old World script, it seemed a reminder that Henri was living in the future while Paul was somehow mired in the past.

The following week, he arrived home one night to hear his phone ringing with such insistence that he rushed to answer it.

A familiar voice, full of excitement, boomed across the Atlantic. "Paul? This is your cousin Henri. We thought you were lost in the war! I can't believe it—after all these years."

"Henri . . . " Paul was at a loss for words.

Elated at the prospect of seeing his cousin again and of the return of Sonia's portrait, Henri continued, "The timing could not be better. You can deliver the portrait personally to Maman in San Francisco when we're together to celebrate her seventieth birthday this month. You must come, Paul! I can't wait to tell them!"

Paul panicked. When Lili learned he was alive, she might think he'd abandoned her and refuse to see him. But he had to see her again. And to see her child.

"You must not tell them. I want it to be a surprise, Henri. And I must be a surprise. Promise me."

"Only because you insist."

"Good. Then I'll come."

•24•

San Francisco, May 1963

"When does the celebration begin?" Henri called over his shoulder, as he rushed out the door.

"Whenever Mimi gets here. She's spending the afternoon in her darkroom, developing, as usual. And where are you off to?" Lili asked from the kitchen.

"I have a couple of things to pick up for tonight. Special things."

"Something more from France you've tracked down? You've become a regular top-notch sleuth, Henri." She'd watched him close down Galerie Claude Bessett by besieging it with lawsuits demanding fines, he had by now recovered about one-third of his missing gallery pieces, and he continued his dogged search for the Matisse portrait.

But he was already gone.

Max was out getting flowers and fresh bread for the celebration dinner, and when they'd finished in the kitchen, Sonia helped Lili set out the champagne flutes, just as they'd always done on family birthdays. Her mother's hands were freckled now, and not so steady as before, but she remained lovely, thought Lili, especially in the white suit she wore, with her white hair done up in a simple chignon. The Limoges dishes with the little birds were the same as those they had left behind in Paris. Lili had been delighted the day she'd come across

253

an identical set in an antiques shop in town, though even Sonia had laughed at the extent of her nostalgia.

"No one but us wants this kind of old thing anymore," she'd said, handling the pieces affectionately.

Sonia lingered to admire the natural light reflecting off the crystal and silver on the table and the prisms in the chandelier. "Lili, aren't you going to prepare yourself? Everyone will be back soon."

There was a knock at the door. "It's probably Max, home early with packages," said Lili, swinging the door wide open.

"*Non, c'est moi. Je suis en retard.* I believe I'm late."

She looked up into a face that was familiarly handsome but much older.

"Paul!"

When she spoke his name, all the air left her body. As she stumbled forward, he caught her in his arms, letting go of his cane, and held her to him. Then she was breathing again and reached to touch his cheek. She quietly searched the depths of his eyes for the boy she remembered.

Then, in a whirl of confusion, she pulled away suddenly. If Paul had been alive all this time, how was it that she had never known? Why hadn't he contacted her? *But why . . . ?* she wanted to say.

Too soon, Henri was up the stairs behind them, struggling with a huge package wrapped in brown paper, huffing, but with anticipation. "I wanted to tell you, but he wouldn't let me. He's been living all this time in Switzerland, and he's found Maman's portrait."

Sonia had followed Lili to the door and stood nearby, her hand on her jawline, overcome with emotion. "Is it really you, Paul?"

"Auntie Sonia, you look as beautiful as always," he said, and went to embrace her.

A tear rolled down her cheek. "No, no," he said, "you'll spoil it, Auntie."

"What I don't understand is why it took you so long to contact us," said Henri.

"Oh, for heaven's sake," said Sonia, her voice full of compassion, "leave all that alone, Henri. My nephew hasn't come all the way here for the third degree. He's here to reunite, and that is enough for me. It's what his mother would want. How I wish that she and Eli and my dear Maurice could be here."

"Remember that birthday, and how we were all together?" said Henri. He began tearing the packing materials to get at the portrait.

"I remember," Paul said softly to Lili.

She turned to him, still in a state of shock. Just then, Max entered the room and jolted her back to the present.

"Paul, meet Lili's husband, my brother-in-law, Max. Our cousin Paul—alive, and he's found us!" said Henri, switching to English for Max's benefit. He was so excited and anxious to see the portrait that he was momentarily oblivious to the drama taking place.

As Max approached Paul with his warm smile, Henri called out, "Aha!" in a volume that no one could ignore. He had succeeded in freeing the painting and was leaning it upright for all to see.

"Oh, Maman, look at you!" Lili said. Sonia looked as beautiful as ever: the red hair, the white dress, the emerald ring reflecting the green in her eyes, the red velvet chair.

"Papa's portrait, home at last," Henri sighed.

"Auntie, how could I forget? Another surprise," said Paul. But he was looking at Lili when he took a small wooden box from his pocket.

"What could this possibly be?" Sonia said.

"Open it." He held the box out in his hand.

She unlatched and lifted the lid to reveal the emerald ring. Its blue-green darts shot out at the group. "My wedding ring!" Sonia said joyfully.

Lili had to reach out and put her hand on Paul's arm, the arm that held the box, to steady herself. She watched her mother take the ring back.

"Happy birthday, Grand-maman." Mimi entered, smiling, her long hair flowing behind her. She kissed her grandmother before noticing Paul.

It took a moment for Lili to say, "Mimi, this is Paul. My lost cousin Paul. He's found us."

Paul took Mimi's hands in his and kissed her on both cheeks, then stepped back to look at her. *Does he see his mother in her?* Lili wondered, as she watched Paul take in the wide smile and light-brown waves that looked exactly like Jeanne's.

"You're exquisite," he said, his voice quivering. He looked to Lili, his expression full of wonder, and waited for her answer. She nodded.

"So, the next generation," he said, his eyes moist.

Afraid she might cry, Lili blurted out, "And more. Mimi's expecting, in June."

Paul's eyebrows rose again. "And the father?"

"Oh, we'll get married soon. Don't worry." Mimi giggled. "He's a French photographer named Julien. We're both photographers. Right now he's away on a shoot, or he would have been here. We've known each other for a long time."

"That's how it is here, I'm ashamed to say. They're afraid of nothing. They think they have all the time in the world," Lili said, her eyes on Paul.

"But we know they don't," he said to her.

"I know," she answered.

Sonia took Mimi's hand and put the emerald ring into her palm. "It's for you. My wedding ring. I want you to have it, for when you marry Julien."

"Oh, Grand-maman! It is beautiful. Uncle Paul," she said, turning, "if it's a girl, we're naming her Jeanne, and if it's a boy, Eli Maurice."

"In that case, I'll come back for the birth, and for the wedding," he promised her.

"Right now would be a good time for a birthday photo of all of us," said Henri, setting up his tripod.

"In a few minutes, Henri. First I want to show Paul our view." Lili took his arm and led him through the back and outside to a small balcony overlooking the bay.

They stood facing each other, a foot apart, against the silence of the open blue sea and sky.

"Why didn't you let me know you were alive? Tell me why!" she demanded.

He looked into the blue beyond her, searching for an answer. "I was hurt."

"Was it really that bad?" she said, looking down at his knee eased by the cane, then up to the hand holding onto it, and noticed there was no ring there. When she looked back into his eyes, to the pain there, she understood

"Yes, it was."

"But I would have waited. I never stopped waiting for you."

"I never knew. Oh, God, Lili . . . I'm sorry."

"So am I."

With a faint moan, he drew her tightly to him. She held him and closed her eyes for a long, lingering moment, to be with him again. She pressed her cheek against his chest and breathed in his familiar scent. It was June 14, 1940, and they were lying under the sheltering plane tree behind Le Paradis. In that moment she allowed herself to remember, and to grieve for all that they had had together, and all that they had lost.

When he released her, he said, "I have something to show you." He pulled a small velvet pouch out from his pocket and, reaching in, withdrew a worn color photograph, faded almost to yellow. "Do you remember, Lili, when you gave me this? Without it I don't think I could have made it through the war."

She couldn't bring herself to answer. There was her father, and Uncle Eli and Auntie Jeanne. Paul's hands entwined with hers. All of them back then, happy and smiling and squeezed in close together to fit in the frame. A family.

"Time hasn't changed you," he said, watching her.

She laughed, then caught his hand. Holding it between hers, her expression serious, she said, "I hope the war didn't do you any damage you can't repair?"

He looked at her with a wistful smile, and finally he answered, "I'm trying. I'm getting married."

An unwelcome pang of jealousy passed through her. She felt it alter her expression momentarily, but then, in her relief for him, it released.

"I'm so glad, Paul. When?"

"Soon," he said, still studying her. "When I get back."

"Okay. Let's get a new photograph," Henri urged, starting to arrange them all in their positions.

Mimi stepped up. "No, no. Let me be the photographer this time."

Sonia was seated in a red chair, the portrait propped next to her. Henri and Lili were right behind her, with Max at Lili's side, then Paul.

Mimi looked through the viewfinder.

"This is perfect," she said, when they had all made their final adjustments.

"*Portrait of a Family*, the second in a series. The next one will have all of us." She looked down to pat her tummy. "At my wedding."

She set the delay and took her place between Max and Paul. "Smile, everyone."

Behind her smile, a lifetime of images and emotions kaleidoscoped through Lili's mind, then settled peacefully into place until she felt their equilibrium, and the camera flashed.

Author's Note

This is the story of an imaginary piece of art, and what could have happened to it in the context of historic characters and events. The Rosenswig and Assouline families are fictitious, but such stories are not.

From 1940 to 1944, the Jeu de Paume museum was a so-called "concentration camp" for an estimated twenty-two thousand pieces of art that the Nazis looted in France from more than two hundred Jewish-owned collections. Hermann Göring, it was recorded, made twenty-one visits to the Jeu de Paume, seeking works for his personal collection. Many of those were sent to his favorite residence, Carinhall.

The secret record keeping of Rose Valland led to the restitution of more than forty-five thousand pieces of art stolen during World War II. After the war, she continued her work to recover plundered art. She died in Paris in 1980. A plaque in her honor hangs today near the entrance of the Jeu de Paume. At war's end, she was awarded the Medal of the French Resistance. She has also received the Legion of Honor and is a highly decorated heroine of France.

After departing Carinhall, Göring was accused by Hitler of treason, stripped of power, and placed under state arrest. Two weeks later, he was captured by the Allies and jailed for a year, waiting to sit trial in Nuremberg for his war crimes and crimes against humanity. He was convicted and sentenced to death by hanging. Shortly before execution time, he was found lying dead on the floor of his cell, one eye open and the other shut. A tiny vial on the floor held traces of cyanide.

Reader's Guide
Questions for Discussion

1. Lili's story is one of love, loss, and reinvention. She begins life as a creative girl in a privileged family but arrives in the United States a pregnant, unmarried refugee. By the end she is again a creative woman living a privileged life, and she is ultimately successful in reconciling her past with her present. Does her ability to reinvent herself spring from her will to survive or her learning to internalize life's challenges, or is she simply a lucky victim of circumstance?

2. Lili and Max have an unconventional beginning to their marriage. In Lili's predicament, would you have made the same choices she did? How does her marriage to Max evolve over their life together? How is it impacted by the Mimi's birth?

3. Paul is a young man of high principles. What aspects of his character influence his choices from the day he is separated from Lili? He waits a long time to reunite with Lili and the Rosenswigs and to become involved in a relationship. Why? Could he have chosen to act differently? In the end, do you think he regrets his choices?

4. Communication in wartime 1940 had none of the advantages that today's social media offers. What would you have done to track Lili if you were Paul in World War 2 France?

5. Claude Bessett's actions seem reprehensible to us. How does he reconcile survival in dangerous times with his personal morality? In his circumstances, what decisions would you have made?

6. Henri and his father Maurice have a difficult relationship, fraught with their many differences. How does the balance of power between them change with their circumstances? How does Henri try to atone to his father for bringing them to America—and do you think he succeeds?

7. Lili's parents, Sonia and Maurice, seem to have a successful marriage. What are the differences in what each one expects from life? How are their expectations challenged, and how do they hold up to these challenges? Which qualities does each one pass on to Lili and Henri?

8. Herman Goring and the Assoulines are both collectors of art. How does the motivation for their efforts to amass great collections reflect differences in their core moral values?

9. Certain objects play meaningful roles in this story. What values and emotions are attached to the Matisse portrait, the family photograph, the emerald ring, the snuffbox, and the family china?

10. The book spans a time period of approximately forty years and takes place on two continents. Consider Lili's journey to find her place in a society with changing expectations for women. As a man, does Henri face changing expectations as well? What about as a gay man?

Acknowledgements

For your encouragement, many reads, and for waiting, thank you: Jim, Jordan, Julia, Jacob, Mom, Steve, Janet Berliner, Ellen Heltzel, Claudine Fisher, Roz Sutherland, Douglas Preston, Yvonne Gionet, Lucinda Summerville, Chris Rauschenberg and Janet Stein, Mary Bisbee-Beek, Juliana Arvai Mcbride and Anne Mcbride, Katie Radditz, Shelley Voboril, Wendy Burden, Cynthia Manson, Edith Davis, Brooke Warner and the team.

Author Bio

©Jordan Winkler

Susan Winkler was born in Portland, Oregon and educated at Bennington College (BA French literature), Stanford University (MA French literature), *L'Academie* in Paris and at the University of Geneva. She was trained as a journalist at Fairchild Publications in New York, and has authored the four editions of THE PARIS SHOPPING COMPANION. She lives in Portland with her family, and has a lifelong interest in art.

SELECTED TITLES FROM SHE WRITES PRESS

She Writes Press is an independent publishing company
founded to serve women writers everywhere.
Visit us at www.shewritespress.com.

The Sweetness by Sande Boritz Berger
$16.95, 978-1-63152-907-8

A compelling and powerful story of two girls—cousins living on separate continents—whose strikingly different lives are forever changed when the Nazis invade Vilna, Lithuania.

All the Light There Was by Nancy Kricorian
$16.95, 978-1-63152-905-4

A lyrical, finely wrought tale of loyalty, love, and the many faces of resistance, told from the perspective of an Armenian girl living in Paris during the Nazi occupation of the 1940s.

A Cup of Redemption by Carole Bumpus
$16.95, 978-1-938314-90-2

Three women, each with their own secrets and shames, seek to make peace with their pasts and carve out new identities for themselves.

Shanghai Love by Layne Wong
$16.95, 978-1-938314-18-6

The enthralling story of an unlikely romance between a Chinese herbalist and a Jewish refugee in Shanghai during World War II.

After Midnight by Diane Shute-Sepahpour
$16.95, 978-1-63152-913-9

When horse breeder Alix is forced to temporarily swap places with her estranged twin sister—the wife of an English lord—her forgotten past begins to resurface.

Water On the Moon by Jean P. Moore
$16.95, 978-1-938314-61-2

When her home is destroyed in a freak accident, Lidia Raven, a divorced mother of two, is plunged into a mystery that involves her entire family.

CPSIA information can be obtained at www.ICGtesting.com
Printed in the USA
BVOW05s1800220714

359791BV00002B/5/P